INJURY TIME

FOR THE VICTIMS.

Julius Caesar and the Roman Empire couldn't conquer the blue sky.

Neil Finn, Tim Finn.

When fishes flew and forests walked
And figs grew upon thorn,
Some moment when the moon was blood
Then surely I was born.

With monstrous head and sickening cry
And ears like errant wings,
The devil's walking parody
On all four-footed things.

The tattered outlaw of the earth,
Of ancient crooked will;
Starve, scourge, deride me: I am dumb,
I keep my secret still.

Fools! For I also had my hour;
One far fierce hour and sweet:
There was a shout about my ears,
And palms before my feet.

G.K. Chesterton

JANUARY 1971

The boy will only speak through his mother. That was the accepted established line of communication. There would be the role play that proved surprisingly effective, good cop versus bad cop. "The game" Shaw called it. What they planned for the interview was that Shaw, as the officer with seniority, would lead with a modicum level of hostility and antagonism that would manoeuvre the mother towards Officer Price. He would then act the appeasing, conciliatory role. Shaw had the kind of personality that made it natural for him to take on that role. He was a ruthless and ambitious man and had no love for the nationalist community and a particular animosity towards Taigs. And at times, he let it show. The officer's experience informed them that the most productive interviews involved a good relationship with whoever they interviewed, no matter what they thought of them and their alleged crimes. This was an unorthodox interview. It was new ground for each officer. Yet they were agreed that whatever the boy told his mother, it could be treated almost as gospel. A boy of ten would not lie to his mother, not in front of the police. They were convinced in that regard.

"Mrs Doyle". Officer Shaw interjected, not concealing the impatience he was experiencing. "Please, if you would Mrs Doyle, would you ask Caelan to confirm the details we have taken down from his statement?" Mrs Doyle took the cup away from her lips. She had insisted on a proper cup, not that plastic rubbish. She 'needed a real cup of tae if she were to get through this', she told them.

"Yes", she said in an agitated tone, irritated by the interruption, "I told youse, he saw a car stop outside McGurks". She crossed herself again, as she did every time she said the name of the pub.

"At the George's Street entrance where a man got out of the car and placed what Caelan, our star witness here", Officer Price paused, having taken up the statement and gave the boy a brief smile to try and build up a rapport, "placed an object that looked like a box or a parcel at the Georges Street entrance to the bar". The boy shrank further into his mother's bosom. He looked oddly ill-at-ease, even in his mother's embrace. The younger officer could not fathom it. The boys discomfort went deeper, stronger than what you would normally find in these circumstances, abnormal as they were.

He had seen that look before, he remembered it from those

personnel, colleagues, who had undergone horrific injuries or experienced events too awful to cope with. He suspected the boy had witnessed more than he would admit to. Or perhaps he was just used to the horror people were capable of inflicting on one another and had seen the effects of violence too often. He hoped that wasn't the case. "And, the man got back into the car and the car then drove off in the direction of Clifton Street. I did not see where the car went to from there. I walked quickly on so as to get home, as it was getting dark."

"Yes. That's what he's been tellin' me and that's the truth of it." His mother said with a conviction. The smell of hair lacquer, pungent and stinging when she first entered the room, was beginning to fade. Her foundation, applied thickly, was smudged from the number of times she employed the handkerchief to dab her face after each line of the statement was read out.

The other Officer, the younger one with a nice smile; the one that had gone out to get her his cup for her tea made a 'hmmm' sound. She squinted her eyes, searching, scrutinising as if to see what was within him. Officer Price had been intrigued by the boy sat on his mother's lap. He was small for his age, undernourished almost; he looked more like a seven or eight than the ten-year-old boy. He had been scrubbed clean; you could smell the soap from his body. His pale white skin shone with an imposed cleanliness. His dirty fair hair had been combed into submission from the right, where a natural fault line in his hair had been exposed. He had been dressed in his school uniform, most likely the best clothes he owned. His mother too had made great effort to look her best for the interview. She wore what looked like a new blue and cream overcoat and blue scarf to keep her hair in place.

"Mrs Doyle, I hope you understand the seriousness with which we are taking this and Caelan's evidence will be essential to understanding what happened and crucially," Officer Price paused for emphasis, "it will direct us to where we need to concentrate our efforts, if we are to catch the men responsible for this crime and bring them to justice."

Mrs Doyle glared at the older, unpleasant policeman who had sat in silence looking at her as if he had trod in something nasty. There was no way in hell he wanted them caught. "Nobody wants these murderin' brutes caught more than I do." She said coldly. "Nobody!" She simmered, her painted lips tightened, imploding into a grimace. "I can direct ye to where your enquiries should start, anyone on the road could. Over there", she nodded her head to the right, "over at the Bay. Everyone knows they planted it. The whole Bay knew about, even the dogs in the street could tell ye that." She finished her sentence in a flourish of defiance that was a show of the contempt she held for them and their enquiries.

"Of course, of course, that is another definite line of enquiry Mrs Doyle," Officer Price moved in swiftly as Officer Shaw sat back in his chair and released a slow exhale of air. He had no time for these people. He was impatient and rude and wanted to get into Special Branch. God knows he was ruthless and bitter enough for them. "But to do that, for us to do our job, we need to be sure of the facts. We don't want some clever lawyer getting these men off when we catch them. So I'd like to ask Caelan to confirm what he says was on the back window of the car. He says it was a Union Jack. Is that right?" He directed the question at Caelan. The boy turned his face fully into his mother's overcoat. She leaned down as her son whispered. Mrs Doyle nodded and looked at the two officers.

"Yes. It was definitely a wee union jack on the back window. It was on the right and down near the corner of the window. He is definite about that. Isn't that right son?" She gently urged. "He's not a liar", she stated with the same defiance, "he's been brung up right to tell the truth." The boy looked at the Detective Constables in solid silence.

"No-one would question that Mrs Doyle." Officer Price said absently, fighting his natural impulse for pedantry and allowing union jack to stand instead of correcting it to union flag. He knew the people of this community had no love for it, and that was an understatement if ever there was one. He recalled the most imaginative description he had heard the flag described to him during a particularly robust interview with an elderly republican who had defied the Flags and Emblems (Display) Act (Northern Ireland) 1954 by hanging the Irish tricolour out of his window at Easter. His was a public demonstration and a gesture that informed to all and sundry he was not for backing down.

He retorted in a measured and contained fury at the repeated request for removal. "I'll fly the flag of this nation to honour Ireland's dead, just as you lot get to fly the butcher's apron on the Twelfth." That description was so vividly striking and admittedly, the delivery so vitriolic, that it stayed with him, as it held such potency and poignancy for the old man. After a particularly robust entry to the house that involved the removal of several screaming women and abusive men, the flag was removed and his arrest for resisting, guaranteed.

Officer Shaw asked again if Caelan could provide a description of the car. The colour even, how many doors the car had. Was it big? Small? A hatchback maybe?

"He doesn't know!". His mother intervened, raising her right arm to shield her cowering son. "It was a dark colour and it had doors at the back. For Godsakes, he's only a chile, and it was dark and after everything that's happened, it's a miracle he remembers anything." She clasped her child tightly with her right arm.

"I know, it's been quite traumatic no doubt, no-one should have to go through such events, especially for someone of Caelan's age." Officer Price commented, smiling encouragingly at the boy in the hope it would induce a response. The boy sat in silence, his gaze fixed to a point somewhere beyond the room.

"Was it a four door, a saloon type car Caelan? A long car?" Officer Price pressed gently.

"That's all he could tell me, I've told ye. He doesn't know anything really about cars, he's only a child." She said in a defensive, comforting voice directed at her son. "We only have the one in the family who drives and that's his uncle. He drives his works van."

"Why was your son out? I mean at that time of the evening," Officer Shaw retreated quickly from his opening accusatory tone, "I mean on his own, that's what I mean. He was a wee bit far from his house and he's very young." Officer Shaw attempted a smile at the boy, who in turn buried his head into his mother's bosom.

"That was my doing, God forgive me. I sent him over to his Uncle Johnsie. He's the one with the van. He lives in Lancaster Street. I needed some nails and a piece of plywood. I wanted a shelf put up in the larder. His da's hopeless when it comes to things around the house. Isn't he?" She smiled solidly at her son. "Johnsie has all sorts of wood," she added by way of clarification, "he's a joiner you see. So I got Caelan here to run over before his Uncle went out. On Tuesdays he goes to the Mandeville club to play snooker. It's something he does on Tuesdays and he goes there on a Friday too after a hard weeks work. He's a bachelor you see. Never had time for the girls nor any of that kind of malarkey."

"Yes Mrs Doyle, that does explain Caelans presence at the time and place. Thank you." Officer Shaw broke in, unable to conceal his impatience, which Mrs Doyle had picked up on by the flashing look she cast him.

"Well you did ask and I'm just telling ye." She replied adopting a defensive pose, shielding herself with her son's body.

"Yes and thank you Mrs Doyle you have been very co-operative and we appreciate that." Officer Price broke in. "We really do." He added in an earnest, heartfelt tone.

"Now would you ask Caelan to tell us why he walked on and thought nothing of the man placing an object at the entrance to the bar?" Officer Shaw asked. His colleague detected the early signs of resentment stirring in Shaw's face.

Mrs Doyle and her son conferred in an exchange of looks and imperceptible body language. "God love him, he thought the man was leaving empties back in a crate he borrowed from the bar. Christ," she sighed heavily, "the innocence of childer."

"Then, I walked on," Officer Shaw took up the statement moving the interview on. "I was near to Victoria Parade and that's when a big bang went off."

"Sweet Jesus, Mary and Joseph." Mrs Doyle said crossing herself.

"I fell to the ground and turned to see smoke and things flying into the air and people were running about everywhere. I fell down because of the noise and put my hands over my head. I stayed on the ground for a while until the sound had gone away then I got up and heard people screaming and shouting. I heard people shouting at me. They were shouting at me asking me what had happened. That was a bomb... Where was it? Did you see anything? I got scared at their shouting and ran across the road and past Artillery House and the New Lodge Road. Then I seen I hadn't Uncle Johnsie's spirit level. I thought oh no, God, mum will kill me."

Mrs Doyle tutted loudly, registering her disapproval at the very idea and made a show of raising her embrace up and around her son's chest.

Officer Shaw glanced at her and quickly moved the statement along.

"I must have dropped it. I ran back and found it on the pavement near to Artillery House. I picked it up and ran back across the New Lodge Road. It was at the bottom of Stratheden Street that I could hear music. I looked up towards Tigers Bay. I saw lots of people were out. There was a small bonfire. I could hear the people singing. It was the big drum beat that was scary. I walked up a bit closer, I don't know why. I wanted to hear what the people were singing I suppose. People from my area were coming out of their houses so I wasn't too afraid anymore. I don't remember anything else. I can still hear the drumming."

"Could you tell us about the drumming Caelan? Was it really loud? Like a band drumming?" Officer Price enquired, keeping his face and tone set in neutral.

"We really would like to hear Caelan tell us Mrs Doyle, its procedure. It's necessary for the law to follow its course. It has to be in his own words for the DPP."

"The who?" Mrs Doyle asked, pushing the sharp features of her face forward to register her question.

"The Public Prosecutor." Officer Shaw did not hide his exasperation as he answered. "He will make the decision when the time comes to take this to court, or not." Officer Shaw told her in a flat, blunt tone.

The boy squirmed on his mother's lap and reached out his small arms, and fragile-looking, bony wrists emerged from the sleeves of his school blazer. His hands were shaking and to stop them he placed his hands down firmly on the surface of the table. He flinched as the table was metal and cold to touch. Slowly he looked up, trying to remember the beat, and began tapping out a rhythm on the interview table.

"da'sda'sda, da, da'sda'sda."

He slapped out on the table. Both officers concentrated on the beat. Caelan tried to sing some words but they came out as muffled sounds held hostage in his mind. Officer Price began to nod and hummed. Suddenly he sat back bolt upright in his chair.

The boy returned to his mother's bosom turning his head inwards. Officer Price sat in his chair silent, motionless. He looked to the boy and then to his colleague who looked perplexed. Officer Price leaned over to his colleague and whispered into his ear. His colleague did not betray any emotion. The boy crumpled into his mother's body and tears fell from his eyes.

"Well? What was it son? Tell us, tell us what was the song them hallions were playing? You know full well now what they were singing. Let's hear it." Mrs Doyle commanded. She was tired and scared. She had sleepless nights with him crying, screaming at times. She had the bed wetting and the tantrums in the morning as she tried to get him to school. She was exhausted, a tiredness that gnawed at her very bones. And she was left angry by it. Her husband had given up caring, he just got angry and hit things like the doors and the furniture. 'He's only a child, it's upset him no end. Just give him some time Harry' she would beg. After another couple of days of the same, he took up refuge in The Phoenix Bar.

"It would not be helpful to speculate at this moment Mrs Doyle. I may be wrong and I cannot go on what I think it may, or may not have been." Officer Price pressed back. "Once we have all the facts, we will be in contact with you and with Caelan."

Mrs Doyle made a sound from a well inside her belly that reverberated around her throat, conveying her deep scepticism. "Whatever it was they were having a right wee hooley, loads of people on the road heard them as well." Mrs Doyle said with a misplaced sense of satisfaction and triumph. "Filthy animals." Mrs Doyle spat the words out angrily, becoming more and more animated, her emotions surfacing and being transmitted to her child.

"That's what sparked off all the trouble on the road since it. Themings and their celebratin'." Fresh tears were squeezed from his eyes the droplets fell from his face onto his school trousers. "All them lies on the news and in the papers. Those people ought to know better. Saying that the boys did it, that it was all a mistake, that it went off inside is all a load of terrible lies. They're spitting on the graves of those innocent people and their families!" Mrs Doyle had reached the zenith of her outburst and fell silent. She took the bundle of scrunched up hankies from her sleeve and dabbed her eyes.

The officers knew best to let her emote, to vent the obvious strong feelings she was experiencing. They knew from their experience not to intervene. They could not afford the risk of antagonising her. That's when the balloon went up and both sides become entrenched in an unproductive warfare of point scoring. She had been freely allowed to say what was on her mind and the emotions coursing through her veins.

"Mrs Doyle", Officer Price spoke, "we are trying to establish the facts to get to the truth of the matter. It's the only way we can catch the people who were responsible for this awful act." He ended passionately.

"Aye, we'll see" Mrs Doyle said with weighted cynicism. A natural silence fell upon the room. It was a moment for all in the room to take stock. The officers were troubled by this evidence. They had not told Mrs Doyle that a couple walking along the road moments before confirmed the sighting of a car parked where Caelan had seen it. They could not see the men's faces but confirmed there were four individuals in the car. They thought the car was a rover model. And brown in colour. They had also had several reports from people in the New Lodge Road complaining, more shouting in truth at foot patrols, of singing and dancing in the Tigers Bay, moments after the blast.

The boy continued to cry into his mother's coat. "C'mon Caelan, that's enough now love. We're going home now. That's us, we're done here. I want to get him to bed." Mrs Doyle said by way of her explaining her movements in the chair. "He's school in the morning and sweet Jesus do I need a proper cup of tae. No offence love." She directed at Officer Price. "It's like bed, there's nothing like your own."

The boy began to shake uncontrollably. "What's up love, what is it?" His mother comforted, rocking him in her embrace. "My poor wee soul. Please tell the nice policeman."

"Is there something else Caelan?" Officer Price pressed. "Something you've remembered? Tell us, it's alright. You're not in any trouble and you're safe here."

"What son? Come on, what is it? Tell us Caelan. Please." His mother cajoled, as she became alarmed at his struggling. She held him tightly, trying to contain the contortions of her sons apparent attempt to break free.

The boy froze and his face became pale. His lips opened and in a small, timorous voice that rippled with fear. "In the crowd..."

The two officers leaned forward to hear clearly the small, frightened voice.

"Yes, Caelan, c'mon tell the policemen. Tell them. Tell me, tell mummy." Mrs Doyle said soothingly.

"In the middle..." the boy's voice faltered and broke, his body convulsed, "in the middle," he sobbed unashamedly, "I...,"

"In the middle..." the boy's voice faltered and broke again, his body shaking uncontrollably, then an eruption of emotional anguish in the middle, he sobbed unashamedly, "I......"

"Oh God, Caelan, Caelan please." His mother pleaded, her voice raised, alarmed at her sons struggling body. The two Officers stood up unable to act, to speak in a scene unique to them both. They waited, poised, expectant of some revelatory information they knew the boy had kept hidden, even from his mother. They exchanged glances at one another in anticipation, fearful too of what they were about to hear.

"C'mon Caelan, tell mummy, please. Please son," she pleaded, holding him tightly as if to stop him rise above into the air, "please God, tell me what's the matter." She demanded, growing angry by the fear she had been made to feel.

"Tell the policemen everything." His mother now ordered, she was exhausted, tired of the arguments with Harry, who told her all he needed was a good boot up the arse was all. And off he would go to the pub to get his head some peace. She was left alone with the child and his silence. His older brother had long stopped talking to him; at least it was better than the fights. He had taken to staying out with friends until bedtime. She was determined now to get to the bottom of it all here in the police station and end what was happening to them as a family since that awful night.

Both Officers had risen slightly from their chairs simultaneously; they remained suspended, frozen in their respective stances, poised for something, some revelatory information. They dared not look at each other; they dared not speak less they break the spell that had descended on the room.

"I......I, the boy stammered, his anguish laid bare and somewhere in the emotional turmoil that possessed his small body; a terrible secret had captured his soul.

"Oh please son, please." His mother's exhorted and then her voice broke. She began to sob due to the exhaustion and fear the ensuing days had taken from her. She experienced a cold tickling chill gather in her chest. She saw the relative security and anonymity of the police station allow the turmoil constipating for days within her; the same turmoil smothering her waking moments, assaulting her sleep, ever since her son had returned to the house on the Godforsaken evening, could now be released.

Seeing his mother cry appeared to give the boy the strength and the courage to reach into his fear and momentarily snatch at the horror, real or imagined, and have it expunged and give answer to those around him.

And in a tiny, terrified voice he blurted out.

"I saw the Devil."

EIGENGRAU

"What's it like? I mean, do you feel anything? Anything at all? Was it really sore when it happened?" I asked, again not expecting an answer. I knew that I wouldn't but I couldn't help but ask. I wanted to know what it was like. Where was he now? Was he happy? Was he in Heaven? I couldn't bear the thought of him in that other place. No way, that could never happen to him. Not to him. He was brave and as mum described at his funeral, honourable. He was long gone now. But it kept him near if I did think about him, and I did talk to him; he would not die. He would always be alive to me. Sometimes I felt guilty for not talking to granddad Brady like that but I didn't really talk to him in when he was alive and he was old when he died, like sixty odd. Anyways, he scared me when he told me ghost stories from the old days and how Banshees haunted North Queen Street where they had lived. I was terrified by them and hated visiting, even with mum, to that leaky old house with its smell of turpentine and soap powder and bleach.

"What's what like young Niall" Lieutenant Tim would then ask. I knew it wasn't him asking but me. And I would ask him the same questions over and over again until I fell asleep or had to get up and out of bed.

Every morning that week he'd had the same conversation with Lieutenant Tim and had been answered with the same silent response to my questions. I dried my eyes on the pillow and tried ways to think myself out of this situation. I thought hard. What was it Blackie had said later that evening at the bottom of Alamein tower. It was their routine after football in the square to stand there and talk about things. Football, school, teachers they liked and didn't like, other boys they liked and didn't like; sometimes girls and men they had heard about who'd been arrested or even shot. That evening only one Person was on their minds.

Lieutenant Tim lay there just like he did from the poster his photograph was on. They stared at it on the telephone pole outside their school. The poster had been pasted on by the Brits the night before the day after Lieutenant Tim's body had been found in the empty shop beside the local MPs house (known locally as Fitt the Brit). His body had been burnt during a fire and he had been trapped in the burning building, so he had been told by his mum who spent the entire time telling him while crying. Someone said he looked like a branch from a big tree. He shouted for that someone to shut the fuck up. But I could not argue with the comment, he did look like that, frozen in that moment of death forever. You could make out his handsome features if you knew what he had looked like in life. He was a strongly built boy, a man really, seventeen and a born leader. You could still make out the torso and the arms that disappeared into the crotch area. Above the photograph, in red lettering, the words: 'See what the Provos do to your sons.'

"Hey you lot, what the fuck's this?" The young man with the really long, skinny legs stood staring at the poster taped to the post. "Youse just gonna stare at that? Get it fuckin' down nigh." The fella demanded. Wee Scullion and Manuel reached up and tore at the poster. "What the fucks a matter with you glipes." He rounded on us as a group, he did not wait for anyone to act on his order, pushing his way through the crowd of schoolboys and snatched at the remnants of the poster the boys could not reach. "Bastards. Dirty fuckin' Brit bastards."

He swore aloud. He was about Tim's age, but taller, thinner, dressed entirely in denim with a studded leather belt at the waist. He wore black brogue shoes that were scuffed and unpolished. I always wanted a studded belt, they were the bees knees. I hated my snake belt now, it kept reminding me I was a kid and not grown up. But mum said studded belts were for thugs and she knew why fellas had them and that was to bop people on the nose; because she knew they used them as knuckledusters. And no child of hers was going around dressed like a hooligan. Mum did talk a load of waffle sometimes, although she nailed it on the head about them belts because the hooligans did wrap them around their hands when they were fighting. Not much got past Mum. I grew cautious of this fella and watched if he made a move towards his waist.

"You see anymore of this shit, you tear it down, or go to the centre and report it. Ya hear me." His thin face, lined at the mouth and corner of his eyes, was flushed with anger and he gripped the strips of the poster tightly in the fist he made. You could see the crooked line of his front teeth when he spoke. There was spit forming at either side of his mouth. All of us made a sound that we would do as he said.

We all watched him walk to the top of Churchill Street, hands in his pockets and waited for him to disappear left around the corner onto the Antrim Road.

"Who's the clampit?" Someone, not me, felt brave enough to commit.

"I think he's from Vicanage" Wee Scullion said.

"Vicanage? What's a wanker from there tellin' us what to do." Big Corbett smarted. He was annoyed at himself because as the biggest amongst us, we had all looked to him to say something at the time. After all there was about ten of us. And Corbett knew it.

"I have a confession to make Lieutenant Tim. You'll listen to it, won't you? Please? I can't tell mum and da's as useful as a chocolate fireguard. I can't talk to anybody. I'm too ashamed. I'm sorry. I could never be like you, as brave or as strong. I want to be. I've always wanted to be. But I'm not like you or Piercy or Tank. Look at me with my skinny arms and legs. My tiny chest. I'm pathetic. Me mum had to get you to take me to big school on my first day. I was so embarrassed and cross with her for doing it. But I was so proud to walk into school with you and Skin and Sars. Even the teachers left me alone. You were brilliant, telling people to pass the word that I wasn't to be touched. You were a man of honour. You did what you promised to my mum you'd do. You looked out for me. You made sure on my first day at big school that no-one shoved my head down the bogs. I have tried to be like you. But I can't, I don't have what you have. I think sometimes the way I look shows what a coward and a liar I am. I'm weak and I'm puny. I cried again. I'm sorry, I've let everyone in my life down. I betrayed my mates. My whole area. I can't even begin to tell you. I'm so ashamed. I'm a pathetic little twat."

I was unequivocal as I was damning. Another big word I learned from Blackie.

I confessed into the pillow how sorry I was and there was no-one who could hate me as much as much I hated myself. No-one. I punched the mattress like it was my own face. My arm sprang back up with equal force. I swear to God. I'm gonna get bigger, stronger and better than I've ever been. I'll be brave and fearless like you were. Will you help me Tim, please? I'll be a better friend, the best; better than I've ever been. I'll make it up to Blackie, I swear to Almighty God. I swore and I cried again, this time for the person he had been and for the person I wanted to be, but would never become.

What scared me more was if I was going to start as I meant to go on, others might start to see what I was really like. I had, as the Owl of the Remove Billy Bunter would say, "been a beast".

I had woken up before the alarm that was set to go off at six. It made a horrible sound so I was glad to switch it off and lie back in my bed with some minutes to myself before I had to get up and face the dark morning. It maybe was rain, but most definitely it was the wind. It was always windy, especially in the early morning. At least it wasn't raining like yesterday. That was definitely the main thing. I hated the rain. You had the extra chore of keeping the papers and yourself protected and dry.

I thought I heard a dog barking across the square. It was low and growly, like it was about to attack. That ginger coloured mongrel called Duke Duffy or that bastard Dalmatian came to mind. My fear was that it was Dylan; the bastard devil dog, with his big angry red balls hanging just below its bright pink arsehole.

Holy fuckin' shit. Maybe it had returned for revenge after we chased it from the area. The thought alarmed me no end. That dog scared the life out of me, it was mad angry all the time. It was always darting about running at people, usually young people, because we were always out in the Barrack playing football or handball. It hated us and we hated it back. I don't know why oul Gerry kept it. I don't know how it hadn't ate the oul git already. He was a skinny oul fella, with greasy looking trousers and hair, who let the bloody thing out all day to roam the Barrack square scaring the bejesus out of everyone when it ran amok, especially if we were playing a big match in the Barrack Square. It never actually bit anyone that I knew of, but it's growling and snarling as it ran towards you was enough to frighten the shite out of anybody. That dog hated everybody.

I made a note in my head to take the big torch, the one that needed three batteries with me just in case.

But we had our revenge. Too right we did. One day after another attack at us playing football in the square; the one that left us holding the doors closed at the bottom of the flats while it ran about outside sniffing the ground and snarling at the doors; we decided we had had enough.

We got together with other boys, younger ones who were too scared to play outside and one or two older guys who gave us ten bob to get rid. So we gathered up a pile of bricks and waited until Dylan left the square and strutted around the far block of the maisonettes, well away from Gerry's house. He ruled the square as a dog and went around the two blocks like he owned them.

He was in the back gardens sniffing around the wall where we played best fallers and sometime lay in the grass watching the clouds. He had found something to dig up and while he was digging into the ground we knew that was the right time to attack.

The bricks, bottles and a metal bucket somebody left out at their porch rained down on the monster. We could all hear the yelps and one in in particular sent a shiver up my spine.

I just knew he was hurt, and hurt really bad. We ran off screaming 'victory' and later met up at the bottom of our flat, about twenty minutes after. I felt deadly about it, I think we all did; but you couldn't say, as we were all in it together. All that day we didn't see Dylan.

Me and Wholenut and Dada went back later in the day to the back gardens to where the attack took place, standing by the small wall that was at the end of the gardens. Wholenut got on Dada's shoulders to see into the grass that was as tall as the wall in parts.

"Nope, he's not there. I can't see him anywhere. He's fucked off. I would've see his big balls sticking up in the air by nye" Wholenut said, making Dada explode into a laughing fit and the two of them parted and fell like a big, broken giant, with Wholenut falling over the wall and onto the grass that was covered in daffodils and buttercups.

We never did found out what happened to Dylan. We never saw him again, nor did oul Gerry who scoured area looking for him. He asked everybody he met if they had seen his dog. I felt really wick for oul Gerry, every night for a weeks he went looking for him. Rumours got around that the Brits had nallered him and took him to be trained to sniff out bombs. When we saw Gerry leave his house to go looking, we all scattered to avoid talking to him. It seemed kinder to me to let him think he was now a sniffer dog for the Brits.

The window in my room amplified the sound of the rain and wind making it sound much worser than it was. I said worser deliberately to defy Mum. We were only two storeys up compared to the big flats. The word amplified made me sad and angry as well. It was a Blackie word, another he had taught me. I needed to think about other things.

I would normally get up right away otherwise I would find reasons not to. This morning I really didn't want to go out, for a lot of reasons that clotted my mind and made me angry and upset with others, but mainly I despised myself.

I got up and went to the toilet, standing squarely on the bathmat to avoid the sticky linoleum that looked like black and white tiles. I didn't want my socks dirty or wet. I'd asked mum why we didn't have a carpet down which would be nice and warm and she said, "what, with two men in the house, no fear". I didn't understand her answer, but was really happy she said two men in the house.

I peed, and at the same time made faces in the mirror to wake myself up. I knew mum was up already too. I heard her lacquering her hair in the spare room. She would put her make-up on in there and then come down to the kitchen and have a cup of tea. I washed my hands and face and raced back to my room. I didn't want to see mum this morning but I would have to. I'd probably have to do a message for Aunt Greta and then mum would want to tell me again what I had to do if I was to go to the match.

Before I left for work, I would kneel at my bed to say the Our Father, the Hail Mary and one to my Guardian Angel. It was so I didn't get shot by the Brits or Peelers or captured by the Orangies. But the last couple of mornings my anger and upset at mum and dad and everything around the bony and Blackie wouldn't allow me to. It was the guilt I felt about Blackie and the bonfire that made it impossible for me to talk to God, who knew exactly what I had done. And he knew too I wasn't really sorry for some of it and was right in other things. That was the worst part. Why did I always have to apologise? Nobody ever said sorry for 'Dirty Joe'ing' me. Everything was changing, I could feel it. I didn't know why it was and I didn't like it at all.

I thought better of it after hearing those dog sounds outside and said my prayer to my Guardian Angel to protect me from Dylan the Dalmatian devil dog just in case he had returned. I would take my big torch with me. It was a good ten inches of metal and would, with the prayer I said, protect me.

I dressed into my jeans and put on my monkey boots, not knowing if it was the effort of tying up my laces or my resentment at them was making my face redden and heat up. I had two pairs of socks already on me in bed for heat and it made getting up and out a lot quicker. I put my check shirt on over my vest and asked again the question making my blood boil: how could they take away my property, stuff that I had bought with my own money? It was the money I earned from my paper round where I had to get up at all hours of the morning and in all kinds of weather. Mum had even said so to Mrs Boyd when she asked what I was up to these days as her son, Gerald, who was a creep and a snob, had just passed some exam in his piano lessons.

So what, he'll be another Gilbert O'Sullivan or most likely Liberace than God forbid, Elton John, who was brill. Frig him, he picked his nose and ate it when he thought no-one was looking. So mum knew exactly what I had to do to get my money and not forgetting the heart and cancer pools on a Friday evening, which covered the whole area, not just a small part like my paper round.

So how could she do it, listen to Da and him saying them things about my records. Something somebody told him in the pub about the bands I liked and the records I spent my money on, my money. I was treated like I'd bought a nudie book or something terrible like that. It was really horrible and unfair, listening to someone slag off AC/DC and Led Zeppelin and great bands like that. All because of some alco in the pub, who didn't know a thing about them and wouldn't know Robert Plant from Englebert Humperdick, the glipe.

You could just hear him slabbering in the bar, aye themin's are all Satanists, they are. All of them, they worship the Devil so they do. And then Da comes in, half bleutered no doubt; telling mum what that alco told him. Some bloody alco who couldn't even spell AC/DC. That was a good line. I would tell Blackie that one. I stopped breathing, my face reddening again. I couldn't tell Blackie. I couldn't speak to him again not after what I had done. I had to move, get out and away from the images from the night before. I got my watch and key to the house from my desk of drawers and put the big ceiling light on before switching off the lamp and ran from the room. I went down the staircase quietly as I could manage. I could hear mum humming a tune in the spare room where she got ready for work. I couldn't make out, but I was sure it wasn't AD/DC or Led Zeppelin.

I got into the kitchen and filled the kettle with water, placed it on the stove and lit the pilot light with the new electronic lighter we got. I put in two rounds of white bread to toast. I would have cereal with plenty of milk to strengthen my bones and hopefully add some weight. I always had my real breakfast after I got back. Sausages, scrambled eggs, two New Lodge steaks, the tasty round vegetable rolls all with four rounds of buttered toast. That would keep me fed for the bus journey to the match. I blew on the bowl I took from the cupboard and shook out the cornflakes and thanked the lord there was more than enough milk for a full bowl and more than enough left for the tea for me and mums tea. I would get milk and bread on my way back from work, probably in Thompsons below Artillery youth club. I always finished my round at Artillery House; it was the tallest of the flats in the New Lodge, seventeen storeys high. But I didn't like it as it was too close to North Queen Street and the Coppers End gang and then you had Tigers Bay nearby as your neighbour.

I needed to leave for 6.30 so I would be in Issacs well before seven so I could avoid Teddy dicknose, who was the true son of a punctured frenchie, not anyone else. I hated him, he was a complete bastard. He had hit me from the side across my nose. We were all slagging him off one night in our place beside the flat entrance doors. But it was me he came after when he found out. How he found out was a bloody mystery to me.

He probably came after me because I did good impressions of people. I was always doing people from T.V. to make Mum laugh. I crunched down hard on my cornflakes, sitting at the small table covered in the plastic sheet with yellow flowers on it. The pain in my jaw from the punch was now a dull pain, not like the sharp, jabbing pain that went round my entire jaw. I squeezed my biceps as hard as I could, hoping to get them bigger and bigger. Hoping one day they would be strong and big enough to break Teddy arsehole's face. They were quite hard, but small, like the rest of me.

The toast popped up, I liked it to cool down rather than have it squishy and get the butter on my hands. I had to wash my hands a hundred times a day with the papers and the pools. Mum had given me some cream from her stock she kept in the spare room for her other job; selling beauty products door to door. She called it beauty consultation. A lot of the time she didn't have to go door to door, the women would come to her, especially the younger women. They really liked the stuff she sold and they could pay it off weekly. Mum wore an awful lot of it herself and she looked and smelled class. She called it advertising her wares. It must be working because she had plenty of customers. And a lot of older girls knew my name and said hello to me in front of the lads which made them dead jealous.

Mum wasn't like most of the mums in the area I liked to think. I knew she wasn't. Most of them mums looked all wrinkled and fatter around the boobs and the bums. Their hair was always brushed up or covered in scarves. They wore slippers and big, long coats and dark tan stockings and all of them all smoked and talked a lot to each other in groups. They all had holy medals and crosses and never seemed to go anywhere except to mass or bingo. They all had jobs around the area or in The Royal Victoria hospital.

Mum worked in town and went out into town on Saturdays after work. She was class that way. I dreamed to have a wife like that one day and I had the girl already fixed in my mind.

I heard mum leaving the spare room, humming a song. It wasn't Satanist song of course. She would go into the bathroom and look in the mirror. That was her final act in getting ready. I had watched mum get ready before on one of the rare occasions she went out with da. It was to the pictures. She told me what she was going to wear: a purple dress, silver choker, mulberry eye shadow with black mascara and peach blusher. All from the stock she sold from the house. Da was wearing mostly Blue Stratos and she laughed. I laughed too, although I didn't know what at. I asked what they were going to watch. She said Kramer versus Kramer, it had the wonderful Meryl Streep in it. Da wanted to see the Deer Hunter not some soppy love story. I would be watching Nancy Drew then The Rockford Files and Match of The Day as mum said they'd be home before eleven.

Mum would have put her make-up on and then the hair lacquer on in the spare room in front of a full length mirror that I only liked looking at myself at when it was at an angle. I preferred to look at myself that way.

She would come down in minutes to the kitchen and have a cup of tea, sometimes with a piece of toast. I didn't want to see mum this morning but I probably would have to. I'd probably have to do a message for Aunt Greta, and mum would want to tell me again what I had to do if I wanted to go to the match. It was going to be another lecture, but I had to take it if I was to get to that match.

I didn't like to think about Da right now, because I felt a hot, angry rage about what he'd done. I could hear Blackie telling me that most of the songs people liked, the ones in the top forty, were all about sex anyway. Like when they sang about funk all night, or I want to rock with you all night, it was about sex all night. They were all sex mad and they're telling us we are devil worshippers for listening to great rock music.

I ate my toast at the table with my tea cooling beside me arm. I held the cup from time to time to feel some warmth as the kitchen was getting cold. I wanted to listen to the radio but da had come in half-snattered so he'd be hung over and needing his sleep. He had overtime in the warehouse in the morning so he'd be up early enough. Even when I promised to play it really low Mum wasn't having any of it. They don't play Satanists on radio one sure. She told me not to be so sarky and behave or otherwise. Otherwise in the last week meant if I didn't behave I wouldn't be going to no match.

I had finished my first round of toast and broke in half the multi vitamin I took every morning to make it easier to swallow. As I gulped it down, I heard mum come down the stairs as quietly as she could in her shoes and uniform. I could be in Issacs in five minutes so I waited for mum to come in and tell me what messages I had to get for Aunt Greta. And also to get the lecture about being safe, staying with Mr Hale and Mr McAlea and not giving any back cheek to them or anyone else for that matter.

I held the mug of tea for warmth, really wanting mum and me to be friends again. I really needed her at the moment, but her siding with Da really made me mad with her. But I had too many battles on my hand I had too many fronts opened up and I couldn't cope with another fight right now. I was fed up to the back teeth with everything. I couldn't wait to get out on my round and be with myself out in the open air doing something. I even wanted to see the boys in the shop who could be a right pain in the arse, but could be a good laugh as well. They were younger than me by about two years. Me, Dada and Peanut were the older boys with a couple of years of paper delivery experience under our belts.

We got the best rounds, the easier ones so-called, not for us the long streets of Spamount, Stratheden, Upper Meadow or North Queen street and well clear of Sheridan flats. Those streets had nasty, snarly barking dogs and some of the owners weren't much better, ha ha ha. I could be dead funny when I wanted. That's what Wholenut told me when it was just him and me at the bottom of the flats. It was a real winter night rain, some sleet and we were backed in against the alcove at the bottom near the doors. No-one was about and I didn't really know what to say to him. I think he really wanted to be my mate. But I had best mates already and you had to keep them. So I started slagging everyone off using my impressions of people and Wholenut thought the it was hilarious. I could be guilty of showing off at times, but everyone was.

I had placed the loose change in my Harrington hanging up on the coat rack in the hall. I normally got a ten pence mix up from Sheila, Issac's wife, who was really nice and had a nice sounding voice that came from the South somewhere. I'd only ever been to Butlins in Mosney, which was in the South. The ones from there that I met seemed nice. But all we ever said about them was that they were almost as bad as the Brits, the Peelers and even Orangies. We sang a song that told them to 'take it down from the mast Irish traitors'. It was because it was 'the flag we republicans claim'. So the song went. We sang it would never belong to free-staters. They were the people who lived in the South. I didn't know what that song really meant and I was heart feared to ask anyone. They might start to think I was one of the free-staters or a friend to them.

I carried enough to get myself a can of coke and a Mars bar or Marathon. The mix up helped keep your mouth wet. My gloves were in the coat not for the cold but the bloody ink that got all over your hands and took ages to get off. More washing of my hands and the skin was cracking on the fingertips. I heard Blackie saying the Harrington was really called a Baracuda Jacket but got the name Harrington from an actor who was first to wear it on T.V. in something called Peyton Place. I have no idea where Blackie gets his information. But I was set on getting back in with him even if it meant buying him a poxy Yes or Rush record. Maybe Genesis or that group he was talking about last week, Joy Divison. I'd never heard tell of them. Blackie's taste in music had changed, the bands he was into were getting weirder and weirder. But I knew it was the best way to say I was really sorry. And I was. I felt really kat about what I did. I had Dirty Joe'd him and I knew more than anybody how that felt.

I thought about the shop on purpose because it cheered me up for some reason. Issac was a crabby old sod with big trousers that didn't fit him around the waist or legs. The trousers were always too short showing off his skinny ankles, where he always wore blue or black socks. He had tiny, small feet that looked too small to keep him and his big belly standing up straight. He was always complaining about the price of things and our wages being too high. We all told him they weren't enough boys and the rounds were getting bigger and the papers were costing more and we were getting pelters from the customers.

We also told him we couldn't read his handwriting or make out his '4's' and his '6's' because they looked like '8's'. He called us a 'bunch of illiterates and ingrates', two words we had to look up in the dictionary. When Squigs found out what they meant, he threatened Issac with a strike. Issac then said we were a bunch of Bolshies, we had no idea what that meant either, but it couldn't be good. Then he went too far and called us a bunch of Stickies and he would get the Provies in to sort us all out. That's when it became an all-out war, with Squigs squaring up to Issac telling him to take back what he called us. It was like David and Goliath; when you saw Squigs no bigger than me and Issac who was like six feet and really big in a fat way.

I had to hand it to Squigs, he was afraid of nobody. People said it was because he lived with five sisters who tortured and bate the life out of him. They were nightmares, you didn't mess with them. Really rough and could bate the bag outta any fella their size, no messing.

It got so bad for him he had to join the Holy Family boxing club to protect himself from them. And now he was being talked about as a future Ulster champion at his weight. I wished I was more like him in the bravery department, but not with having all them sisters. That would be a real nightmare.

Sheila stepped in with that big smile of hers and said she'd write out the addresses on the papers from then on. Issac grumbled that was alright but wanted us in earlier by quarter of an hour and anyone late two days in a row would be out the door. He was as a good as his word when a week later he sacked Fungus for that exact same reason. We were all happy about that. Fungus was a stinker, his whole family was. The only thing that didn't make him an Onion was that there was only five in the family, Dada said. He also said their house had to be evacuated once when a bar of soap was put through their letter box. We all laughed and Fungus ran out of the shop crying his lamps out. Issac was as happy as us with Fungus gone, the not so phantom raspberry blower he called him. It was a lousy thing to do to anyone, let off and never let on, even though Issac was a big farter as well and sometimes blamed Fungus when he had released a SBD, a silent but deadly one in the shop. We all knew that. He'd have to find a new sucker to blame it on now.

Mum would be in the kitchen very shortly, she'd been fixing her hair, looking herself up and down in that uniform for work which made her look like a nurse, if it weren't for the make-up and smell of perfume and hair lacquer. It was Elnett she used and sold in the area. There was Blasé and Max Factor Metallic Atomiser which had blue stars on it and her other big seller was Mulberry eye shadow. I knew all this because mum let me help her stack and count what was in the boxes she brought home. She let me tot up her figures and confirm them on my own calculator. She used her own. It was silly she said, but she felt better if we did our own adding up on our own calculators. She let me double check her figures and tote up what was paid and what was owed in the big red ledger book that had loads of lines on the pages. Mum was good at figures and helped me with arithmetic in my schoolwork. I had to work extra hard for things like sums and equations to sink into my head.

She used a thick jotter that had graph paper as it was best for sums and columns and stuff, so I got one from Easons in Royal Avenue to count my change and put in the amounts. I collected my change in the Roses sweetie tin that had a slot cut in the lid. Total amount from last night £9.46. I had the number of comics, 107, marbles, 203 and records, 31 LP's and 29 singles. Mum had around £30 in stock in the spare room more of course at Christmas, that's when mum got me a bottle of Denim in a small wee bottle with a black top filled with yellow liquid that smelt really strong for about the first ten minutes. Christmas was brill, I really looked forward to new clothes, a new record and books like, Billy Bunter, The Hardy Boys and Nancy Drew mysteries. Last Christmas I bought her a bottle of Cot'y L'aiment and da got a bottle of Denim. This Christmas coming, I know it was miles and miles away, I wasn't going to spend so much on mum and even less on me da.

"Morning my wee man, and how are you this fine morning?" Mum was cheerful and breathing out a fresh mint breath from brushing her teeth. She walked in and went over to the kettle and brought it over to the taps and began filling it up with water. I didn't say a thing. I was still angry with her for siding with da. I was for giving up saving to buy the Blue Raleigh Racer with ten speed gears in McGarveys and packing my bags and running away to Mosney to get a job as a redcoat working for Tara House. I wasn't telling her I'd given up the dream of saving up and when I got older and got a job, I'd get us a house up the Antrim Road either. Probably best job for me was a postie as I knew the area dead well and all the different letter boxes and where the bad dogs and even worse people lived. I was going to save up and by a house up the Antrim Road for myself now, where there was trees and front gardens and no riots and no Teddy boakface, but I wouldn't say that word with mum in the room.

"Are you still sulking young man?" She asked, nowhere near as cheerful now. "You know if the wind catches that face."

"No". I said, knowing full well that she knew that I was. I was going to tell her if I'm listening to Satanists, then she was listening to sex maniacs and she didn't even know it. Except for Marc Bolan and T.Rex because no-one knew what the hell he was on about. She went to the larder to see if we needed anything in and I would have to go and get it. All her singers sang about was sex, having it, losing it and wanting it back. Blackie had pointed it all out and when we listened to some songs on the radio I knew he was completely right. She blew out a big breath that made her sound really tired, making me feel bad.

"Do we need anything?" I asked because I felt a bit bad for being cross with her. I knew she was tired because I heard her and Da talking in the bedroom very late last night.

"Not really". She said in a long voice as she scoured the larder looking for something we didn't have in. "Just the usual, milk and bread." She sighed like she was really tired and I felt terrible for sulking with her. "We have the meat in for Sunday and the soup is ready. We'll have that chicken breast, the legs are in for the soup. We love that soup Dad makes don't we?" She said without looking round from the larder. She sounded really tired and I don't think she meant what she said. Mum was no way a Fanny Craddock. I had to admit Da was the better cook. "At least your father is making dinner tomorrow, eh son?" She said with a wide smile examining the larder again. She had tiny teeth like child's teeth. I thought they were cute. I stared at the back of her head and her nice brown hair that was all shiny and straight. The one thing Da was really good at, Sunday dinners. His vegetable soup and his brisket with turnip were the bees knees. His dinners were really great, fair dues to him.

I always liked the way she called me son so I said "I'll get them right after work."

I was told to get a bap, not too black, his mum cautioned; sometimes the crust was practically burnt and it stuck to the roof of your mouth for ages and your teeth had black bits which you had to brush off with a toothbrush. At that time of the morning he would have a large selection to choose from. "And get the Mirror" she called after me, "there should be enough money there". "Yes mum", even if there wasn't I would buy it with my own money. I raced down the seven hills that stooped and sloped its gentle decline, until it stopped abruptly yards short of the wall marking the start of Artillery House. It was the tallest of the seven tower blocks that dominated the area. Everyone was in a distinct neighbourhood. Churchill House was the farthest from his house and the one which I rarely visited and didn't know anyone who lived there. I looked upon it like you would an alien landscape, with alien names and all the potential dangers from the alien inhabitants.

Then there was Alanbrooke, Alexander and Dill Houses clustered together. Alexander would remain in my mind because of the feud between the Provie side of the IRA and the other, 'the stickies'; they were commies who didn't go to church and didn't even believe in God. We were told by bigger lads they had surrendered years ago and there was only a few left in New Lodge. We sang "take it down from the mast Irish traitors" at them and at the people in the free state. I had read all the writing on the walls of the staircases inside the flats, stopping at times to read who was gonna get shot next, how the latest gang 'Ruled OK' or how it was to be 'better dead than red'. I'd take any colour rather that being tatty bread. And of course, the things Genghis wrote about all the birds he bucked.

The Stickies didn''t put pins through their Lilies to attach to their coat lapels for Easter. Their parade was much smaller than the Provies' one. The Provie one was massive, they marched up to the Falls cemetery with loads of bands and flags and the men and even the women looked class in their sunglasses and masks and the leather gloves and jackets. I only ever got as far as the bottom of the New Lodge, because mum would never allow me to go to anywhere outside the area.

Any further and you were having to pass through Coppers End and The Moffat street gangs territory. And if that wasn't scary enough you had Unity Walk then the Shankill. I would have to bring out Iain Craig, my alter ego who would come to his rescue in case I was ever captured by the Orangies. I had learnt The Sash off by heart and memorised what King William had said before the battle of the Boyne, 'let ambition fire thy mind'. I had practised to pronounce my H's just like them.

She made a small laugh and touched the top of my head as she went past to get something from the bread bin. "I'll leave the money on the mantle, my wee man." She said still smiling. She stood looking at the wall can opener. "Mind when your opening cans with that son, I think it needs tightening." She placed her hand on it. "Doesn't feel that secure, must get your dad to look at it. Perhaps he could get us a new one. This ones been up for yonks." She said going to the bread bin to get one of the scones she would be taking to work. She cut it in half and I could see the currents that I didn't like. "Aunt Greta, I'll leave you out the money for your Aunt Greta's milk, her bap, ciggies and the paper".

I was going to tell her I had the money but I hadn't completely forgiven her yet. So I let her use her own money. I must have pulled a face and didn't realise because mum said. "Here, and you can cut that out. Your Aunt Greta dotes on you and she's been plenty generous. So less of the face young man. It doesn't suit you." she said, but not in an angry way.

That's when I thought it the best time to apologise and make the peace so I didn't have another war on my hands. "I'll get them for Aunt Greta and bring them round to her mum. No worries."

"Thank you, son" She said in a weary voice. "Your Aunt Greta hasn't been in the best of health" Mum said, and drank from her cup with milky tea. And I wished then she had never met Da in that Romano's ballroom with some band called Amen Corner playing. Mum liked to tell me they were number one in the charts when they played their song in Romano's. Some sex maniac song, no doubt I thought. What did she see in him, the man who gave me his skinny girl arms and legs, baldy hair probably when I'm a lot older and with sticky out ears. I boiled again with resentment and raged at my life. I could have told mum about last week when he was supposed to take me to the Waterworks on Saturday lunchtime, but didn't. Instead he took me into the bookies on a day when the sun was splitting the trees. Inside the bookies it was dark, smelly and full of smoke and oul lads who stank of smoke and BO and worse.

Mum left the kitchen with the cup in her hand. I could tell from the noise she was in the living room. I concentrated on the last round of toast as I heard her coming nearer. She came into the kitchen and stood at the table with her hands behind her back and smiling. She said nothing, she just smiled and it made me laugh out. "What? What are you smiling at mum?"

"You know you really are the sugar in my tea" She said, with the smile still etched across her mouth.

"Mum, c'mon." I used the moany voice I had when I was fed up but didn't want to start an argument.

"It's come on, if you have to use the expression. None of that guttersnipe talk in this house, you know that."

"I'm sorry, I know." I knew it only too well. She was always telling me off for what she called lazy and ignorant talk. Like fousand, it's thousand she would scold me and pronounce it in a very long way. It's not hing, its thing. It's not windy its window. She was raging with me the time I caught her out saying tarl instead of towel when she asked me to fetch one from the spare room. I pointed out she already had a tarl on her head. She laughed when I said that.

"Right, my little Charles Atlas. Oh God, I'm sorry love." She apologised when she saw the look of wrinkled consternation registered on my face. "Oh, you don't like that, I forgot son, sorry, but you work so hard on building yourself up, with your Bullworker and weights and that." And she gave me slight hug of my arms. "I'm really proud of you for that. I am." She said as if I had said I didn't believe her. "Keep it up, but try not to kill or injure yourself. Girls like brains more that brawn and they like manners more than brains. Anyway, I have something for you." She left the kitchen and I could hear her in the living room. She came back to the kitchen and went 'Ta dah!' loudly, like she was a magician's assistant and took from whatever was behind her back and held them in front of me.

There they were. Angus standing his mouth and shirt covered in fake blood and beside it was the Led Zep album they were all dressed like world war one pilots.

"I'm getting them back?" I stammered. I actually did stammer. A small tremble of excitement made me. I was really shocked. Once mum made her mind on things she never changed it. "Does Da know? Did he say anything? " I don't even know why I asked about him.

"Your dad had a change of heart and thought it was wrong to take them off you and he didn't really believe what he was told anyway."

"Why'd he say it for then?" I asked because I was really upset and really confused. I held the albums and set them down on the table.

"You have to admit he has a point. I mean this album here is called Highway to Hell and there's a guitar sticking in his belly with blood everywhere and you have songs like 'Hell ain't a bad place to be' and here," she said running her finger down the back cover, "Rock and Roll damnation. Good lord how do you listen to this? If there is music in hell, this'll be it. No doubt." She said.

"But it's just a bit of fun, you know it's not real." I protested, as I thought she was about to change her mind as she stared at the front cover. I liked the Atlantic record label the album was on as the colours on the record were green white and orange. I was so relieved when she set them down on the table. I moved my arm slowly towards them and rested it there to hide the picture on the cover.

I could never understand why he did the things he did at times. He could be a real bullroot. Like that time I was supposed to go to The Waterworks to catch spricks. You were in town with Aunt Greta and Teresa Rabb, your best friend from work. I felt really stupid in the bookies with my yellow net at the end of the bamboo stick and my glass jam jar with the lid on it. All the men were talking and got really excited when the man on the T.V. was talking very quickly as the horses raced one another. There was shouts and bad names shouted and then the big man with the white shirt and black braces who looked a bit like Issac, with a big belly and skinny ankles and tiny feet; he was writing on a big blackboard and that reminded me of school so I wasn't happy at all.

Some man came up to da and asked if he had the name of some bulbs. Da shushed him and took him over to a wall near the door and then they talked. Da came back and gave three ten pence pieces to go out and get a can of something and some crisps. I asked him what time we were going to the Waterworks but he didn't answer. When I came back from the shop, Da was laughing and cheering. He had won money on a horse called Kestrel Kling and the man who asked him for bulbs then asked him for the lend of a pound. I saw da crunch up a pound note he got from his coat pocket and hand it to the man and told him he wanted it back on Monday mind, that's when he would get him the 'you know what' he said.

'Your da's one jammy blurt, if he fell into the Lagan he'd come out with a Salmon in his mouth. He's some operator, I'll give him that." Then the smelly aul bullroot winked at me with his wrinkly eye. I sat all afternoon in there, looking out the window slits at the sunshine on the buildings across the road. I was nearly asleep on the floor in the corner beside an old friendly dog when an old man who had come in with Da told me to 'get up, we were heading home'. I was to say nothing about the bookies and he gave me fifty pence piece to 'seal the deal' he said.

"He did it out of the best of intentions. He really did son. But we know you are a good boy. You work hard at school and with your jobs and you help a lot around the house. That's good enough for us." My brain was still in that smelly old bookies when Mum ruffled my hair and leaned down to kiss my head, which was free of nits after Friday nit night last night.

The newspaper was spread out on the floor on the pages you never needed and the steel comb tearing down my scalp ploughing into my head like a tractor in a field. All I could think was that this was the night that was going to make me a wingnut for definite. The little nits would hit the paper. The only way to really see them was with the big light on in the ceiling. You could see tiny bits of blood in their bodies and you used the handle of the comb to snap the little buggers to death with a tiny crack. Thank God they were getting less and less. In some houses they had nits, fleas and ringworm. Jesus, I shuddered.

"Oh, and don't forget those items, your dad has left out in the hall, remember hon."

"I know. I won't forget them. I've to go over to Mister McCollams with them." I said brightly, I was so relieved and happy to have my albums I would've agreed to anything she asked.

"Right my wee man, before I leave. You know what I'm going to say don't you?"

"Yes." I said in a way that did not please mum. I said it like I was sick sore and tired of the last couple of days. If I'd known I'd get this much grief I wouldn't have gone to the stupid bloody match.

"This is important. I want you to listen up and pay attention. Are you listening to me young man?"

I nodded. I was dead tired of being told the same thing again and again. But this was important if I was to get to the match. Mum was deadly serious about it.

"Right." She said, wiping herself down and looking at her shoes her feet close together. "Glad we have that business out of the way." She leaned in a bit, getting a wee bit closer to me. "I want you to promise me that you're going to meet with Mister Hale and Mister McAlea outside that club and you're to travel with them to the match and back again. You're to stay with them at the match and not lose sight of them. They have both kindly agreed to take you. They will tell me if you mess about and you know what that'll mean. Don't you?" She said and she was deadly serious, she wasn't smiling at all.

"I know." I said quietly.

"And what is that?" Mum asked leaning down her face inches from my own.

"I'll never get to another match." I said in a low voice letting her know I was not happy being treated like a baby.

"Exactly. And I mean it. You won't get to another match, not while you're under this roof. And that, my young man, is a promise." She had her serious voice on, the real mum one that was serious and full of threat.

"Mum, I won't mess about. Honest. Swear to God and shame the Devil." I told her, to get her to stop badgering me and to let her know I would do as she bid. I mean, did I have a bloody choice? And I hated that tone of voice when she was really serious about being a mum and not my best mate.

"Right," Mum said, standing up straight, "we'll leave it at that. Don't let me or those two gentlemen down and most importantly. Don't let yourself down. Okay?"

"Yes." I had to play it straight with mum. I couldn't mess about, this was deadly serious.

Mum went back into the hall where she would put on her coat, fix herself up for the outside and then she would say a wee prayer at the sacred heart and open the door from where she would say, loud enough for me to hear whether I was in the kitchen or the living room, "Oh, listen, my songs come on the radio, can you believe it and I have to go." She sounded really disappointed as I could make out the song coming from the living room on our Waltham record and cassette player. "Oh, I love this song" and she began singing "come up and see me, make me smil-l-l-l-le." She was swaying to the music, damn, "I have to go. Oh, the money for Greta's messages are on the mantelpiece love."

"Okay, right. I've to scoot. So hon," she said, I looked up knowing exactly what was coming next. "See you later alligator" she shouted from the hall. And she blew me a kiss which I always caught and placed in my trouser pocket.

And I would always say back. "See ya around crocodile." I heard her still singing that song as she closed the door and walked past the window of the kitchen waving in. I waved back smiling that she was happy on her way to work.

I got up and went into the living room and turned up the radio, not by much as I didn't want Da getting up and coming down slabbering about the noise. In fact I wanted to get out on my round without seeing or hearing him at all. I went over to the small window where the TV sat and pulled aside the lace curtain, watching mum walk past the Grotto touching the stone from Knock where Our Lady had appeared to someone and blessing herself. I did it every time I had cause to pass the Grotto and would always put something into the wee money box above the blessed stone. I always gave the most valuable coin be it a two pence or a five. Once I got caught out with a fifty pence piece and searched all my pockets and thanked God I found ten pence to put in.

Mum walked down the paved path towards Victoria and past Alanbrooke Flats towards the Reccy, which had been the big recreational hall the Brits in the past used as a gymnasium; and then she'd be gone from my sight. It was lovely to keep a watch on her without her knowing. I felt like her Guardian Angel for those moments and a bonus this morning was seeing her with her music on in the background. It actually was a good song. The instrumental bit was a really good piece of guitar like it was Spanish or something. It made the heart soar. A good piece of music like that always made me feel closer to God. It was like a language, a prayer in itself. So how could it be Devil worship? I should have said that and how it made me feel inside. She disappeared from view as she walked the path separated the two sets of trees either side and I felt like I had fallen through a trap door into a well of sadness and loss. I had to think of something happy. I thought about mum's music.

Mum loved that song that had just finished on the radio. She also loved ABBA and Roxy Music, because of the lead singer who reminded me of a fox. She loved The Carpenters, especially the girl singer. She had one album I really liked. It was from Bob Seegers and The Silver Bullet Band. It was really rocky. It was called 'Stranger In Town' and had really cool songs like 'Old time rock and roll'. Mum always played the songs 'Still the same' and 'We've got tonight' to death and I got a real sickener of them.

She also had a Rod Stewart album that had that stupid Sailing song mum loved to play. She watched crappy shows like Dallas and weirdly the Sunday politics show presented by a sickly looking man called Brian Walden who talked like he had marbles in his mouth. I hated politics it was so boring and I hated him, he talked more that the guests. He got on my wick. But when it ended I heard the best music I had ever heard on a TV show ever. It was really heavy rock, mum went to turn it round but I wanted to hear it so she went in to make herself a cup of tea. I listened hoping they would say who it was or tell me at the end of the credits. Nothing. I rifled through the Radio Times down in Marshalls Bookshop after mass the following Sunday. Nothing. I had to ask someone, I needed to know who had made such a great sound.

That guy was Frank Munroe, known to all as Enroe. He knew more about rock music than Blackie even, he lived in Templar House on the third floor. I didn't know him only to nod to or say alright to as walked past. He seemed friendly, like you'd expect of a hippie. He wore flares and check shirts with a waistcoat and had longish dark Curley hair and was always walking into town and coming back with records. I planned to accidently on purpose, bump into him next time he went into town.

It turned out I met Enroe on my paper round, shortly after hearing the song on that programme. He was leaving for work and was wearing a long parker jacket with overalls and big black safety boots. They must've been steel toe cappers. I would love a pair so I could kick Teddy fanny face's head in. I would've thought he would have gone to work in a record shop or even Alcatraz or Just books where all the hippies went. I said hello as he closed his front door behind him. Then I summoned up the nerve to ask him if had ever seen the politics show on Sunday. Only it's the music at the end of it I want to know about, I said quickly. I worried I had offended him in some way from the look he gave me. He had a long nose that seemed to point in towards his mouth and crooked teeth but he had a kind face and gentle voice. He seemed to be always nodding his head like he was listening to music in his head all the time.

"Ahh," he said, "yeah that's a band called Mountain, man. Great track." He placed his hand over his long, pointed chin. I saw his fingernails were spotless clean, like a woman's.

I didn't know if he meant the band was called Mountain Man or not. I liked the way the rockers called the songs tracks, Duffer did it too. He was well into his music and he knew Enroe I saw them talking to each other a couple of times most likely about tracks.

"Yeah, Mountain. Good tune. The albums called Nantucket Sleighride." He stood with his hands in his pockets. "You're into your music, good man." He gave me sly smile and I felt well made up, plus he called me man like I was one of them who knew their music.

"Oh yeah, I love AC/DC, UFO, Zeppelin, Purple, stuff like that." I liked the way he didn't call me kid at all. Plus I was conscious to say it the way music people talked about bands. I didn't want to say I liked Krokus or Preying Mantis or even Kiss. I stuck to the classics.

"You like the Zep? Good man!" he said again. He smiled showing up his crooked front tooth in the bottom row of teeth. "I'm heading to see them at Knebworth in August." He said like it wasn't anything brilliant. "Got the support acts rhymed off to a tee." He thought for a moment. "They are, The New Barbarians, which is really Keith Richards and Ronnie Wood." I loved it that he didn't try to explain to me who they were. "Southside Johnny and The Ashbury Dukes, Todd Rundgren, Fairport Convention, man, what a line-up." He said to himself as he checked them all off nodding his head.

"You're going?" I paused and had no idea how to continue my sentence. "To see Led Zeppelin?" I yammered on in disbelief, scundered that I sounded so breathless with shock and admiration. I felt my cool stock losing value. I felt a real tingle of excitement give birth in my stomach. I couldn't believe someone from our area was going to see the greatest rock band that ever was. No way, it couldn't be. Someone from the road? From this hell hole? I didn't like thinking it, but maybe he was just messing me about because I was way younger.

"Yep. I got to go. Talk is they're going to split after this gig." He said simply like it wasn't the biggest deal ever. "I'm heading to see the Pope too when he comes." He smiled and I saw his bottom two teeth were crooked;

one fell over the other but they were dead small and you didn't notice until you were up close. "Two very different gigs, eh?" He laughed at his joke. I suppose I laughed too, just to be nice and keep in with him. I usually did with people, so they'd like me.

There you go mum, I thought, a Zep fan who loves the Pope. How could he be a Satanist then? I thought in triumph.

"Gotta get to work bro. Gotta earn the funds for those gigs. Ciao."

"Yeah, okay sure." I said, not knowing what to say next. I was worried I might say something stupid and look uncool in front of him. So I left it with my lame reply.

"See ya around."

"Yeah, definitely." I said in all earnest. He opened the door to the staircase and disappeared. I was stunned. I had to look and see if I had delivered all the papers on the third floor before moving on. I had, so I followed Enroe out the door onto the staircase to the second floor. Unbelievable, he was going to see them in person, live on stage. I felt sick with envy. He didn't look like much out of his hippie clothes, just like all the other fellas going to work. That's why I hadn't really noticed him before this I supposed.

It was a bit disappointing to tell the truth. I thought he'd be a musician or at least working for Smyths Records or Caroline Music. Even them weirdo places like Alcatraz or Just Books where all the hippies and punks hung out. But he had something none of those wasters could have. What did he mean by split though? They'd go on forever for sure. Too big, too good to ever call it a day. There'd be riots bigger than the ones in the New Lodge. And I would start one! I smiled at the idea of me trying to get the numpties around the road to care that much about an English rock band that they'd go ape shit and start burning buses and vans. He was a great fella, talking to me like he knew me well, like I was his equal. He was an instant favourite of mine now, was old Enroe. I was definitely gonna ask him for a programme of the concert. At least I would have a souvenir. But I felt like I'd just been kicked in the plums. I'd never see them live now. Never.

"Stop picking that willick of yours Junior. Do you think people want to get your snatters on their papers? And you, yes you Scallions, get your hands away from that Sun paper, you mucky little walloper." Issac was in worse form than ever this morning. Though he was right about Scallions; he was a real hornball, who would crawl along the ground where girls were sitting to see up their skirts. It's all he talked about most of the time.

Issac was sweating buckets again and working like a madman behind the small counter, trying to get the papers into the piles for each of the paper rounds. We could never understand how he stayed so fat after all the sweating he did.

Sheila, his wife sat smiling in her corner of the shop. I gave her a small wave as I stepped into the shop and she gave me a little nod. She was so quiet compared to Issac, who was always shouting, always sweating, always on the move in that tiny area behind the counter.

"Listen you lot, that's them papers sorted, get your bags and get on out with yees. Where's the rest of them for the love of God?" Issac let out a loud sigh like he was knackered. "There's only the three of youse in so far."

"It's only a quarter to seven Issac." I said looking at my watch. I was trying to be helpful, but Issac didn't see it like that.

"Only? Only?" He stared at me like he'd swallowed a wasp, "I 'm here from half five." He shouted back all over the shop.

"Issac calm down. It'll be alright." His wife Sheila said and the voice was so calm that you believed everything was going to be alright. Issac grumbled and muttered something only he and his jumper shared and lifted a bag.

"Scallions, you're up. Here's your round, you've an extra customer with this round, wee Barney Higney. He can't get around anymore. Diabetes." Issac said to his wife, who nodded as if she knew all there was to know about the condition. I just knew it had to do with fat people and sugar and Barney was not fat, just the opposite, he was as skinny as a rake. We all called him Barneys boots because of the shiny tan Chelsea boots he always wore.

Scallions grabbed the dirty canvas bags we used for the rounds. They used to be white or cream but were all sorts of colours of smudges of ink and wet ground. "Bout time. I'm bloody Lee Marvin. My belly thinks me throat's been cut for Godsakes." Scallions moaned and rubbed his stomach.

"Shut up Scallions, you're doin' my head in." Issac bit back. "That goes for all of youse. Keep quite and collect your round, and," Issac leaned on the counter and paused, "in an orderly fashion."

"Yawhol!" Scallions shouted. He made a fisted salute and turned to Sheila to order a ten pence mix up.

"Half wit." Issac said after him.

I went over to join Scallions at the counter to get my own mix up. Nobody knew why he got called Scallions, he sure didn't look like one or smell like one and his name was Paddy Burns so there wasn't anything obvious there.

Sheila, who was on her stool, was beside the two bar electric fire with her overcoat on. She didn't have any wrinkles and had a nice, wide smile with really good even white teeth. She was quite slim and all of us who worked for them agreed she was much younger and nicer than Issac was. I asked for a ten pence mix-up and she took one of the bags she had stacked up behind her. Sheila sold the bread, milk, ciggies, firelighters and bundles of sticks, all two or three pence dearer than anywhere else. But there was nowhere else open at that time of the morning for early workers or people coming home from shifts needing milk or bread, matches, even combs and shoelaces.

People said they made a fortune in candles and batteries during the UWC strike in '74. They also said Issac had a contact with a loyalist and that's how it got the stuff. They said he cried when the strike ended. But people round here didn't like you getting on too well. I noticed that with Scone Caldwell, a friend of mine in school; when his ma won money on the pools and it was enough to get a deposit for a house on the Cavehill Road, everyone started calling her a snob, that she thought herself too good now to go to mass in Saint Patrick's. No, it was Saint Gerard's for her now. So I didn't believe Issac would deal with Orangies, even for a thousand quid. Sure the boys would've shot him for that anyhow, no problem.

Sheila sold everything from candles to the little petrol tubes for Zippo lighters. She sold tobacco for pipes, ciggies, hairclips, combs, matches and tins of snuff that made me sneeze lot when we tried it once in Genghis's house.

"Right, who the hell let off again and never let on?" Issac shouted. "Thought we seen the end of that with Fungus. That's mingin' you. You're Abe Lincoln Junior, have you been eating dung again?"

"It wasn't me." Junior, who wore big thick glasses and had the beginnings of a moustache shouted back, his face all red and the veins in his skinny neck were bulging. "That was you. Whoever smelt it, dealt it, remember." He picked up his bag and slung it over his shoulder. He just stood and glared at Issac, who walked the few steps to put a couple of lumps of coal onto the fire.

"I'm afraid it'll reach the flames and take us all out." Issac said.

"What's up with him? He's in a worser mood than usual." I said smiling, nodding over towards Issac.

"Ah wind yer neck in." Junior shouted back over at Issac, who hadn't heard or didn't care, as he just got on with the papers. "Alright squint, listen to that glipe will ya." Junior said. "He's the one letting off. He's being a right head melter today." Junior said quietly to me.

"He's gonna end up in Purdysburn one day alright." I said back to Junior just as quietly. "Yeah. I'm not bad. What's up with you? Any craic?" I asked, smiling, nodding over at Issac.

"Same day, different shit Squint." Junior replied.

I got Squint as a nickname for no real reason. I didn't have one. I knew that I got so wound up I had Mum and Aunt Greta look in my eyes. No. They were certain. "Who's going around saying you have one Son?" Aunt Greta asked, sounding really annoyed and offended. I said 'no-one really just some boy shouted it at me'. "His heads full of sweetie mice, he's the one with the squint" she said, sounding exactly the same.

I still was wound up and Mum knew I was worried and got me over to see Doctor Moore at the health centre at Unity flats. No. "There's no sign of Strabismus or Tropia" he said waving his little tiny torchlight into my eyes. There you had it and all in big medical words. He was a Doctor who had brains to burn. So I wasn't worried by the nickname. I'd be more worried not to have one as that meant that nobody cared enough to give you one.

"So, nah, nuthin much." Junior said sourly, "except he's getting on my wick, he is. If I didn't need the money, I'd be outta here pronto. It's bloody him, he's been letting off SBD's since I got in here. He's just like a big, giant fungus." Junior said back, turning his head to face Issac, zipping up his lumberjack jacket with the big furry collar. I noticed Junior never cursed, not like we did. He was a bit of a holy Joe, an altar boy, who served at ten o'clock mass very Sunday.

"Stop acting the maggot you two. Junior get on out there and start deliveries, get some work done. People want their news on today."

"Bloody hell, wise up Buckets, I'm heading out nye." Junior sounded really fed up and didn't seem to care what he said, even using the nickname we had for Issac. We called him Buckets, for all the sweating he did in the shop and for the size of his big head. His official name was Bucket head.

"For flips sakes." He wheezed out from his lips that had crinkled into a kind of smile. "See ya later Squint. Take it you're away till the match today?" I nodded back that I was. "Good luck. I wouldn't thank you for a ticket to that. Not my thing mate, but good luck anyways."

I said thanks and Junior leaned down and craned his neck to look out and up at the clouds. "Thank the good Lord, it's not going to be baltic and its stopped raining. Me and me da have to go up to a wake for me mum's aunt. I couldn't be bothered, but da says we have to go and show our respects. A great woman she was, so he was tellin' me and I said, here Da, how come it's only good people who ever die, never any of them glipes we're surrounded with? He clipped me round the ear for that." Junior laughed and then he let out loud sigh through his lips as if he were dog tired. He eyed up the outside through the cracked window.

"Junior, will you get the hell out on your round?" Issac shouted.

Junior smiled back at me and waved goodbye to the shop.

I rarely looked at the ground anymore, it always appeared wet anyway. I just prayed it wasn't really windy with the rain, as that was a deadly combination for the paper delivery.

"Stay a glipe, eh Junior? Then, you'll never die." I said and Junior laughed, saying I was right on the money.

"Gotta skeedaddle. Here Squint, at least it's payday eh?" Junior just rolled his eyes in those big, black glasses that made me laugh. He looked like yer man on the TV, Harry Worth. He didn't give a hoot how he looked or how he spoke to people, especially if they gave him gip. He was a bit like Squiggs in that way. In fact, everyone around here was a bit uppiddy. Nobody I knew would take stick off anybody else without slagging back or squaring up to you. Suppose you had to, to survive this place. I did my impressions of people and mimicked them to get the right side of people to get a laugh and make them friendly towards me.

I had paid Sheila the ten pence and made my helloes to Jay, one of the younger ones who was always early and always quiet. Everyone said he was thick as champ, but he delivered to the right houses and on time. Oul Mrs Shaw from up the road said he was the nicest, pleasantness fella on the road. He was putting his wages in his jacket pocket; they were in the small brown envelope that Sheila made out in our names. And she made it out in our proper names. We discovered Jay's real name was Jeffrey, which made us all laugh at the time and put on snooty voices when we called out the name. And we re-nicknamed him Fontolroy after Lord Fontolroy from off the tv. It only lasted about a week as Jay was dead on about it and took it in good heart. That made him one of the boys for definite. Jay said hello back and pulled on his paper bag. They were adjustable to your size which was handy as Jay was only about four feet in his socks.

"Now make sure your pockets are zipped, you don't want your money to fall out. Oh, I wish you would let me keep it here for safe keeping and you can collect it after your round." Sheila said to him. She was so kind and thoughtful especially with the younger, smaller boys who could be a bit scatter-brained and weren't allowed to collect money off the customers. Issac did the collecting around lunchtime if they hadn't come in themselves. I saw him sometimes, charging about the streets as late as three or four him and Sheila driving around the streets, hunting people down for their paper money.

"I have to be home early Mrs King, mum's taking me to town to get new trousers for school from McManus's and she needs the money for them. So I won't lose it, it's zipped up and I won't be opening my pockets 'til I get home."

"Good boy." Sheila smiled at him. It was the most I ever heard Jay say in one sentence. He turned and walked out to do his round without a word.

"For Godsake Sheila, you treat them boys like babies." Issac said, shaking his head and going over closer to the fire. He stood right beside the fire and using the toe of his unpolished brogues, positioned a briquette on the very top of the fire. He stared into the fire and Sheila went back over to her chair and stared at the electric fire she had to keep her warm.

"You're off too then Scallions? Where's your round start?" I asked him, and just at that moment I realised I had never knew the route Scallions took. I had a general idea of the areas he covered. It was quiet enough. No real bother or black spots we called them. They were the places where there were known to be dangerous dogs or regular foot patrols.

"Trainfield," he said his mouth full of midget gems, "then up Upper Meadow and down Spamount, then finish bottom of my street."

I knew his street was Stratheden Street. "Well, all the best wee man. Watch out for them dogs and Brits."

"Will do sure, and the same goes for you. See ya's. Wouldn't wanna be ya's." Scallions said to all and made to leave, though he had to side-step past a young man who was coming into the shop.

"See ya round, if not square." I said back as it seemed the natural reply to his 'see ya.'

I stood aside, leaning against the wall where the paint was peeling off, to let him out the door into the shop. I liked Scallions because he was fun and he was as skinny as me. He looked younger than twelve. And he was a bit too young to be hanging around with us in the flats. His bag's strap, like all the rest of us, had to be tied up in the middle so it didn't drag on the ground. That was another reason to hate the Saint Mal's boys, they were all taller and bigger than us, even some of their first years fucksake. Some fella wearing a black monkey hat came in steeping past Scallions and trapped me between the door and the counter.

"Sorry there kid. Won't be a mo. Here Sheila love. Twenty Player's and a packet of firelighters. Much is the Players?" He asked, looking at the money he had in the cup of his hand. He was wearing big, black workmen's boots and a jacket like Scallions, but the fellas coat was mostly red tartan. I stood with my ten pence mix up delicately balanced in my hand.

"Sixty eight pence." Sheila replied in that quiet, calming sweet accent she had.

"Bloody hell, least Dick Turpin wore a mask." The fella said and he made a sarky laugh and rummaged in boiler suit and took out a pound note. "Gonna have to give these up at this rate" He said. He laughed the same laugh. It was the kind of laugh we all made when you don't want to fall out with someone or get into a fight but you want them to know you thought they were taking the mick out of you. Sheila smiled her smile that never seemed to change and gave his cigs and firelighters, and some change he looked at in a curious way. As soon as he left the shop, Issac planted my bag on the counter.

"Now you, here's your round and your wages." His voice was quieter than usual and his eyes glistened under the bare electric bulb hanging from the ceiling. "Here, before you're off. Just like a word on the QT." Issac looked over at Sheila who sat on her stool without a word. She had just placed another strip of black tape on the ply board stuck to the window to cover the crack on the window sill. A stray brick must have got through the wire mesh that protected all the windows on that side of the riot as it was a favourite place for the Brits to stop and search people. I had never known the window to be without the scar from that stray stone, so that was over two years ago. I looked at Sheila half-expecting her to say something, but she just rubbed the side of her face.

"Yeah Issac, what is it?" I was comfortable talking to him, even though he was a grown-up man and my boss.

"You ever fancy earning a bit more in your rounds? I mean it's no big deal. You know Vicanage? Up near Thorndale? And Adela? It's just we've got some new customers who are wanting their papers delivered, me and Sheila think you're the very man for the job. It's just the type of people who are a wee bit." Issac stood at the counter, his arms folded. "Well, there's like teachers and civil servants, you know people like that up there. Only if you fancy it, mind." Issac was talking to me, like man to man. "Some of them read papers like The Guardian. Bit of a different world really." Issac's small shoulders seemed to get smaller inside his big patterned coat as he finished saying what he said.

I didn't know what to say but yes was on my lips. This was the opportunity to get more money and do more saving. This was great praise from someone like Issac, who was usually telling you off and I felt really made up and proud that they saw me as good enough for the extra responsibility and for 'these type of people'. I really wanted to say yes right away, but I couldn't as mum was always banging on about school work not suffering and if it did she'd stop me doing the round.

And I really wanted to get out before Teddy puke face got to the shop for his round. Teddy cock nose face would be really pissed off too, it would melt his head. I couldn't wait to tell mum. I would tell her I would work twice as hard at school. I really, really wanted this now, when I thought of how it would piss Teddy puss head face off.

"I'll have to speak to my mum, Issac. I'll have to run anything like that past her, because of school." I said, careful of my wording because of what had just occurred.

"Sure, sure. No problem. Right then, get yourself on out and I'll see you Monday." Issac said in a hurry. "Try having a word with your mum over the weekend. Early mind. Try and let me know by Monday."

"I will, I'll speak to her about it. Bye Sheila." I said, and in a much lower voice. Sheila's smile saw me off as I placed the strap of the bag over my shoulder.

Adela! Holy good Jesus, that's right on the border between us and the heel and ankle. The really scary Orangies, that's where the butchers came from. The big union building was there, the one that looked like a Lego block. The AEU, that was it, right beside Saint Machs. Not a chance I was never putting myself in that position again. Ending up getting caught by the Orangies; no way Jose. Mum would never allow me to go there. No chance. I was saved.

I breathed out the scared air that had built up in me when I thought about delivering there. I loved the early mornings at times, especially when it wasn't windy or lashing with rain. It was quiet and peaceful, most of the time and you could get your work done without all the slabbers and wallopers about.

I felt like I owned the whole square as I ran from block to block across the ribbed concrete where there was only three cars parked, freeing up the square for the big football games that usually involved about thirty of us shoving each other around. There were few rules except no bladgers, no toepokers and definitely no Oxfords.

One oul lad who was watching us one day shouted, 'there's no danger of a football match breaking out here'. We all told him to clear off and somebody kicked the ball at him and missed and we all laughed as the oul boy turned and shouted he was the safest one in the square because the ball was aimed at him. That stopped him from getting debagged as two or three of lads were talking about doing it.

None of us had any idea what Issac charged for deliveries. It was like everyone, including the customers had sworn a secret oath not to tell. Issac and Sheila went out on a Saturday evening in his crappy Mazda's1300 saloon, that had been yellow or mustard once. The rust was all along the bottom of the doors. They went out to collect the delivery money and deliver whatever Saturday Nights had been ordered. It had all the football results and match reports and photos from a lot of the local games. I was hoping to be in it tonight with my scarf up in the air in both hands celebrating victory.

The school holidays weren't far off but none of us in the gang was looking forward to them, not after all that had happened. I tried cheering myself up thinking about the money I had saved and the bike I would be getting when I got to saving the fifteen pounds I agreed with mum. I was just shy of three spondoolics.

My first customer, if I didn't take the lift, was Mrs Boyle. She was lovely, always asking about me and my mum and how we were. She had a real smiley face and soft manner about her. She had four kids, two were twins, blonde boys, one thin, one a regular size. They freaked me out a bit because they looked like those kids in that real scary movie, The Village of the Damned and they spoke this weird language to each other as they toddled after their mum to the door. I asked Da about Mrs Boyle's husband. He just called him a waster. He called most people in the area wasters. I wondered why he didn't work harder or more to get us more money and get out of this dump.

With Mum's two jobs and my saving we could get a deposit for a house out of the area in no time, two years top. Mum was earning easy an extra eight, nine quid a week. Her Denman hairbrushes were flying out of the house she said. Mum had loads of stuff in boxes she came home with from work with. All manner of womens perfumes and make-up, I noted them all down in a jotter of graph paper I got from Easons. I counted her stock and how much it cost to buy and what she sold it at. Then I would use my calculator to count up the figures she had already counted up and she would smile at the jotter she held in her hands. 'Another good week, for Kathleen and son limited.' I liked that she didn't use our surname because it would mean involving da in some way.

Mum generally wouldn't have a paper in the house and she didn't watch the news. She said there was no need for bad news to delivered to the house and certainly no need to watch it to be entertained. It was something I felt I understood when she said it. But there was a downside when I got over to the flat; they'd be talking about some bomb or shooting that I had no idea about. That's why I listened a lot, which was a good thing, after all, didn't granda's Hennessy say that's why God gave us two ears but only one mouth.

Mum had loads of toiletries, or cosmetics, I heard her correct me. She didn't like that word. There was No 5 Chanel Paris Eau de Parfum, a yellow liquid, Blackie would understand what that meant in French. The brainiac. Evlon - red lipstick. Nail colour in vamp - nail varnish, deep, dark red. Mason Pearson hairbrush, the ultimate grooming tool, 'how do I look dahling' mum said in a snobby voice, making me laugh. I could write the names but never pronounce them and when mum asked me she would go into a wrinkle of laughter which made me try even harder. She also had Rosebud Salve, which soothes chapped lips, dry skins and minor burns, which mum made me wear in the winter on my lips.

Me and Mum were a great team.

Then I could really ask Francesca out and I could take her up to see my Mum. Francesca and her family lived in one of those three storey houses in Thorndale Avenue. They were big family houses and although they were just across the Antrim Road, it felt like a million miles away from the New Lodge when you were up there. That was another reason not to take on that round, imagine me delivering to her house and she sees me all scruffy, with wet hair and all dirty from the papers.

I wanted Mum to have a real kitchen, a proper sized one. The ones in the flats were bigger than ours. I wanted her to have fully carpeted house with a Hoover vacuum. We'd have a garden at the front and back and a place where we could keep a dog; somewhere where we didn't have to put up old newspapers against the windows to keep the real cold out in the winter. I would stop buying kids stuff, no more comics, no more marbles, Lego or music magazines. I would have to stop buying records too. That's why I had renewed my library card so I could tape the records and get the loan of books like The Hardy Boys and Billy Bunter instead of buying them. I mean a washing machine cost two hundred quid and a house like the one I wanted was around twenty thousand easy. I checked one day in an estate agents window one day when me and mum were in town. They had a house for sale where Jim Johnstone, another schoolmate of mine lived.

He was really good at art and I was good at drawing things that were in front of me. I had gotten really good at drawing my superheroes, but that wasn't enough for Mister Carter. I lacked the imagination, but I could be very good at reproductions. I didn't really care. I wanted a job that could get me and Francesca a house where I could come home after work, walk the dog with her and come back have dinner, she would be a great cook and we would listen to records or go to the pictures down to The Avenue.

After that we'd go to Robinsons or The Europa and I'd have a pint', I'd pay more than the seventy two pence it was. Then we'd go home and watch The Old Grey Whistle Test and The Two Ronnies. I would make the Sunday dinner, I'd get Da to show me. I'd have a car and my own Walkman. I'd have a room with all the weights and a punch bag hanging from the roof like in the boxing clubs. I'd have the best Omega watch I could buy. And if I wanted another Bullworker I'd buy it right off, eighteen pound fifty and save two pound twenty. I'd wear my best brogues and navy cords for Mass on Sunday. Come home to Sunday dinner, to the best record collection I could buy and Francesca, the best wife in the world.

As Mum said I'd need to buck up my ideas about school. I'd need to study harder and try to get a job in the Civil Service or a Bank like Frank and Margaret O'Connor. They lived only three doors down the balcony. They were dead quiet, never went out except to work, Frank always in a suit, shirt and tie and Margaret with nice officey type clothes. I knew I hadn't the brains to be a teacher or an architect and all the engineering jobs were for prods. I fancied being a trainee lawyer after watching The Paperchase on T.V. which was about trainee lawyers at college who solved crimes as well as studying. I thought that would be class.

I walked along the face of Templar. I never used the back entrance, which would've saved me a bit of a walk, because you couldn't see if anyone was behind it or as I thought, because the Brits sometimes used it during raids and riots that the Provies would booby trap it one day. That morning I walked straight into two Saracens. Two very large Saracens that looked like giant metal Rhinos. One sat at the front of the flats, shielding the entrance. I saw a soldier standing at the back doors looking over at me. I carried on walking, unable to ignore his "good morning". I said it back and felt kat for talking to 'the enemy'.

I had seen this before, with a new shift of soldiers to man the look-out posts or when they were getting supplies. Sometimes they would use a helicopter to deliver material and food. The noise was incredible and you'd stay well away in case some nutcase decided to shoot at it. The soldier had an accent that sent a chill down my chest and into my balls. I had to say something back. "Hello" I said back, sounding pathetic, and feeling like a real traitor.

I walked past the Land Rover and saw a load of kit bags lying on the ground, just at the double doors. I stepped up onto the entrance and through the door into the ground floor that was tiled in shiny tiles that became dead slidey in the wet weather.

There was movement and voices at both lifts; one soldier was standing guard at the door to the stairs and one was throwing a kit bag into one of the lifts. He was the one who looked up at me. "Och aye, who's the wean then?" He stopped dead with a kit bag in his hand.

"He's just a bairn, looks like he's delivering the papers." The guard at the door said, taking a look up the stairs as he held the door open with his body. He looked right through me, never smiled, never a second look.

"Right ye are pal. Ye can join us in the lift up then." He stood upright and carried the last bag towards the lift. "Ya comin then?" He said. It sounded like an order. I couldn't say a word and just walked over to the lift. My first stop was the eleventh floor. Mrs Taylor, Winkie Taylor's mum. He worked in the Executive barbers in Castle Street. I thought it was Castle street anyway. I didn't know what to think as I joined the two soldiers already in the lift. They stood with their kit bags and guns lowered by their sides. They stared at me. Clean shaven with big jaws and both of them had blue eyes and similar faces. They wore caps with a big band of tartan around them.

"All the way ta the tap?" The one holding the big kit bag said to me.

He had stood at the side of the lift to allow me in. I normally liked to walk the staircases to build my legs up. I would deliver from the bottom up and then race down the stairs taking them four at a time. Now I just stepped inot the lift and stoof dumbly facing two of the scotchies. The one who had asked me if I 'was going to the tap' turned his back on me. As the doors rattled to a close, a terrible thought entered my head. What if the provies knew about their arrival and had planted a little welcome on the roof of the lift? I'd be blown to pieces and everyone would wonder what I was doing with the Scotchies in a smelly lift that smelt of pish and cigarette butts and sometimes vomit. That would be until Issac got his say, being interviewed on BBC by Nicholas Witchell, who looked like a ginger walnut. I could picture him, standing at his rotten counter, sweating buckets, telling everyone at home that the real victims 'was the people who didn't get their papers that morning'. Why couldn't I have said 'No, I'm using the stairs because I start at floor one?' I was so slow at times.

The one with his back to me was really tall and you could tell he was their leader I guessed. He looked really muscular and his neck was really clean, no hairs at all. "Alight wee man, deliverin' the papal paper. Here boys, this is the stuff we'll be up against?" He let out a snort of laughter I knew was about me.

"The weans? Don't be kidding yourself. Thon's the future gunmen" the one with two stripes that made him a corporal said. The two other soldiers didn't laugh.

They sounded a bit like the way we spoke but more nastier and scarier.

"Eleven." Was all I could manage to say, then I forced myself to speak again. My mouth was so dried up. I rolled my tongue around my mouth to say. "Please."

"Jesus, am gonna need the cludgie when I get out of this lift." The shorter one said.

I stood staring at the floor. I tried to shut them out. I just knew they were looking me up and down, hating me for being a Taig. Mum would certainly have had something to say about their pronouncing words, they were worse than us. "Awfy, reely, wally?" What the hell did that mean?

"Here lad, let us see a copy of that soup takers bugle, youse read."

"Leave the bairn be McCaig." The Corporal told him.

"Ah just wanted to see if Davie Cooper was playing today and if Dawson and McDonald were on." The one called McCaig, talked back drawing a look from his senior. "They probably don't even mention the teddys." He grumbled and for a moment, he sounded just like a young boy who couldn't win an argument with his mum.

"You'll be listening to it on the wireless, no doubt." The Corporal said firmly.

"Am fair peached. I need a dram." The other one with sweat beads on his forehead said. "It's hoachin in here, smells rank."

"What's the bint like round here? I'd love tae git me hands on a big pair of hebs."

"It's not like Bangor or Coleraine. The bint round these parts wud cut yer balls off as soon as look at ye."

"You feart McCaig?" The sweaty one laughed.

"Well, we canae all be from Gallowshields." McCaig smiled back.

"Bawbeg." The sweaty one answered back below his breath.

There was silence and I could feel they wee all looking at me again. I could tell them my favourite Rangers player was Sandy Jardine and that I knew the Sash and if I found a juicy piece of morsel I wouldn't bless myself and pick it up, I would use the ten second rule just like Orangies before popping it in my mouth. My name would be Iain with two I's and my surname was Craig after the leader of the Vanguard. I pronounced my H like 'aitch" and I knew that King Billy had said: 'let ambition fire thy mind' at the battle of The Boyne. I needed to know all this if I was ever captured by them again, like that sunny afternoon in the fish and chip shop on Duncairn Gardens.

I had gone with Wholenut as he had to see his Gran, who then had to get him to do something in her house, leaving me to walk back to the barrack square on my own. I didn't like the long streets, too many people I didn't know. And you were in their area. It was then some oul doll came out from her door and asked me over. "Here son, wud ye go and get us a fish from the chippy over there. I can't walk, I sprained me ankle going tae the shops yesterday." I looked at her skinny legs with the dark brown tights and could see her left leg bandaged up to below the knee.

The chippy was over in the Gardens, Hun territory. I would've walked all the way down to Poolios on North Queen Street rather than go over the road. 'Here son' and she handed me a pound note. "It's forty five pence," she told me like I was going to cheat her. I looked over again at the chippy. It was empty. "Salt, no vinegar son," she said with her face all full of wrinkles. I took the money and walked slowly towards the chippy. I turned and seen she hadn't left her spot at the door. She was watching me the whole way, the oul shite didn't trust me. I was shiteing myself. Go on in you oul bat so I could run round to The Savoy and get you yer bloody fish or get Tucker Kelly to get her the bloody fish.

I felt like running, but there would be crowd after me for running and stealing an old womans pound. And everyone saw me at Wholenut's Grans house so they'd identify me straightaway. I was already at the pavement to the Duncairn Gardens without realising it. I could feel sweat running down my back and the back of my knees. I looked up and down the road, there was no-one about and the chippy had remained empty. I could see figures moving behind the counter. I took one last look behind me, praying she had gone in but I could see her at her door, leaning out, staring up at me. Bloody oul goat, I raged. I ran quickly across the road my heart pounding, my head hot and light. I was in Orangie territory. I looked back again and could see her tiny wrinkly head, with those wrinkly eyes boring a hole into me. An ice cream van went flying up Duncairn towards the Antrim Road and I wished I was in it or on the sofa lying upside watching TV with mum. I wished to God I was anywhere else, yet instead I was at the first and only step into the chippy.

There were two big fat women behind the counter, one was much taller than the other. She had bleached blonde hair under her blue hat and clips holding her hair in place. She wore a lot of foundation and had large gold earrings dangling down from each ear. The other woman was way at the back lifting white boxes with symbols of fish and chips on them. She looked at me and then I could see her look out onto the street.

"Yes son, what'll it be?" She asked, staring down at me and then out over my head onto the road.

"Fish please. With salt, no vinegar." I said as pleasantly as I could. I wanted. No, I needed her to like me.

She went over to somewhere in the big stainless steel area that sizzled and placed what I knew to be a fish into the fryer, which crackled with an explosion of fizz.

"Forty five pence love." Her voice wasn't unfriendly, or unwelcoming. She sounded nervous but nowhere near as much as I felt. She kept looking out over me to the outside. I had decided not to turn round and look again until I was leaving. I had to act like this was my chippy and that I belonged there. But I couldn't stop my leg from shaking and I felt I was going to start crying at any minute.

"Pam, do you need any more pasties out?" The other woman shouted from the back of the chippy.

"No Doris. We've enough on." Pam said back, opening the till with the press of a button. She closed the till and put the change onto the counter.

"Stick that in yer pocket love, in case you lose out getting across that road."

"Thank you." I said ever so pleasantly and smiled, even though my face was freezing over with fear.

I placed the change in my pocket struggling with my sweaty hand to release the change. She knew rightly I was a Fenian. I could end up a deep fried Taig soon. I couldn't keep my feet from hopping from right to left, then left to right. I wanted the toilet. I could feel my guts filling up with an icy chill. I was minutes away from getting that fish for the wrinkly old bat and I'd be out of there, never ever to return. Then it happened. The door opened. I heard a male voice, older than mine, yet still young.

"Pam, where's our Doris then?"

"What is it you want Darren? Usual? Pasties and a small chip?"

Darren stood at the counter about two feet from me his arms resting on the counter. He must be about sixteen. Out of the corner of my eye I could see he too had bleached hair and a stud earring in his left ear. He was wearing one of those cricket jumpers that was popular with girls in our area.

"Aye, the usual. No fish for us, eh boys?" He laughed and there was someone behind him who laughed back.

This is it I thought. They've been called for to get me. I was ordering fish and it was a dead giveaway that I was a Catholic. I was choking with dryness. I could feel that I was moments away from wetting myself.

"Here, where's Archie, you three are joined at the hip." The woman called Pam asked.

I knew where Archie was, if Archie was the fella on the tiled floor beside me and grabbing my privates. He squeezed really hard. I fell back a bit not wanting to but I was so shocked and scared.

"He's around." Darren laughed.

Pam must have suspected where he was when she lifted the opening to the counter and came out onto the floor.

"What the hell are you at Archie? Get away from that wee lad this instant. Get yersel up and stay well away." Pam roared at him. He scrambled to his feet laughing. I heard Darren say 'Fenian lover', under his breath.

"I was tying me laces is all" Archie said, all innocence like.

"Right son, you stand here at this part. I'll get yer fish." I was so relieved I thought I might faint. Everything was a blur as Pam handed me the fish, all wrapped up in white paper and in a see-though plastic bag. Next thing I knew I was on the street again, standing by the road with Pam watching the traffic like the Green Cross Code Man. "Right you, now get across that road. And don't be coming back here, it's not safe. Ya hear me?"

I got to the other side of the road and waved back at Pam to thank her but she had already turned to go back into the chippy. The three fellas were giving me the fingers, with Archie drawing a line across his throat with his finger.

I ran to the oul dolls house where she had now got a chair in the hall to sit and wait for me. I handed her the bag.

"Me change son? You got that?" She said taking the bag and getting up groaning as she did.

I slid my hand into my pocket, it was the wrong pocket. Then into the right one and scraped the change out of my pocket and handed it to her. She counted it out. Then said, ach, thanks son'. She handed me two pence that she had already in her apron. I took it without a word and she closed the door. I stood in silence. My goolies were now really starting to hurt. Two pence! I raged inside my head, saying things I no way could say out loud. I could've been deep fried and covered in brown sauce or skinned alive, served up in the chippy with the sausages and pasties. The wrinkled oul bat. I hoped she choked on a bone in that fish. As I walked home, I got the brill idea then to create myself a prod version of me. And like the superheroes I would have another identity. That was the day Iain Craig was born.

I went to bed early that night and cried into the pillow, making sure Mum couldn't see me and especially Da. Mum would shout at me for my stupidity and for making her frightened. He, da, would probably laugh at me for being a WaWa. I cried because I was small and afraid most of the time. I cried because Mum would be so disappointed that I never heeded her advice and warnings. I knew she would be crying her lamps out at the thought of me lying dead, thinking of the deep-fried parts of me being found all over Tigers Bay and no-one would know why on earth I had been in that area. But I took comfort in the fact that I now had another personality that could protect me, just like the superheroes in my comics.

The big metal door of the lift wobbled open with a dry squeaking at the eleventh floor. At long last I would be free. I jumped out over part of the kit bag that had fallen flat on the floor of the lift.

"Here lad, tell the Provos that the boys are back in town, will ye." The one who was called McCaig, who stood with the kit bag, had stuck his neck out of the lift. I said nothing. I hurriedly left the floor. I would double back as soon as the lift closed and they were gone on up to the top floor.

I wish I could have shouted back 'chucky ar lar' or something smart but I ran the real risk of bumping into them again on me round. So I held my whiste as we say and popped two midget gems in my mouth and chewed quickly to get some spit going.

I had finished Templar and was bursting with the news that the Scotchies had come back to the area. There was definitely going to be blue murder now. There'd be more rioting and trouble with them back. Before I left, the right hand side opened but no-one came out so I ran over and pressed as many buttons on the panel for the floors as quickly as I could, hoping that would slow them down. Have that I thought, you beasts, as The Owl Of The Remove would say.

I thought about the last time they were here. Genghis' da was given a right beating by a squad of the bastards coming out of The Felons club. He was pissed and fought like a Trojan and they still couldn't get him down or into the back of the Land Rover. I remember all the women screaming and shouting at them to stop and they came out, like hundreds of them, even my mum who never bothered with the troubles. The came down from our Maisonettes and out of the flats and the houses on the lodge and went towards the Scotchies, who called the mums and the women really dirty names. They began threatening to hit the women with their batons and one shouted he would shoot if they didn't get back. Women were screaming for them to shoot, calling them dirty cowardly bastards, the scum of the earth. 'Go on home you British bastards, go on home' they began singing like they were at a football match.

That's when the fellas came out and I could see from the veranda's where mum told me to stay that the Scotchies were shiteing themselves. They were all fired up, their faces white as sheets, shouting and screaming at the crowd surrounding them. They really were the scum of the earth threatening women and beating up poor Jim, Genghis's da. And what they did to Terry Hackett, beating him to a pulp outside his own house and in front of his screaming mum. You couldn't even see his face for the blood and they dragged him off and flung him into a sixer. That was the last time I saw Terry. People said when he got out of The Kesh that he went down the South and then to Australia. Some said he was a coward and should've joined up and got a few of the bastards back. Fair play to him for getting the fuck out of it I said to myself.

Shite. What the hell was I gonna say to Genghis? I was calling to his flat at half twelve to listen to his new Steve Millar Band LP. Fuck, his da would have a meltdown.

It was getting much lighter as I walked over towards Alamein House across the square, bursting with my news. There was always nosey nabes out this time of the morning but where were they when this time I had something to tell them and watch their faces light up with excitement and fear. Even oul Bridget the midget, who hated the army with a passion because they killed her son years ago in a gun battle at the bottom of the road; even she wasn't about. I was sort of glad because the Brits were used to her and laughed her off and her fist shaking and threats. I think the Scotchies would treat her different. They wouldn't see the funny side of her slegging and would probably have lifted her or give her a kicking for her troubles or both probably.

The only person I saw was a kid about seven who was going to the Thompsons shop. He was singing that song from the TV advert, it went 'if you like a lot of chocolate on your biscuit join our club'. He stopped to ask me if I had doot he could eat. 'Naw mate', I told him 'I didn't have an apple on me.' I felt so bad for him now that the Scotchies had arrived to make all our lives worse. He looked half starved so I handed three of my midget gems. You'd have thought it was Christmas. He beamed a great big smile and said in a loud happy voice, 'thanks mate' through his chewing and walked off waving to me. Poor little sod, he looked hungry and really poor, like Harding or Moffat Street poor. I noticed he hadn't a shoelace in his left shoe and his trousers and jumper were boggin. He had come from the direction of Lepper Street but he didn't look like one of the onion clan.

I was on the fifth floor and shoving the paper through 5b's letter box when Joe Porridge feet came to mind. He was called that because of the big grey woolly socks he wore in all kinds of weather. He was the oul boy who cycled around the area delivering the 'Tele', The Belfast Telegraph, a protestant paper that Mum wouldn't have in the house nor would ever, ever let me deliver. So I wouldn't be taking over from him when he retired. I'd have liked that job, flying around on me blue racer, using all the ten gears for the hills. All of us in the shop worked out one morning that he must be worth a fortune because he got 2 pence on each paper.

I had no idea who came up with that. But working on this figure and the number of deliveries, Junior said he delivered up as far as the Limestone Road and scallions said he saw him riding through Unity. If he delivered one in every four houses, that would be around a five hundred two pences he was getting everynight. How much was that? Ten quid a night! Six nights a week he did it. Sixty quid a week! And he probably earned more than that. Couldn't be, no way, that's ballicks. We all sneered until wee Fake Eddie, who was not a spoofer by no means because he rarely talked; but when he did he said he had saw Porridge Feet one Sunday up the Falls near the

Royal getting into a big silver Merc.

Wee Fake Eddie was there because he was up at the school of dentistry to get a tooth out. You didn't go up there unless you really had to, because they were a bunch of butchers up in that school. They had all these glipes who were training to be dentists or butchers and they'd experiment on you there. Bit like Lincoln Avenue where we were marched over to have our nappers examined for nits and have our teeth drilled and pulled out without any anaesthetic.

If I were to go to Mum with those earnings she might well change her mind. I was caught up in this thought as I went across to five D, folding the paper in a tight oblong piece like a stick. I knew five D had a wire basket on the door and you had to shove it right in and then down.

Something caught my eye lying on the tiled floor. It was a magazine, a real glossy one that shone under the big lights on the ceiling. I delivered the paper as quickly as I could, praying Mister Denvir didn't come out to say hello or anything. I looked at the magazine again and held my breath. Just below the glass partition, before the big veranda's outside where people could hang out washing I think. I looked around the floor listening for doors being unlocked. All four doors were quiet. I was alone with the magazine. My heart was beating quickly. Then I thought, was this a trap? Left by some dirty old perv it for me to find and then pounce?

I couldn't get Goldie out of my mind. The fifth year from last year who had work experience in a garage, Fiat cars it was and he had found a load of nude books in the toilets just left there by the men working in the garage. That was the spring when dirty pictures flooded the school and the teachers hadn't a Scooby Doo about it. At first, whole pages were floating about by the Fifth years, then smaller pictures and ones that had been cut up were sold to the rest of the years. Whole pages were going for like fifteen, twenty pence. Then it all came crashing down when a first year had gone to a teacher to complain that he had spent ten pence on a picture and he didn't know if it was a woman or not. Who'd he complain to? Bryce, of all the bastards in the school. A Maths Teacher? He was the worst bastard in school after the Brothers.

Assembly was called and the issue was raised by Brother Cassidy who found the whole thing depraved and disgusting and said that all those who had the disgusting pictures should hand them in forthwith and nothing would further would happen to them. If not, anyone caught in possession would be expelled and the Police informed. Also, there would be indefinite detention for the entire class of the boy who had distributed the pictures in the first place; if he or his classmates didn't come forward or his name was not forwarded to his form teacher. Goldie had been given to the end of the day to come forward. He was persuaded to go forward by his entire class. By the end of the week he never returned to school. There was talk he ended up in Rupert Stanley across town. I don't think he became a car mechanic.

I swallowed my disappointment, telling myself it was a blessing in a way that it turned out to be one of those women's magazines called Honey and where they weren't naked; at least from what I could see, before quickly shoving it in my bag anyways. There might be something to look at, like in the Littlewoods or Kays catalogues with the womens underwear pages, but Mum kept a close eye on them and kept them in with her toiletries which was a horrible word because it had toilet in it.

I completed the deliveries in Alamein and the two Maisonettes were dead easy, only two storeys, four staircases and you could slide down the bannister because they had a red, hard plastic coat on them. I saw Artie Musgraves da come out to look at his car; it was the only one of the four cars parked in the barracks. Two belonged to the Allsopps, they were mechanics. One of them never moved though. They were always under a car, you rarely seen them on their feet and when they were, they were bent over an engine. You recognised the da's from the son because of the different shoes they wore. One belonged to Chuck Redding who was called the Apeman by all the kids and he really looked like Mick Jagger with a big greasy quiff. I think he was a binman but he never talked to kids or got the paper or went out except in his car, so I didn't know him at all. Artie's da was an undertaker who had buried Lieutenant Tim, even he cried that day and it scared me to see a big, grown up man cry. I never had before.

I waved to him from the back of the Maisonettes when I was on the second floor, near Mister McColloms house. I would have to go back to later with the lights that were sitting in the hall. Artie's da waved back, I didn't have the heart to tell him the Scotchies were back, not after what happened at the funeral. He'd be worrying about the next round of funerals they would probably bring. Anyway, people would find out soon enough I thought; as long as I knew it was me that first saw them, I was fine with that.

I had finished at the Russells, number 46. Sean and Hugh were boxing mad, they were always heading down to the Holy Family to train.

They were dead on, always said hello even though they were always in a hurry to the club or some fight. And I was always dead nice to them because they could knock my ramp in, easy. And it was good to have guys like that on your side. It was funny, I thought that I was someone who delivered papers, even though I never read them. Well not the front part, it was all Gerry Fitt and Jim Callaghan, then the bombs and the riots. I stayed with the football. As mum said, there was more than enough grief outside your door, why would you want to invite it in.

I made my way over to Jimmys to get Aunt Greta her bap and milk and her ciggies. They were cheaper there than Issacs, you'd save easy nine or ten pence. I had to tread carefully so I wouldn't be seen going in there by Issac or Sheila. It felt like I was betraying them and the shop.

I walked up to the crossing at Lepper Street and crossed there and walked the thirty yards to Jimmy's shop that used to be painted red but most of it had come off the wood. I had never known the shop to have windows. It was always boarded up with big sheets of plywood and wire mesh padlocked at the bottom and top. I felt sorry for Jimmy and his wife, they were both ancient and we tortured them sometimes when we were in a big group, coming in and asking for 'spunky bonbons' and 'a quarter of seagulls waterboots' and us laughing our heads off as Jimmy stood leaning on his bare counter with his big bony hands and the biggest thumbnails I'd ever seen. He always wore a jumper, red or blue, with a tie, no matter the weather. He never had anything on show, but whatever you asked him for he would trapes round the counter, dead slow and go through a door to the side and come back with what you ordered; except for spunky bonbons or Seagulls waterboots.

I didn't like going in by myself in case he pulled me about being one of those scitters who takes the proverbial. But anytime I did go in he just said 'Hello, what's it to be?' from way down low where his head met his throat and neck and sat over his shirt and tie. His big watery eyes stared right through you; it was like he thought, like he knew, everyone coming in was going to act the wanker. I placed my order and off he went, slowly towards the side door and entered it. I imagined his wife who was probably the same age, was stacking all the shelves with all manner of stuff, sweets, ciggies, tea and syrup, the only thing they didn't have was fruit or veg. That was the shop at the opposite side of the street and on the opposite corner. A lot of their stuff looked old and stinking. But inside when I was asked to go get an emergency box of Oxo cubes or something like that, they had tons of fruit, some I'd never seen the like of before. They looked like spuds or oranges, like normal fruit that had been subjected to gamma radiation and become like the Hulks of the fruit world. Me mad spud, me no happy. "Arrrggghhh" they'd say, if they could talk.

I paid Jimmy who stood at his counter holding onto what I'd ordered like grim death. He looked at the money and then dragged it across the counter and dropped it into a drawer beneath. Then came the change which took an age. He slid the coins one by one towards me and in one swift move, like a magician off the TV, the stuff you asked for were in front of you.

I put them in my paper bag and went out to get to Hartwell Place and the four doors to Aunt Greta's house, which was really Granny's old house but she was in Musgrave hospital after she was found walking the streets in her nightdress looking for her daughter. That was me Aunt Geraldine who had died as a kid from TB. Poor Gran, she went doolaley after that, so I heard them talking.

A big green door, number six, the paint was shiny and new. Da had brought it over from work, though he didn't do the painting. Aunt Greta did that. Truth be told, Aunt Greta scared me a bit. She was dead manly like that, painting, even plastering a hole in the wall when she got some new sockets in. She had great big arms and a square jaw with short, really curly hair that was dead brown like that guy on top of the pops, Leo Sayer. That's what Da called her behind her back and I'm ashamed to say, it made me laugh and I felt rotten because Mum got so upset that she threw her big bag of cosmetics at him.

Aunt Greta had a long nose but a good heart, she was dead kind and generous and all the kids in her street liked her. Not like a lot of people about who so stingy they wouldn't give you the top of their egg. And they were usually the people who had money.

And although she was big and strong she was always sickening for something. She never missed work as a stitcher and she sewed the patches on my old denim jacket. I only had three patches; UFO, AC/DC and Deep Purple. You were supposed to iron them on but Aunt Greta said they would stay on forever if they were sewed. I had a key to let myself in. I opened the door to the long hallway, which smelt of strong tea and cigarettes. She worked Saturdays late from ten to about four down somewhere near the Irish News building. I was always curious how she didn't look a bit like Mum, except for her eyes and ears. They all got that from Grandad who used to be a Stevedore down the docks. I thought that meant he was a bullfighter when I first heard that word. And I got real excited and was about to ask where he killed the bulls and could I see his Matador outfit. Thank God Mum could see my confusion an explained what he really did. Thank Christ I didn't say those things out loud, da would've had a field day and pissed himself laughing.

I walked along the hall that was tiled with tiny black and white tiles a lot of them were cracked and some parts of them missing. At the bottom of the hall was the tiny kitchen with the big stone sink and the cupboards da had got for Gran from the warehouse. Mum used to tell me stories about me getting my first baths in that sink with either Gran or Aunt Greta drying me off. It was well before her and Da got a place of their own. The thought of it still makes me squirm.

I knocked on the living room door. There was no answer I put my ear up to the door. Not a sound. "Aunt Greta are you in? I've got your messages here. I'll leave it in the kitchen if you like." I was beginning to worry. I knocked again and then I heard a low voice say something I took to be come in. The first thing that hit me was the heat, it near took my breath away.

"Aunt Greta, you here?" I stepped into the room, it was boiling. My face was blazing and I could hardly catch a breath. "You alright Aunt Greta? I got your messages here." I said holding them up in the flimsy plastic bag. She was lying on the sofa in her dressing gown and she had a giant towel wrapped around her head. It's a tarl I thought, making me snigger.

The electric fire she had was in front of the fireplace and all three bars were on. I stood wondering what to do. "I have your messages here Aunt Greta." I said quietly as I could but still be heard. A blind man could see she wasn't well.

"Aw thank you son." She said with a gasp, as if she were breathing her last. She sounded terrible and looked horrible, with her big towel on her head and her feet up on cushions.

I could see her big slippers were beside the sofa pointing towards the fire. "Do you need anything? I mean are you alright Aunt Greta?"

"Fine, fine son. Just leave the messages on the table. The moneys on the mantle son. You're a wee star so you are." Her voice faded away as she lifted her large hands to her face. "I'll be alright, I've just been to the doctors and saw Doctor Murtagh." She stopped talking for a moment and breathed in heavily.

A martyr to her nerves Mum said, da said the only thing she didn't have was hypochondria. If she found a plaster, she'd cut herself. I looked that word hypochondria up in my pocket Collins dictionary and it made me laugh when I thought of what he had meant with the plaster remark. I had got that dictionary because I was fed up asking Blackie all the time about words he came up with. I think he was a bit fed up too, telling us wawa's the meaning of them.

Mum said she had heart arrhythmia that she got from Grandad who smoked like a chimney and drank like a fish. It was a miracle she didn't have it as well, she said. He had been in the merchant navy, not deep sea, just to Liverpool and Southampton on the coal boats I heard. But he had been in the army for a while and was never the same when he came back.

"Would you like me to make you a cup of tea?" I asked as I had nothing else to say.

"No son, there's a pot there on the table, just made. You're an angel for asking. I'll be up on me feet soon enough."

"What'd the doctor say? Doctor Murtagh, whad he say?" I asked, getting worried at the state she seemed to be in.

"No son, that lovely young Doctor Murtagh. He's an angel. I always go to him. Even if I have to wait a day or two, it's cos' he's so busy. People are always wanting him, cos he's such a nice doctor. Not like the rest of 'em, they haven't a minute for ye."

I moved slowly toward the mantelpiece that was covered in brass ornaments and I took the money in case I forgot. Mum never liked too many ornaments, clutter and dust gatherers she called them. That was another difference between her and Aunt Greta.

"What'd he say?" I asked, to cover my sliding of the money into my pocket.

"Oh son, I went cos my head was pounding all week, no amount of

Paracetamol would shift it. So I made an appointment and saw him." Aunt Greta stopped to gather her breath. "After he examined me he said he couldn't understand what was wrong with me and I didn't want to be going to no hospital. So he says to me 'Greta did you wash your hair recently' and I said yes. Then he says 'did you go out after washing your hair and it was still wet'. Yes, doctor I did. 'And was it cold outside, were you out for long?' Why yes doctor it was freezing that night, Thursday and it rained a bit and I was out for near half an hour doctor. 'Well, Greta I think I know what you've got'. I said oh doctor Murtagh what is it I said. 'Brain freeze'. You've got a bad case of it, I'm afraid."

"God doctor, is it fatal? I said. 'No Greta all you need to do is stay in and keep your head well wrapped up and warm and it'll pass in twenty four hours. The freeze has gone from your hair in through your scalp and into your brain. There's no lasting damage but you need to get home as soon as and get that head of yours warmed up." Aunt Greta let out a big, deep gasp and dug her head into the bed pillow she was resting on.

I was mortified. How many times had I run the risk of catching that? With me out in all weathers with my round and sometimes without a hat or a hood covering my scone. Brain freeze. Bloody hell, it sounded bloody awful and really sore. And dangerous no matter what Aunt Greta said. Poor Aunt Greta, I really wished her well and soon. I felt really wick when I remembered the times I would avoid her when I was with me mates. I knew they'd slag her off. I remembered them saying 'isn't that your uncle over there?' saying she was a man. And Wholenut saying her hair looked like she was wearing a woollen hat. I hated him for that. I tried never to slag their families off, even though Wholenut's da looked like an old Joe ninety and his ma looked like Parker from The Thunderbirds.

"So son, don't you be going out with your head wet, out in the freezing cold. Keep your head warm" Aunt Greta advised.

"I will Aunt Greta, I definitely will. Are you feeling any better now?"

"Oh Gawd, yes, thank Gawd. Plenty of hot tea and get the heat inta me. I've the hot water bottle in here with me. Wrap up warm Doctor Murtagh said. I feel a whole lot better. How's that Mum of yours?"

"Oh, she's fine Aunt Greta, great. She's away to work. She said she'll be over with home made soup tomorrow as usual."

"Ah, that's dead decent of her. She's an angel that mother of yours. Best sister you could ever ask for." Aunt Greta sounded dead tired she rested a hand on her head and let out a big breath. I needed to go I was boiling to death in that room. The windows were covered in water that ran down the glass. I had things to do; I had to get to Mister McCollums and had to get ready for the match, then go to Genghis and his house and listen to the new record that Duffer was bringing over. It was an album by The Steve Millar Band. Genghis said it was brilliant but then he was the biggest spoofer on the road.

"Right then, if you're sure you're okay then Aunt Greta."

"Yes son, get you on. Don't be wasting your time here with an oul doll like me."

"No, I'm not." I said, not knowing how to finish what I wanted to say without lying. I was dead relieved that she didn't need me for anything. I wanted to get out of the room before I fainted from the heat. "I'll get on then. I have to get ready for the match and have messages to do for da. As long as you're okay."

"Aye", she said in a growl. "No, you get you on son. I'm fine."

Bloody hell, brain freeze. No way did I want to catch that. I'd make sure it never happened to me I thought to myself, as I closed the front door as quietly I could behind me. It was hats from now on, duffle coat and parker during the winter and me monkey hat for the wet days in spring and summer. I wondered how many people caught it in this dump, where it was always windy and raining.

I walked back to the house hoping Da was up and already away to work. I deliberately took my time walking back. He'd only say something about the albums, like he did when he said the devil has all the best tunes or maybe he'd say that he was sorry, again.

I opened the door my keychain rattling as I turned the key. Some of my mates didn't even have a key to the house because they couldn't be trusted with it. I stepped into the hall and the next thing I heard was Da's voice behind me as I closed the front door.

"Hello, hello, hello. Here's our own wee Phil Spector now." Da said, impersonating that old peelar on Dixon of Dock Green. He was holding the cassette I had made for Francesca in his grubby paws. How could I be so bloody stupid? I had left the tape in the unit from yesterday evening as I sat listening to the radio for songs I could tape. "What's this?" Da asked, looking at the writing on the cassette. He laughed out loud. "From The Blue room recordings. Where's that? Up in your room?" He laughed again. This time to me it seemed forced, like he was deliberately trying to wind me up.

"Give it back, will ya please." I pleaded before he read what songs I had recorded onto the cassette. It had taken me ages to get those songs. It was weeks of listening to the charts, trying to cut out the DJ's slabbering at the start and end. Getting the right songs, imagining what Francesca would like to hear.

He laughed again. "Oh my. Boys oh boys, you got it bad." He was smiling like a Cheshire cat and I believe I hated him then. I prayed he'd would choke to death right there and then in the middle of his laughing.

"Gimme me, gimme it back please". I almost screamed it out. My head was raging hot along with my face.

"Various artists," he read out, "The Real Thing. Oh, I like that song." He said, with a stupid smile twisting his gob. "You to me are everything, the sweetest song that I can sing." He sang, moving over to the big window, like he was dancing to the song. He stood at the living room to get a better look at the writing on the case. I had to make really small to get the artist and the song title on the back of the cassette case. "What's this one? The Bellamy brothers. Let your love flow? Dunno that one. Oh here, now we're whistling Dixie. Stevie Wonder." He read out what I had written with my best Biro. "I believe when I fall in love it will be forever." He sang out, really out of tune. He was destroying the whole idea of the mixed tape. I know I was hitting a real beamer, I could feel my face on fire with rage and embarrassment. I felt really stupid now. I hated myself for leaving the tape for him to see. I began to cry, as I hated him for what he was doing and for what he had done. He couldn't hear me crying and I quickly dried my eyes with the cuff of my jumper.

"Come on son. I'm only pulling yer leg." He said handing me the cassette. "Your girlfriend wouldn't want to see you gurning now, would she?"

I took the cassette without word.

"Who is she anyway? Must be a right wee belter to go to all this trouble. It's not wee Donna Duffy?"

"No it's not!" I shouted back, really angry he would think I would fancy that tomboy, who threw stones at the army and had spots and a snattery nose.

"Woah, easy tiger. So there's a girl then." He said like he had won something. "Who is the lucky lady?

"You wouldn't know her." I shouted back, really angry with him and with myself for being so stupid and leaving it for him to get his hands on. I wanted to get out of the room and get up to my bedroom.

"Come on," he said in a funny wee voice, like he was really trying to be my mate, "who is she? You know, making that cassette was a really classy thing to do. It really was. Any girl would be really made up with that."

"You think? Really?" I said wiping my eyes completely dry. Thinking it not well be the end of my world. It was good to hear. Da would definitely know more about girls than any of my mates.

"Yeah, she'd be putty in your hands after getting that. If you tell me who she is I might know her Da and put a good word in for you." He said and winked.

"No, no. Please don't say anything to Mister Fusco." I blabbed out and right away I knew I had told him who it was I had made the tape for. I was about to cry again. I felt like a complete twat and I hated him there and then for making feel like that.

"Fusco? The ice cream people? They have the parlour on the road?" He gasped and coughed a bit. "Hold on, it can't be Angelica, at least I hope not. She's married with three kids. And one of thems older than you. Not Elizabetha? No, she's in her twenties and she's dating that nutcase Brasso. God only knows why, nah, let's think. It's not Mario?" He laughed.

"No, stop it, just stop." I shouted and I felt the swell of tears that I knew to be behind my eyes come flooding out and down my face. I felt the words swimming around my head.

"Thank God for small mercies." He said making a big sigh of relief sound. "Here, here, no need for the waterworks wee man. I'm only codding you on." He said and handed the cassette over.

I took the cassette with my hand that trembled and felt sweaty and greasy. "It's Francesca." I sent out her name into the room where it fell flat at Da's feet.

"Gerry Fusco's wee granddaughter?" Da whistled. "Here, they're worth a few bob. Hold the phone." He clicked his fingers. "Francesca, she's the wee one with the bob and big smile. I saw her once serving in the shop. She's a wee honey." He brushed back the long fringe from his face and said. "You're punching well above yer weight there son. She'll be fighting the fellas off with a hurley stick."

I felt sick, like my stomach had been emptied by a big vomit. It felt like I had been Judas punched again. Like I had thrown the Judas punch, which felt much worse than getting one to be honest. I wanted to throw up. My heart actually hurt it was burning at my chest and I was going to cry again. Then I said 'no, don't do it'. I turned my feeling to anger and a rage for my dopey Da and it stopped me from feeling sorry for myself.

He grabbed his stupid sheepskin jacket, which I'm sure cost a packet, the song went off in my head. He looked at his stupid face in the mirror on the wall above the sofa. "But don't let it stop ye giving that tape. Faint heart and all that stuff. If you get in with that wee Francesca, you hold on for dear life. We'll have free ice cream for the rest of our puff." He laughed into the mirror. "See you later Romeo." And he made his stupid laugh again. "Romeo, that'd be right for an Italian girl."

I thought he was being a real glipe and I didn't feel the least bit bad for thinking that about my own da. But I almost forgot that I had my revenge already.

"Here, before you get on. I've news to tell ye." I said, all innocent like and trying to look and sound helpful.

"Yeah? What is it? Come on, I've to get til me real work here." He said fixing his shirt collar down over the big furry collar of his coat.

"When I was out on me round, I bumped into the Scotchies, they were going up in the lift to get to the look-out posts on top of Templar. They're back in the area and they told me to tell everybody."

"What?" Da's face was a picture, like he'd lost a pound and found a penny. He was shiteing himself as the news sunk in. I was delighted and nearly laughed. "Are you sure it was them. The Scotchies?" His voice was so full of fear now. I could swear he had gone a funny colour and I had to stop myself from laughing.

"Yes, definitely they made me go up with them in the lift. They said tell your mates the boys are back in town." I didn't try and do it in a Scotch accent as I'd be shite at it and I didn't want to give him something he could laugh at.

"Ffuc.." He breathed out as he pulled the zip up on his coat. "Right, must get on, and you." He said, stopping dead in mid sentence that startled me a bit.

"Yes?" I said without realising I had said it. To hell with him he had crossed a line with Francesca.

"You watch yerself at that match and get home pronto right after it. With those scumbags back, anythings likely to happen. Ya hear me?" He said. He could be deadly serious at times.

"Yes, I do. I promised mum I would." I hoped he knew from what I'd said and the tone of my voice that it wasn't him I kept my word with.

"And don't forget to get them lights round to Matt."

"I won't" I said. Matt was Mr McCollom to me.

I stared at the list and songs I had picked, they looked really stupid to me now. What the hell did he do that for? Why the hell did I leave it in the stupid cassette player. I was a real clampit. Francesca would laugh her head off if she could see it. Best of my love, The Emotions, Baby I love your way by Peter Frampton a bit of classy rock just to show I wasn't all soppy. I'm not in love by 10cc and the classic, 'I want you to want me' by Cheaptrick. I was sure Francesca would like it. She had class in spades, the way she dressed and danced at the youth club with her friends. No, it had taken me ages to get the right songs. I would keep it and I would get it to her. Never mind Da and his waffling, I would wait for the right moment to get it to her.

My first thought was to post it to her. Then I thought, no, give it to her friend Deidre who looked really nice, she would understand and not take the piss. She wore nice girly clothes, long dresses with colourful patterns and she was really clean and wore big glasses and went to Fortwilliam, which meant she was smart too. Not a millie from The Little Weed which was our joke name for the real name The Little Flower. You would never see her out in the riots. She and Francesca had class. But I was afraid she might laugh at me and thought it better to bite the bullet and hand it to Francesca myself if I ever got the nerve up.

I went to my room I wiped my face down with my towel that was in the room before I had left for my round. I still felt a bit like crying. I would get round to Mr McColloms and leave in the lights, then I'd count my savings and my comic collection. That always cheered me up. I would read the match news at the dinner table in the living room. I was going to have two eggs and three sausages with the soda's I had kept over from the day before. I would wash it all down with a big mug of tea then I'd get my kit bag ready just like a footballer. It really was just my school satchel. I'd bring a can of coke, a mars bar, a bottle of water in my Fanta bottle, my notebook and two pens. Make sure I had plasters in there too. I put in a small purse that Mum had bought me. She insisted it was a man's purse, she had got it from some promotion in work and it was man's deodorant. It had the word Faberge on it and it was black and it was really tight when you closed it. It turned out it was perfect for the extra change. I liked to take in case of emergencies. It was around one fifty in case I ever needed the bus or a taxi. I had three plasters to take with me too. Maybe Aunt Greta would like one I smiled, trying to cheer myself up as I cleaned my face and got ready to go outside again.

But I was miserable. I had been since the raiding party by Piercy and his hallion battalion. That day changed everything. Actually, it was weeks before that really with Lieutenant Tim's death. I dreaded the summer now. They were going to be deadly long and I almost wished them away and we could move straight to the end of August and going with mum to McMurrays in North Street to get my school clothes.

I walked round to Mr McColloms with the three long lights

wondering if he knew his nickname around the area was NTB. It stood for Not Too Bad. He always said it when he was talking, if you mentioned anything to him it was 'not too bad'. It made me laugh as I always tried to get him to say it. I was sure I could as I climbed the four stairwells to the second storey of the block of maisonettes he lived in. Number forty six B. I wondered why we needed letters when we had numbers but nobody could ever tell, not even Mum. The worst time was when Da asked me to take round two toilet seats. They weren't in boxes, just covered in this plastic sheeting and you could see what they were. I walked round cursing him for making me take them round. I was praying no-one would see me and I'd get away scot free.

Then I heard: "Here Squint, you got the two bob bits?" It was Wholenut and his cousin Drooper. He was called that because of a lazy eye and he had to wear a patch from time to time. We called him Captain Drooper because when he wore the patch he reminded us of a pirate like Captain Pugwash.

'You need to take the toilet with ye nigh, is it that bad?' Wholenut laughed again. I had no answer for him, he'd got me by the balls so I just gave him two fingers and walked on as the pair of laughed their heads off. Of course, for about a week I was called everything under the sun, like W C Fields, Bogman, things like that.

I used the letterbox to rap the door and waited, hoping his son Maurice wouldn't answer. He was well older than us, about seventeen or eighteen and he wore big flares and went to dances in the clubs. We all slagged him John Revolta after the movie star in Saturday Night Fever, that none of us had seen because it was an X movie. He was wearing a white suit as he raced along the garages they had and up through the hole in the wall. He was wearing big platforms and he nearly fell over several times as we shouted abuse over at him. So seeing him right now would be dead awkward and potentially dangerous.

Thank God, it was his Da, the NTB.

"Ach, hello there son. Them the lights for me? Let me take those from you." Mr McCollom asked, smiling as he did so. His big round face got rounder. His head looked like a giant egg, he had no hair at all except round his ears and back of his neck; but you could hardly see it as it was really fair. His face and neck were flushed red and he had some foam under his right ear. "Just been shaving", he said, wiping his face with what looked like a tea towel draped over his shoulder, "getting meself presentable for work. Here, let me take them from you son." Mr McCollom took the lights in both hand. "Aye, not too bad, they'll do the trick alright". He said looking them up and down. He placed them behind in the hall and delved both hands into his trouser pockets and I could hear the change in his pockets moving. He always gave me his shrapnel. He was always very generous and I had to look away as he made a count of the money in his right hand. "There you go son, that's for your troubles."

"No trouble at all Mr McCollom, sure we're only round the corner."

"Aye, you're a good lad". He said as his hand hovered over mine. "You'll need both mind". He said referring to my hands. Brilliant, I thought. This would be going into the purse for the match for extra security I was thinking. Mr McCollom dropped the money into my cupped hands. I could swear I saw a fifty pence piece amongst the change. "There you go son. That's great now. I'll see your dad this evening more than likely". He pulled up his trousers to above his waist as they had slipped down, probably due to the weight of all that change.

"No problem Mr McCollom. I'll get on then. I'm heading to the big match today."

"Oh aye, that's right, the Reds are playing in the cup. They're not doing too bad this season."

"No, they're doing alright. Not too bad at all" I said, feeling really smart that I had said what he always said.

Mr McCollom looked at me, his face at a slant so you could see several folds of skin in his neck and with his eyes that were dead small and really blue in his big white face. He blinked both eyes and said "Aye". Dead slow like, like he knew I had just slagged him off. "You mind yerself now." He said and I didn't know if it was to do with my slagging or the match.

I couldn't wait to get home and count what I had earned so I went flying up the last two stairwells two steps at a time. I looked at the open door of the big room where people put out their washing. There was Mrs Patterson, bent over her wash basket on the ground and I had a flash of a dirty thought about her daughter's underwear being in there. She was really attractive, a year older than me and she looked like she was about eighteen when she had make-up and a skirt on.

I got my coat off, flung the bag onto the table in the kitchen, grabbed a glass of water and went up the stairs carefully to avoid spilling anything onto the new carpet. There was a fifty pence piece. I separated that and the ten pence pieces from the two and one pences. There wasn't any five pence pieces which was odd but I didn't care as I counted out fifty pence piece, three tens, seven two's and nine ones. Total, a princely one pound and three pence. Haroo! as Hurree Jamset Ram Singh would shout in celebration of a postal order arriving for The Remove. Although I always saw myself as Harry Wharton, form captain and natural leader and founding member of The Famous Four before Bull joined, that would be Wholenut in our gang, he joined late. But he was most welcome, loyal but pig headed. But I felt like Skinner, a bluffer and a chancer at times.

I quickly gathered my earnings and separated them into my left and right pockets and made my way down the staircases, sliding on the thick red plastic for people's hands. I would get home and get myself ready for the game. I would have extra money to put into my Woolwich savings account. I was getting ever closer to getting that ten speed racer. I had to get it before the summer ran out. It was getting near the end of April now, five weeks from Lieutenant Tim and two from Piercy's raid on our tyres and wood. It had been nearly a week since Blackie. I ran round to the house, taking the stairs three at a time.

I was walking back towards the house when it hit me like a punch on the face from nowhere by a dirty Judas.

It was at Wholenut's request that Blackie started his story. Wholenut had been away to his grannies in Glengormley because of the rioting. They lived in the corner house at Edlingham Street, a spot where the rioters gathered and their windies were always hoarded up at night because of it. The rioting had gotten much worse recently because of the shootings by the Brits and the loyalist killings. And their house always smelt of C S gas.

Blackie obliged. We had all shuffled into a tight group to hear what for some of them would be the second time the story of Genghis and the riot had been told.

When Blackie spoke we all listened. There was usually about eight of us, sometimes when we weren't football training, kept in, not allowed out or having to do homework. Blackie always wore what looked like his school trousers, that he constantly pulled up to settle on the little belly at his waist. And he wore real da's shoes, black brogues shined within an inch of their lives. His smile made his face fat at the cheeks and chin but he was still pleasant, like his voice which was warm and on the verge of laughter. He could do a load of voices of people in the area that were hysterically funny. He used them all the time to tell his stories so they sounded so real.

It was the bottom of our tower block which was Alamein. We called ourselves the flat dwellers. It was better than the 'never get yer hole gang'', from over at the land of the Erps. Who would call your gang that name? Especially an area run by the loonies in the INLA. It was our area, the Barracks. We were known as the flat dwellers to everyone. So Wholenut, who had heard the news about Genghis but not any of the details, asked the man who told the best yarns by far, Blackie, to tell him the story of what happened and leave nothing out, all the juicy details. Blackie duly obliged. As per the usual. They had all shuffled into a tight group to hear the story of Genghis and the Riot.

"The mob moved as one, a solid mass of darkened shapes treading carefully, quietly, under the cover a natural darkness lent to them by a moonless sky. Everyone knew strict silence and stealth was the key to a successful mission. The element of surprise was their greatest weapon. They shuffled along Churchill Street, a cold chill swept across the mob reminding them that the night could be deadly. Sinews stretched to breaking, muscles steadied, hearts steeled and minds set. The moment to attack, to fall upon the enemy was nigh. Mouths went dry, hairs on necks went up. Bottles and bricks were gripped and caressed. The moment had come. They were at the corner, the enemy in sight and unsuspecting. The shout went out and up into the night sky." Then Blackie stopped talking and the place went deathly quiet.

"Snatchies!" Blackie shouted out. Startling all of us gathered around at the bottom of the tower block. After tellin' him he was a bastard and that he near give us a heart attack, we burst into laughter. Even those of us who had heard the story the night before laughed loudly, as the images in their heads from that night before came flooding back. Blackie continued with the story. His voice deliberately low, almost in a whisper as he spoke.

"The crowd broke and burst into smaller groups, some towards home, their hopes and dreams dashed of vanquishing the enemy. Some raced back from whence they came; others were unsuspectingly and now dangerously close to an alerted enemy. There were shouts and cries trying to calm the situation. Natural leaders called for a halt to the retreat, shouting encouragement for those clamouring away to return. Those who raced away began to stop and turn, realising if a snatch squad of Brits had been employed they would be upon them by now. They regained their courage and slowly but surely they merged and began the march back to re-engage the enemy."

There was a moments silence and some sniggering.

"Peelars!" Blackie's shout went up and into the darkening sky. Those in the group who had recovered their composure from the first fit of laughter broke again into prolonged and louder fits of laughing.

"Blackie, for chrissake." I said, feeling he was dragging the arse of out it now. I'd already heard his version of what happened. It was funny the first time. I'd started to see Blackie different recently. The St Mals boy who hung about with us wawa's just so he could look and sound smarter than the rest of us. Using big, brainiac words. He was the one who explained, in a St Mals way, about what Piercy had done to us on that day that seemed to change everything. He was collecting tribute. Like the Romans did to the people they had conquered. In return, not to get beaten again, they paid them off with gold and silver and even their own people as slaves. "So you're saying we're conquered Blackie," Dee asked. He looked at Blackie in a funny way. Like dead suspicious. "Not saying that Dee, just he can bully us people about because they're by far the biggest and nastiest gang in the New Lodge. Sure they've even got stuff off Pinkerton and North Queen Street." Blackie explained looking at Dee to think it was alright. "Suppose." Dee said.

I could see Dee was starting to feel like I did. I knew he thought Blackie was the Brussel sprout, although we had decided it was wee Tackie, the boy with the lisp who came from Ludlow Street, which was a stones throw from Sheridan. He had scarpered off to Omeath with his Ma and Da. In his absence, he was found guilty as sin.

"Go on Blackie, go on with the story, this is beezer." Wholenut told him.

Blackie looked at Dee and then at me before he went on with his story.

"The shout went out in alarm, no-one was sure if they were surrounded by snatchies or peelars and everyone ran in flight in all directions, bottles smashed and bricks fell to the ground, any hand holding a weapon would, maybe, be shot and definitely scooped and taken to the cop shop for interrogation. Men without fear, warriors all, scattered for their dear lives, for their dear freedom as the alarm 'snatchies!' rang out in night air, causing terror in the bravest heart. The fiercest of warriors discarded their weapons fearing imminent capture and arrest."

I watched Blackie staring him up and down from his stupid Da-looking shoes, all polished like they were new, and then to his school trousers and jumper and shirt. Didn't he have any after school clothes? And he was getting into bands called New Wave, whatever that meant. It was Nerdy wee bands like XTC, Brinsley Swartz and Elvis Costelloe; an ugly looking brainiac who looked nothing like the real Elvis. He was shite too. They were really boring. A bunch of moaning minnies, bloody jessies who'd never heard a bomb go off, never got stopped by a foot patrol. What the hell were they complaining about? I was sick of Blackie's smartness, sick of being the only one singled out for slegging off by Teddy diddynose, sick of being afraid. Sick that I was going to get caught out as the one who, accidentally on purpose, told Piercy and Lieutenant Tim about our hoard of tyres and pallets because I wanted to impress them. Piercy had dirty Joe'd me and Lieutenant Tim.

Everyone but me and Dee burst into laughter. Dee kinda did smile, I sorta did too; because it was funny, funnier for those like me who had seen it happen. I was busying myself hating his stupid da-like shoes that were polished to death, but you knew they were old and his school trousers he always wore and the blue v neck sweater or the black one he always wore one or the other. I don't think he even owned a pair of jeans. There he was, always talking, always smiling, always centre of attention. He never bought books, always got them from the library. As soon I bought 'The Hardy Boys: The secret of Skull Mountain' he was down at the library looking a copy. He was a bin hoking blue lamp. I felt the rage from Lt Tim, the loss of our tyres and pallets and Teddy pissflap ears and his Judas punch on the side of my head boil inside.

"Blackie, holy sweet Jesus." Dada squeezed out from his laughing fit, doubled over as he held onto his guts. "Where'd ye make this shit up, ya head the ball?"

"Bloody hell how do you think this stuff up Blackie." Wholenut sneezed out from his nose more than his mouth. "Weeker, absolute belter. Ghengis, what a bloody heel and anchor. A complete dick."

"I don't have to make it up. You provide me with the best material." Blackie smiled, opened his arms and showed the palms of his hands as if he had invited us all into his company.

"Here Wholenut, ease up on the swearing." I nodded over in the direction of the group of women who were still saying the Rosary for peace.

"Fuck, sorry. Shit." Wholenut sniggered and the others sniggered with him.

I could sense some of the women gathered on old Jimmy's porch were looking at us even as they prayed. I think they used Jimmys porch because he was never in. After his ma died he went on the drink and was never out of The Circle or Lynchs bar. They said he had been a good upholsterer and it was great shame what happened to him, so da said. It was one of the few times he actually felt sorry for someone without slegging them off.

And also Mrs Burns lived in the maisonette beside Jimmy so they wouldn't be disturbing anyone next door because she was with them. There was the usual crew of Mrs Wiggins, Mrs Duffy. Mrs Madden, Mallon, Young, Hackett, Connolly and the aul Mrs Burns, a tiny wee women with orange hair and who hated us playing football or cribby or tennis or handball. I didn't know any of the other women by name as they came from outside the area. Mrs O'Connor didn't go and she went to mass every Sunday with her kids Frank and Margaret. They were dead private that way I guessed. I liked them, they were always saying hello to me.

The bombs were still going off; people were still getting shot and murdered. The rioting was getting worse if anything. The Brits and the peelars still stopped you on the street to ask you about yourself and your family. I even saw someone getting shot, well after it just happened. So the prayers weren't working. I don't think Jesus listened to us anymore. He was fed up with all the shite we did.

It was in Dill House. The day of the shooting I saw. I had been over at Danny's, he was the only person I knew in the entire tower block. He was a schoolmate who wanted to sell me his studded belt. But it was too big, even if I cut it with a knife as Danny suggested. We heard the shots at his front door and we ran to the stairwell and looked down from his third floor bannister. 'Will we go and see?' He asked, I could tell he was all excited. "I dunno Danny, it could be really dodgy." "C'mon, ye big froot ye" He said, I knew he was still annoyed I hadn't bought the belt. We ran down when we heard all the shouting. We opened the door to the ground floor and a guy was lying there, his head all blood and purple and black looking.

This kid, who was about nine or ten and had a ripped brown slappy joe on; he was at the front of people looking down on the guy. Someone had gone and got a towel and put it round his head and covered his face. The kid walked past us telling his friend that he saw the man shoot the guy and the blood didn't come out at first and then it went whoosh!, it came out like pish, right out of his head. They both ran up the stairs and they disappeared but you could hear him shouting whoosh! over and again.

But the praying went on and on. It was like they were repeating the same words over and over again for ages through wind, hail or shine. They were sure to go to heaven, like my cousin Kevin, from the song by The Undertones. Blackie had managed to get it taped on the radio by that weird John Peel, who always sounded so bored to me.

Mrs Wiggins was always there with Mrs Duffy, Duffers mum, and Mrs Young whose daughter Donna was beautiful; she had long blonde hair and blue eyes, who we called Custer after the general, all the others followed their lead as they started the praying. It was their voices you heard the best, the clearest across the barrack. When they finished they dispersed very quickly after their Rosary was said. We never paid them much heed, we just thought they were a bunch of holy rollers who thought they were better than us because their husbands did the collection at mass and they knew the priests by name.

"Tell us the story about best fallers Blackie. Go on, tell them." Wholenut pleaded. "Have youse heard this one. Ah Jesus, such a geg it was. Go on tell 'em." He prompted.

"Let me finish this one Wholenut." Blackie answered quietly smiling his chubby smile, warming up to the end of his story of Genghis and the riot.

"We all know, what happened. Genghis got fucked out of the riot before he got his ramp kicked in. The end." Dee said in a real nasty tone.

"Fucksake, whad'ya wanna do that for? Ya bloody needler." Wholenut directed at Dee, he was disgusted that Dee had spoiled the end to the story, especially without a laugh.

"Wind yer neck in. Whay'd want to hear about his spoofing, fucksake all he does is spoof and make shit up. I'm sick of this, I'm off home." Dee walked across the stone floor we stood on, the stones sat up like eggs above the cement and you couldn't stand for long in guddies. You had to be careful of some of them, they would make to slip and fall.

"Fuck me, what a sickener." Wholenut said when Dee had got into the lift. "C'mon, Blackie, give us more stories about Genghis." Blackie looked to me.

"Naw, best leave it for tonight. Some other night Wholenut eh, what do you think Squint?"

I just shrugged. What's my opinion matter I thought. You'll just go on and tell the stories anyway because you just love an audience and all the attention, ya smart arse, the thought boiled in my head. Thoughts were burning around my head, the words lit up like flames.

"C'mon, it's early yet. Nobody's awanted for anything yet, come on. Until we're called inta the house." Wholenut pleaded. He never wanted to go home. He always waited for his little sister came to the hole in the wall and shout for him to get home. His da was known to be a hard man and had been involved in a couple of scuffles with the boys in the past. And we'd seen Wholenut with bruising before when he said he fell. He always seemed to fall on his face. "C'mon." Wholenut was almost begging now.

"Alright, alright then Wholenut, hang onto your cacks." Blackie caved in, not like his arm had been forced up his back like.

I listened to Blackie catalogue 'The misfortunes of Genghis' as he called it. I listened and I was thinking who the hell was he to slag off Genghis about the riot? I mean, at least he was out in it. He even was out with me 'til dinner time when Lieutenant Tim died. Where were you Blackie? At home with your mummy probably, reading and doing your homework. Getting yourself ready for some brianiac job no doubt. He was smartarse that was all. He hadn't even helped with the bonfire, not one piece of wood had he collected.

I was eaten up with resentment as he told the story about the time Ghegis invented a sister for himself, telling us she never went out and that was the reason he had two big bags of winegums, crisps and two big bottles of coke. One bag of each was for each of them. He wouldn't back down even when we asked his cousin Kevano over to give us the full SP. Kevano laughed like rattling gun when we asked. We confronted Ghengis, who still insisted he had a sister and that his cousin wouldn't know as they didn't talk to his side of the family.

Then there was that time he was in America and he killed someone when he dropped a dime off the roof of The Empire State Building. Like most of us he hadn't been further than Omeath. We all just got used to his spoofing. There was no harm in it most of the time. He was only a danger to himself, like the time Blackie was blabbing on about right now.

"So Genghis, seeing the power and glory of the home made catapult, shoves wee Morgan aside and says he wants a go. So he gets a brick, puts at the end of the plank. He positions it carefully on the concrete ledge and slams his big Yeti foot down on the other end. And whack! Straight into the centre of his his forehead."

"Is that when he ended up to The Mater and shagged all the nurses?" Wholenut piped up, tears rolling down his face.

"Oh Jesus, remember that? This is better than Jackanory. No, that was when he and, it was with you Squint wasn't it?" Blackie turned to me smiling. "You'd better tell it. You're good at his voice."

"You tell it Blackie, you're the best at it. No offence squint." Wholenut said.

"None taken." I said, knowing full well Blackie was going to tell it anyway. "He tells a yarn better than anyone" I said, wishing Dee had heard me and he would know what I had meant.

"The two of them were out and heading over to oul Jimmys shop, wasn't that it?"

I nodded.

"That was the time the boys had knocked out all the lights to stop the Brits getting about, remember, you couldn't get about without a torch in between the flats, pitch black. But they'd also taken the manhole covers and used them in the riots. One minute Squint here, is walking along in an amiable fashion without a torch, using the lights from the flats as their beacon. Talking to his dear friend Ghengis esquire when. Crash, bang, wallop. His companion disappears. Right down the manhole the cover that had been lifted. Below him, he hears an awful moan as poor Genghis is at the bottom of the manhole lying like his dad on a Saturday night with a ruptured knee and a fractured wrist."

I thought Wholenut's head was about to explode and Dada's went into a sneezing fit that set them off laughing all over again. I think at that point I hated Blackie for his free and easy way, his total acceptance with the gang in spite of going to St Mals and being from outside the Barrack.

I had all this guilt from the bonfire, from my action to Teddy ballsack nose's sneak attack on me that I had to keep hidden from mum and act like my face wasn't in agony and I could hardly eat my food and insisted on soup everyday saying it was part of my exercise regime. I felt like everything was falling apart and no-one was to be trusted.

Wholenut said a gloomy 'cheerio' as soon as his sister appeared at the hole in the wall. Dada went with him as they lived in the same direction. Blackie and me were left alone. Normally that wouldn't be a problem but the way I was feeling it was dead awkward. I knew Blackie felt awkward too because at this stage we would both be talking about The Hardy Boys or Billy Bunter's adventures. We'd talk about music all night if we were allowed to. I didn't know what to say without it coming out wrong. I was still blazing mad at him for going into town with Dada and Dee without me. I saw them come up through Victoria from the living room window. There they were, in broad daylight all three of them walking side by side laughing amongst themselves in the sunshine. I could see Blackie had a bag from Smyths Records at his side. And me in all afternoon. I had to content myself with talking to young Rory at the bottom of the flats, talking rubbish with an eight year old who was more interested in dissecting worms and drawing circles round their cut up bodies.

"Well, what record did you get in town the other day? More of the alternative, indie shite you're getting into?" I felt I had to ask. And I felt the need to be mean about it. I didn't even mention it was the Saturday.

"It was rock lobster by the B-52's. Waited an age to get it. It's quirky but well balanced song. The girls can really sing."

"Yeah, I know what it's like to be waiting. Waiting that is." I said. "I mean I waited all day Saturday for you to call." I felt as if I was going to sob.

"I did call, just after one."

"Yeah, you must've rapped my door with a bloody sponge then." I replied savagely, not able to conceal my anger and upset.

"But I did, honest." Blackie insisted, his hands widened out showing me both palms. "I stood outside for ages. I even shouted through your letter box."

"I never heard a thing."

"You must have been out somewhere, maybe delivering something for your dad. Maybe." He said, trying to make me out like I was lying.

"You calling me a liar?" This time I said it with anger. I could feel my face flush up and my body going rigid.

"No, honestly mate."

"Don't be using four letter words like that to me."

"What? Blackie now looked startled and worried by my tone.

"The four letter word, you're using." I waited a moment, enjoying the brainiac's confusion. "Mate. You're the big lad with all the brains. Surely you know how many letters are in it. For the record, you're no mate of mine." I said it dead cold and flat. But inside I was boiling hot. Like there was a fire inside my chest. I couldn't help not feel the way I felt and I really meant what I had said at that moment.

"Look, I'm going to get on. It's getting late." He said, looking at his stupid wee watch that was out of a lucky bag probably. He said good night and turned to walk towards the hole in the wall and that's when it happened. I don't know how, I know why but I couldn't for the life of me tell you what exactly happened. I felt the shock of pain shoot through my clenched fist. I saw Blackie's face in complete silence without a sound or sign of pain. He just stared at me, his eyes looking straight into mine. I knew instantly that we would never shout haroo! to each other as parting as Huree Ramset Jan Singh would in the Billy Bunter books we loved to read and talk about.

I thought a lot about Blackie since that night. I tried to explain what I did to myself. I could not stop feeling a sickening guilt and a crushing urge to call round and apologise and beg for his forgiveness. I wanted him back. He was my friend, probably my best friend. Now he'd go on to get a great job and move out of the area and I'd never see him again. But if his mum was anything like mine she's tell me to go chase myself or words to that effect. That's why I never once mentioned the Teddy fannymouth incident to my mum. She'd be round to his house faster than a scalded cat, screaming and squealing the house down.

What was that strange, weird word only Blackie could have come up with? He and none of the others gathered had ever heard the word before and hadn't a Scooby Doo what it meant. The thought of Blackie brought his image to mind and made him smile sadly. Blackie was funny, not in a Billy Connolly or Two Ronnies way, but the way he said things. It was always with a smile. He was a bit more like Dave Allen, dry and observant; at least he wasn't like them real English bin hokers in Monty Python. I hated them and their cleverness, it was ever so English. But the English we knew weren't a bit like that; they were nasty, stupid, violent thugs. And the Brits were hoodwinking the world with their comedy shows and their fair play and jolly hockey sticks. They were so bloody smug and maddeningly condescending. These are words I had learnt from Blackie.

It was because Blackie went to Saint Malachys, the grammar school on the Antrim Road, I knew that. They were all the boys whose da's had big cars and office jobs, or were lawyers and doctors. But Blackie was like them, from the road just over the hole in the wall in Hartwell Place and as working class as they were. He wasn't a snob, he didn't have airs or graces and even though he said some strange things, he said them like they would say them. He wasn't rich, they didn't have a car and his da worked in the fruit market and his ma was a home help. Everyone wondered where he got the brains from.

We were sure we were working class. Some of us had TV's and washing machines, even a tumble dryer. We all had radios and record players. But like, the Onions would never have those. The Onions, that wasn't their real name. They were just called that because someone had said once they all looked like onions with big, round, expressionless faces. They did all look exactly the same, even the girls who looked exactly like the boys but they had long hair that grew straight down from their heads onto their shoulders. No-one really knew how many they were due to the fact they were all different ages and they were never all out together. Yes, we may have no bananas but we've onions galore people joked. I would feel sorry for them from time to time. That was up until the eldest one ended up joining the Sheridan Hallion battalion because he was one of the best stone throwers you'd ever see. He could throw for miles and he was deadly accurate.

Alamein flat was ours only due to the fact it was closest and several members of their gang lived there. Dee was on the tenth, Genghis on the twelfth, the very top of the flat, and our hangout from time to time because his da worked in the Dockers club early in the afternoon and didn't get home to very late and more often than not very drunk. Three of us came from the maisonettes and they could all see their houses from there. We were easily the worst gang in the whole area. Worst that is, in terms of rioting ability, size in numbers, reputed hardness and most importantly in the summer, the size of the bonfire for the ninth of August to mark the introduction of Internment.

I shuddered with a cold chill within my chest when I thought back to that day. It changed everything. It got me hating Blackie. I think it was Dada saw him first. I remember him going sweet Jesus preserve us. We all looked round at once to see what he was looking at. There he was standing dead centre of the hole in the wall. I couldn't make out his face but I recognised that head from anywhere. Piercy. Even his name sent a chill down the spine, one that made me shudder. My first thought was what the hell was he doing down here? I mean it was well known throughout the area the Barracks gang was the worst in terms of fighting, rioting, collecting for the ninth, anything really.

That's when it hit me like a punch out of nowhere and without warning. I knew why he was here and I knew what he had come for. My great fear was that he was going to tell the rest of the gang. There he is. My little Gypo Nolan.

He sauntered out of the hole and down the slope of tarmacked open ground. He had his head shaved and wore a white tee shirt that showed off his big chest and muscled arms. He was brown from the weeks of sunshine and the sunlight glinted off the round specs he wore. He was wearing denim shorts and great big bovver boots like DMs but harder, hob nail style. His legs were like, tree trunks, like those of my superheroes in Marvel all muscled and proportionate to a man of great strength. I read that somewhere and it always stuck in my head, not like in school.

I could hear myself pathetically following Lt Tim and Piercy, struggling to keep up with them on the path. My schoolbag was near the same size as me and near the same weight too. They didn't carry any books and didn't even wear the school uniform; they wore the jumpers with white shirts but with jeans and DM boots. I followed up the tarmac path that gradually rose to meet the porta cabins that were dotted around the main building. At the top of the hill there three stuck together and behind them the art class. Right beside you was the start of the Cave Hill, which was a great place to go on the beak and bunk off school.

I couldn't hear what they were talking about but I was dead excited about our delivery of four tyres and six pallets for the bony this year. The Allsopps had got us the tyres from somewhere and Geordie O'Neal had asked Wholenut if wanted some pallets. And if we did, we'd to come and get them early, as he was fed up chasing youngsters from his yard this time of the year looking stuff for the bonfires. We got up extra early, me Wholenut, Dada, Dee, Tacky and his kid brother who was called Skin. We dragged them down with the rope we had tied onto them at seven in the morning. We'd never have got past Sheridan or the long streets any other time.

Geordie's scrap metal yard was across the Antrim Road at the top of the New Lodge. It was massive and was teeming with burnt out cars, trucks and an Ulsterbus he got from the top of the road the week before. He hauled the dead vehicles past the army post that sat looking down the New Lodge. Everyone that passed it shouted abuse or hurled stones at it. All that work, all that stuff to look forward to burning on our fire was about to go up the Swanee river.

I just prayed that Piercy wouldn't rat me out and let on it was me who told the two of them about the best bony the barracks was ever going to have. If he said anything, I'd get my pan kicked in and would really have to bugger off to Mosney to live.

"Oh bloody shite." Dada said in a low voice. "I thought, I thought he was just heading through to Pinkerton or somewhere. They've got a good pile of tyres this year. Shite, he's looking straight right at us. Holy fuckin' hell."

"Shut up Dada, sit down will ye. Nobody say nothing to them. He probably doesn't know anything." Dee said, but his face looked worried and he was biting his bottom lip. I was glad I was at the end of the concrete ledge and no-one could see how worried I must have looked.

Then we heard the rattling and in a moment it seemed like someone had opened a can of hallion battalion. They came pouring though the hole in the wall some were dragging large metal cages. The kind you saw outside Stewarts supermarket as the men brought in the milk and bread and stuff. There was dozens of them spreading out over the open ground.

"I say we get stuck in. I've got a black belt in Karate." Genghis said, moving his arms like he was Karl Douglas dancing to Kung Fu Fighting.

"Snakebelt in Hi Karate, be more bloody like it." Dee snarled back at him making us all laugh. "Shut your cakehole Ghegis."

"Share the joke lads." Piercy said as he stood before us. His voice never sounded the way I thought it would. It was deadly quiet, calm; polite even. He was half smiling like he knew something was up. "You." He said. And everyone went deathly quiet. I prayed it wasn't, but I knew he was talking directly to me.

"It's nuthin' Piercy, honest to God. We just wondered what has youse down in our neck of the woods. I mean we've got to have the worst bony on the road. It's hardly The Warriors round here." Percy's smile widened to show a row of tiny white teeth that looked strange in such a big lad. Smiling didn't much suit Piercy's face, his eyes practically disappeared when he did so. Thankfully his smile disappeared as fast as it came.

"Your, ah," Piercy paused as he thought, "McDonagh's wee lad, yeah, Brendy McDonagh's lad. He was in the Kesh not so long back. Nor meekly served his time either." He gave out a loud, sharp whistle from his lips. "Here Bap, this one here is McDonagh's lad. Your uncle served time with him on the blocks."

The one called Bap who was built like the Hulk or The Thing and looked like he could give anyone a good clobbering time, gave a short salute and said nothing. "Fair play til ye kid for doing what you're doing. I know it's a ballicks but that's the way the cookie crumbles. Your da's a decent spud. Harp and a vodka and coke man if memory serves."

Piercy worked in The Felons club as a barman and served most of the da's who had been inside. "I like your style, but I don't have time for small talk. So this is the way it's going to be boys. Youse will be kind enough to go and get the tyres and pallets you've got hidden and bring them out for the lads over there with the cages. And we won't have to knock yer malts in. You and laughing boy here can go bring them out from wherever you have them stashed. It's too warm to start fucking around. And I'm getting tired and hungry. You won't like me when I'm hungry." He made a point of stretching out his giant arms, and sticking out his chest like he was some kind of gorilla in Animal Magic with Johnny Morris, and let them do the talking. I could hear Johnny now, big gorilla to the little chimps 'I'm the king of the forest, the jungle VIP, get me your firewood or you'll swing from the nearest tree.' And we all reply: 'Yes O mighty king gorilla of the forest, the jungle VIP, we will carry out our firewood because we're all wimps and yellow you see.'

So one little chimp gets up, me; and I found out who my chimp partner is as Wholenut gets up to join me and we walk towards our hiding place like two dogs beaten by his master. We were joined by the biggest gorilla in the forest as Bap tagged behind us. We didn't speak a word until we reached the bottom of the stairs inside Alamein. Bap waited at the lifts. He didn't need to say a word. We knew what we had to do and we had no choice in the matter.

At the bottom of the stair case was the hidey hole we had for loot. We had covered most of it in an old carpet we had found at the back of the garage roofs outside the maisonettes where a little water ran behind it and their was a slanted wall all the way along the back of the garages. We hardly ever ventured in there because of rats. Sometimes if we saw one scuttling along out or back in we would attack it with rocks that we had deliberately stored in the stone basin where flowers had meant to be.

"How do you think they knew about this stuff then?" Wholenut hissed over to me as I lifted the carpet off the pallets in a cloud of dust that made me cough.

"Fuck if I know." I managed to get out during my cough, attempting to sound really sore about the whole episode. I dragged the top pallet.

"Watch out for scalfs Squint." Wholenut advised.

"Aye, I know, I just wish they had given us gloves for their dirty work."

"You serious?" Wholenut giggled.

"Course not. Just being sarky." I said.

Wholenut took the pallet I slid along the tiled floor. "I'm never collecting again. Never. Not a lollipop stick, nuthin'." He said like he really meant it. "It's a fuckin' joke this is. They just sit there and get it handed to them."

"Come on, let's get and done and dusted" I said as sadly I could.

"You think we could getaway with just giving them some of it and stashing a tyre or two?" Wholenut asked from beneath the staircase. "Squint? Squint? Whadya think? Well?"

My face must have given me away. "What is it?" Wholenut asked, without looking up.

"No." I said simply.

Bap, who was directly behind me laughed. That really pleased me that I had made someone as hard as him laugh.

"Jesus, Mary and Joseph, Bap, I thought I was away for me cornflakes there." Wholenut placed his hands over his chest. "I nearly had a heart attack there."

"I'll tell what you'll be getting, if you don't get a move on getting that stuff out to us." He said in an sinister tone. "Come on, start shifting it." This time Bap was deadly serious, the smile dropped from his face.

"Right ye are Bap, let me get this one through the door and I'll leave it against the wall outside." Wholenut told him. I couldn't help myself from staring at the size of Bap. His chest was almost as wide as the door frame.

His arms and legs looked like they'd be carved from tree trunks. I wondered what he ate at meal times and what sort of exercise he took. Probably all he needed to do was his clobberin' time just like The Thing. God knows he was big enough.

"Good lad. Right you" Bap said, looking right at me, "start getting that gear out to him quicker." He instructed.

"Yes, sure. No problem, wee buns." I said, in a cheery tone that made Wholenut look at me like I was a complete stranger. I lifted one of the car tyres and rolled it to the corner. I may have well saluted my commanding officer as I carried out his order as quickly as I did. By the time we left the flat we were both covered in marks, smudges and dust. Our hands and fingernails were boggin'.

We stood like dummies watching The Hallion battalion march towards the hole in the wall with our pallets and tyres captured by their thieving hands. They rattled up the slope and trundled through the hole with the cages. And they were gone.

All but for Piercy and Bap who remained with us.

"Alright lads, I know how you're feeling right nigh. It's a kick in the goolies you don't need. I know you hate our guts right now."

"Naw, no way Piercy." Genghis shouted up from his seated position. Everyone of us turned on him at the same time and told him the same thing.

"Shut up."

"Yeah, what they said." Piercy told him. "But I'll tell ye this. It's all in a good cause. The reason why we're doing this is to honour an old comrade who died for Ireland. And we're gonna make sure he gets the biggest bonfire the New Lodge has ever seen. And it's gonna be in his honour. You all know who I'm talking about. He was your neighbour and a mate to youse. A better man this place will never see. So I just wanted you to know that and we're not being big dicks for nothing. Just hope it takes the sting out what's happened. Alright lads?"

He turned to walk away and Dee shouted his thanks out to him on all our behalves.

"Just so there's no hard feelings lads. You're all invited to come up and watch the bonfire on the night. You won't have to sneak up like youse do every year. No-one will touch you. Okay?"

I watched Piercy as he spoke and I filled up with pride and admiration at the way he was treating us like we mattered. He looked like some kind of giant bird of prey as I followed his gaze towards the maisonette, my maisonette and my balcony. You could imagine he could see through the walls and God help anyone hiding their bony collection from him. They would need to be behind lead-lined walls.

He'd be a great friend, if he was your mate and you could tell he was serious and sincere about you know who. I could see his eyes fill up before mine did. I drew attention to my tears by wiping my eyes, hoping Piercy and Bap would see how much Lieutenant Tim had meant to me too. Then they'd never feel like telling on me to the others.

"Cheers Piercy that's really brill of ya. If you hadda said that at the start what it was for, we woudda gave you the gear no problem."

And we again turned to tell Genghis to shut up.

"Sure where's the fun in that." Piercy coughed out a small laugh. "C'mon Bap. We're not finished yet. No rest for the wicked". He made a small laugh and they put their arms across each others shoulders walked up to and through the hole in the wall.

I watched them walk out the Barrack with the greatest sense of relief I had since escaping the chippy with my life. None of us there said a word. Even if they found out now it was me who, accidentally on purpose, told him about the tyres and pallets I could say it was for Lieutenant Tim that I did it. They told me what it was for and I had to tell them. He was my friend, my avuncular as Blackie explained, he took me to big school on my first day; he lived on our balcony for Godsake. Who could blame me? I think we all left one another shortly after, again without a word. Except for the big hole in my story. I had told Piercy when Tim when he was very much alive and all three of us walked up the path to school.

I had my big breakfast, two eggs scrambled. I couldn't poach them to save my life. Two vegetable rolls or New Lodge steaks we called them; two sausages, Cookstown of course, after Pat Jennings on the TV. Two potato farls and a soda bread. It would set me up for the day and see me through 'til dinner time after I got back from the match. I only ever ate Shredded Wheat, Weetabix, as Rice Krispies and Cornflakes didn't have enough of what I needed to build myself up. I had to add the extra money it cost or I'd have to listen to mum moan every time she saw the boxes or saw me eating them. And I hated porridge it was like that semolina muck they dished out at school dinners.

I went up the flight of stairs and to my room where I intended to lie down and digest my breakfast but when my head touched the pillow Blackie's face appeared, all sad and teary-eyed. It was like he was haunting me, pointing a finger and calling me Judas. I sat up and decided to run the bath. I put in some of the blue powder mum used and poured in lifebuoy from the bottle and watched it bubble up. I would leave the bath to cool down and went to my room to get undressed and wore the big towel I had around my waist. I pulled a few poses in the mirror in my room laughing at the puniness of my physique. Although I had noticed recently my shoulders were getting a shape either side of my neck and some muscle showed even when I didn't flex. Walk before you run I heard mum's voice say.

I placed my hand in the water it needed more cooling so I twisted the cold water tap and allowed it to flow for several seconds and then I swirled it around the bath. I stepped in the water was about four inches above my ankles. I sat down in the bath. The water was just right, it didn't scald me like the last time. I dragged the bath rack towards me for the flannel and soap and began washing my face, arms and chest. I ran the flannel down my legs and then dabbed my goolies. Ever since the capture in the chippy they had never felt the same. I was dead careful around them. I even moved them so they sat flat on the seat of my bike, most of the time I rode my bike without sitting on the saddle. I knew they had been hurt in some way but I could never tell mum as it was dead embarrassing. She'd probably want to see them and then she'd get mad at me for being so bloody stupid to go across Hallidays Road.

I thought about cribby and that trebler I made that day against Dee. I'd never did one before plenty of doublers hitting one side square on the edge of the pavement on bouncing onto the other. Of course, Dee said it wasn't because the moment you got one, you won the game hands down. It cheered me up to think of it and then I thought about the match to come and what the players were doing. On their way to the ground after a good breakfast similar to my own maybe. Getting to the ground early to check out the pitch, get a feel on how to play. They'd be out passing the ball and making runs, stretching their bodies like I'd seen them so many times at the Solitude before kick-off. Learning who was on and playing where. I'd watch their exercises and make notes in my head how to do them as they did. I did these things on the quiet I was too scrawny to join the boxing clubs or the weight lifting club down by Saint Patricks, they'd laugh their heads off at me walking in with my kit bag.

I lay back against the bath feeling the chill from the plastic and sank further down in the warm water. I felt a sense of ease I had not known for a week of two. I had intended to read the paper after my bath but time was running short if I was to get my exercises done and get to Genghis's as I said I would. I'd kept up with the team news all week and gotten some great photos to cut out from my scrap book. A couple of photos of the players when they signed for the club and one had had a christening of his baby boy called Charles Eamonn. There had been no major injuries thank God. McCusker, Bell, Platt and my favourite player, Largey. They all had clean bills of health.

Defenders always got the raw end of the deal, they never got the credit they deserved when they played well but were slaughtered when they made mistakes cause they usually proved costly. It was always the front men, the glory hunters who got the praise, not the guys who supplied them or who put their boot in where Angels feared to tread to get the ball. Eamonn did that with a big smile on his face, he was hard but never dirty. He had great muscly thighs and a long lean torso. He reminded me of Johann Cruyff to be honest.

They'd probably play four, four, two with Bell and Platt up from and wee McCusker playing in the middle. Sinky would get on the score sheet, I had no doubt of that. And we'd sing 'C'mon you reds' and 'We won't be mastered by no Orange bastard' and chant SS RUC and slag off that wee twat Jackie Hutton who hated us and our club because we were Fenians and Nationalists, even though our board was as black as your boot. Seventy years since any silverware, it was exciting to think we could win something this year. I'd stay in the cage, cramped up with the crowd, standing, trying to stay on your feet, fearing you'd get trampled, fearing the RUC were about to attack at any time. I would stand near the back, close to the wall, always hoping for a chance to kick off a chant myself.

It was time to get out of the bath as my fingertips were shrivelling up and I had to exercise and get my routine done to bring us luck the last time before the game. Ever since the first game of the cup against Linfield away and we bate them four three I had started the routine. It was one game and ground in Belfast mum would never let go to. I was glad really as I don't think Iain Craig would even have saved me if I'd been caught at Windsor. I dried off in the bedroom and put on a fresh pair of trunks and socks. That was the start of the routine. Then jeans, boots my ankle boots with the DM sole, then my football shirt number six. I would use Right Guard and then touch the statue of Christ. I didn't ask for a win, just that we played well and no-one got injured on or off the field. Mum had told me never to ask for things for myself; 'that's not how prayer works love' she said.

I counted my Lego bricks, three hundred and twenty nine, marleys, 'marbles hon, say marbles', I hear mum telling me. Sixty three, including nine bullers. My change, I kept in a big bottle da brought home yonks ago that was full of some gunk to unblock the sinks in the kitchen and the bathroom. Mum told me to rinse it out thoroughly before using it. When he'd finished he just put it in the cupboard under the sink and I rescued it a week later; washed it out in the bath and took it for the change I was saving in a tin up until then. The bottle was great to save in as it was twice the size of the big lemonade bottles and I never got close to filling it all the way up. It was a pain to refill but I had to count it all out if we were to win this afternoon.

I had exactly three pounds and forty five pence in silver, and four pound and eighteen pence in coppers. I always waited until I got five pounds in silver and five in coppers before asking mum if she would take me down to The Woolwich and hand my savings over in bank bags to put in my account. I had thirty three pounds in my account, enough money if I ever needed to get away quick from the house and with selling my bike and marbles and my paper round I could live down south for a couple of weeks 'til I got another job delivering papers or being a milk mans or lemonade man's helper. I nearly always had those thoughts when I counted my money and thought of my savings. What I really wanted was to have enough, me and mum between us, to buy a house up the Antrim Road.

I needed to wash my hands after I had made my count as they stank of metal and had like a rusty smell on them. I headed to downstairs to get the stereo. We'd had it forever, a Waltham stereo system. I remembered when mum had it delivered. I thought it the best thing ever. It had the radio and record player and a built-in cassette player that you could tape the charts off. Even though the DJ's were dense enough to talk through the start and end of songs, you got most of the song taped. I read the instructions cover to cover and would take charge when mum wanted to use the record player or use the tape machine which I called the tape deck. I showed her all the radio settings she needed Radio 1, Luxembourg stuff like that. She was dead impressed with me.

I unplugged the speakers and placed them on top of the plastic casing protecting the record player and carefully carried it up the stairs counting each one as I climbed. Fourteen stairs. My arms ached as I carefully set it on the bed. I then set the speakers on the ground and then the unit. I plugged everything in and then decided I would do half of my normal exercise regime. But I couldn't it wasn't part of my routine to bring luck. I hadn't done any exercising the morning of the first cup game. That in itself was unusual. I couldn't remember why I hadn't exercised that morning. I always made time for it even on school days. I would do some, usually fifty for each arm and twenty squats on the big bar for my legs; much to mum's frustration as she shouted from the downstairs kitchen for me to get a move on. I mean I had already done my paper round and had got another wash and would change into my school uniform after my exercises. She never left the house until I had appeared downstairs for the school inspection. That annoyed me as I thought she treated me like a child in that. I mean I got myself up for work everyday even on Saturdays, she had trusted me with a key to the house and Aunt Greta's which I kept on my key ring an old one she had from work.

Anyway I wasn't going to annoy myself with that. I had music to listen to. My top ten rock tracks in the exact same order as the first morning of the first cup game when I played them to take my mind off the game and the fact I wasn't allowed to go. Up first, We will Rock You by Queen, I loved the guitar piece at the end where I would play it to perfection in the mirror with an old tennis racquet I had. It had "c/w, We are the Champions" on the cover. I played that last. I had no idea what c/w stood for and I wasn't going to ask Stevie or Duffer. Then Cheaptrick live at the Budokan with I Want You To Want Me, then came UFO with a serious piece of guitar with'Rock Bottom'. I even struggled to keep up with that on my tennis racquet with the plastic strings. I took a break after that one and got a glass of water to take up with me on stage. I'd pretend it was Bourbon, a drink rock stars seemed to like from what I'd read in music magazines.

Next a track that cheered me up no end because they didn't seem to take themselves that seriously and like the Who's My Generation, it had the singer stuttering. Bachman Turner Overdrive and You ain't seen Nuthin Yet. I always sang the chorus even though I was playing lead guitar. Next, one of my favourite tunes ever with a fantastic piece of guitar that went unnoticed by most. I think it was because the radio always ended the song too early. I wanted it to last forever when I played Rainbow's, Since You've Been Gone. I really dug my fingers in to get the screaming sound of the chords reaching into my soul and singing upwards towards God Himself. This was the language of true prayer. I never felt close to God at church only when I listened to songs like the next on my listen the mystical beautiful sound of Lynard Skynard playing Freebird. I found it impossible to imagine how anyone could write such a thing, how you could think up the words and tune and then break into the twin guitars of Rossington and Allen who I had made a point to read about once when I had bought the 45. A terrible tragedy happened to the band a couple of years back with the singer Ronnie Van Zant dying in a plane crash that always made me tear up when I played the song. I did it in remembrance of him and of Lieutenant Tim.

I was in another world, a world where I could be anything, anyone I wanted. These people weren't ordinary, how could they be, writing and playing such wondrous songs. I was dead jealous. I wanted so much to be a guitarist and play in a band like this. I was wrapped up in the glorious screaming guitars my heart on fire with electricity flying through my body. It was pure joy I was feeling. How could that be Satanism? I would grow my hair long and wear leather jackets and have a beard. I would rink Bourbon and shout out on stage, Hello Belfast, are you ready to rock? And the crowds would go wild and girls would smile at me and blow me kisses.

The antidote to such sad thoughts was next on the list: Led Zeppelin's 'Rock n Roll. From the crazy opening strings that opened up a great track that exploded into life with a thunderous sound of, furious wailing guitar and Plant's voice soaring into the heavens with a beauty I could never have made up. Then I had a moment to rest and sip some water before I put on what I am not ashamed of and stand by my choice even against Stevie and Duffer if they disagreed. The Osmonds and their cracking track, Crazy Horses. An absolute belter of a tune. Who would have thought those big toothed do-gooders could come up with something so great. The singing was all rock, full of shouting and about as much anger as The Osmonds could muster about those Crazy Horses.

Then once I had drank some water I put on Kansas and their monumental track, Carry On My Wayward Son, the extended version with the long guitar action at the end as it built up and up to it and I went into a head banging session that almost made me faint. I thought I had damaged my brain at one stage. Finally, it was Queen again only for the match on the flip side of We Will Rock You, We Are The Champions. It was the most stirring and appropriate song I had to end the concert and get me ready for the game.

After all that I was exhausted but happy and confident that we would win. I dismantled the system and brought it down to the living room and set it up as it had been. I checked my bag again for the items necessary for travel. I checked my money and my other pocket for my emergency fund. I was still too warm to put on my scarf in the house. I tied it around my left wrist and buried my hat deep down into the back pocket of my jeans. I had washed, was wearing fresh socks and underpants. I looked in the hall mirror and with my right fist shouted come on you reds. I blessed myself with the holy water at the bottom of the Knock Shrine and prayed for a good win and a safe journey there and back.

I left the house making sure all the sockets were out, the kitchen window was locked shut, the stove was off and checked the door was closed and locked behind me. I was across the square and pressing the button for one of the lifts less than three minutes later.

The lift arrived and it smelled of piss and tobacco as usual. I had to stand there all the way up to the twelfth, trying to hold my breath was impossible all the way to the top. I used my scarf to cover my nose and breathed in and out of the wool feeling the cold spit build up on the material. I jumped out before the door fully opened and inhaled a big breath that made me feel dizzy.

I approached Genghis's door, it was blue like most of them, some had put their own doors on with letterboxes that were vertical not horizontal like a letterbox should be. Pains in the arse sometimes, especially with those wire baskets on the back and they filled up. I just rolled it up like a stick and shoved it in with as much force as I could muster.

I remembered his door well. I had good cause to. There was me, Dee, Dada and Wholenut with Genghis messing about in the flat, we were on the balcony standing around spitting onto the barracks. There were always empty crates on the balcony from the club his da worked in. They were always empty. That day someone and no-one to this day ever admitted to it; someone dropped a bottle over the balcony. Thank Christ no-one was hit especially after Genghis killed someone in New York by firing a cent coin off that Empire State Building.

But people in the square below were pointing up at us and we cowered back and closed the door to the balcony shiteing ourselves. We waited an age in the living room not making a sound. We kept peering up the hall towards the door listening for sounds. Nothing.

"Thank fuck. No-one's coming." Dada said, placing a hand over his chest as if he had survived a heart attack.

Then there was this great big bang on the front door.

"Fuck you Dada."

"What? It wasn't my fault. It's whoever fucked that bottle. That was you Dee."

"Clear the fuck off, it wasn't me. I can'tell ye that for nuthin. It was you Wholenut, you'd think somethin like that was dead funny."

"Wise up. I never threw nuthin. What about Squint? Why's he not in the frame for it?"

"I didn't do it. I was at the back. It would've whistled over your heads if I'd have lobbed it. I was nowhere near the balcony when it happened."

"How'd you know what happened then?" Wholenut was being really sly and serious.

"Go to hell Wholenut." I told him. I was bloody raging with him. "I'm not the one who thinks that kind of thing is funny."

"Everyone shut the hell up." Dee said, in a hushed, scared voice that was hard to ignore. And we did. Then the door was banged again. 'Get out here, ye wee bastards.'

"Aye right, we'll go out and get our heads kicked in. Go on Genghis, get out there and talk to them. It's your house. You keep saying you're as game as a badger."

"It is your house." Dee reiterated. "Tell them to fuck off away from your door."

"But don't open it, just talk to them from the hall." I added, trying to help us all out and keep us all safe. Genghis didn't look too sure. Genghis walked to the glass fronted door of the living room.

"Lads we're real sorry it happened. It was an accident. The bottle fell off the balcony. We didn't mean it. And no-one was hurt. That's the main thing." Genghis looked back at us and made a thumbs up sign.

"Open this fucking door or we'll kick it in." The door monster shouted.

"C'mon lads, you need to stop banging the door." Genghis pleaded. "My da's gonna be back soon."

"Yeah, we'll give him a fucking kicking an all." The door monster told him.

"That didn't cut much ice. Wait 'til superalc does arrive." Wholenut sniggered.

"Oh yeah, whadya think he'll do to us for causing all this shit." Dee warned.

"Jesus, you're right. He'll use his superpowers of alcohol to knock us all out." Wholenut laughed.

"Hopefully with his fists not his super smell." I said and to my great satisfaction, everyone apart from Genghis laughed. Genghis was engaging with the door monster that was getting more belligerent and issuing blood curdling threats to our persons.

Although Genghis's da was a bit of a hero after that incident with the soldiers and his courageous stand against a whole foot patrol; behind his back we had made him a superhero called Super Alco. That night as we relived the incident and watched it on the news we invented Genghis's da into a man with the fighting strength of ten alco's as soon as he had his vodka. It was a bit like Popeye and his spinach. Once the drink touched his lips, Boom! Super strength, and super powers.

He could knock over any man with his breath from ten yards. He could pish over tall buildings and slabber for Ireland. He could fart at anytime he wanted and with such great accuracy he could knock a man out at twenty yards with the stench. He could outrun a sea of diarrhoea that would escape his legs and engulf his enemies in a tide of slimy shite that would kill you stone dead. We had a real laugh inventing him a new identity that night and Genghis never knew we had ripped his da to shreds.

Genghis moved down the hall towards the door monster with its letterbox of a mouth demanding the door to be opened. Genghis moved hesitantly down the hall. He walked sideways like the men you saw in a duel. He was dead slow and stuttering like he was walking the plank.

"Hurry fuckin' up, and open this door." The door monster demanded.

"Please lads, look let it lie lads. No-ones hurt c'mon please." Genghis was walking towards the door monster who threatened to knock him out if he didn't open allow him in.

"Here c'mon yousings." Wholenut said in a whisper, using his hand to cover his mouth away from Ghengis. He nodded his head backwards. "We'll get onto the balcony and lock ourselves out on it this time."

"Good thinking batman." Dee said and I followed reluctantly because it was Wholenut's idea and we were abandoning poor Genghis. But the door monster was getting angrier, the banging noises it made got louder.

Wholenut locked the balcony door from the outside and we all hunkered down so if the monster came roaring into the room it wouldn't see us. We waited forever without making a sound. In total, it was probably about five minutes before Dada said the blood had stopped circulating to his legs and he announced he was standing up. Everyone felt the same, sometimes you just get sick of being frightened. Dee ventured to open the balcony door and listened for noises. Nothing.

"Shit. Do you think they got him?" Wholenut asked.

"Come on, let's have a Jeff duke." Dee said.

"After you" Wholenut said with a big smile.

"Dick." Dee said stepping into the living room as quietly as he could. We let Dee walk across the room to a point where he could look straight down the hall. We kept the door to the balcony open to allow just in case the door monster had broken through and into the flat.

"Genghis!" Dee shouted out down the hall. "C'mon out lads, Genghis is lying on the deck." Dee got to Genghis first who was lying on the ground. He was crying and holding his face. "What happened mate? What'd the fuckers' do til ya? Bastards." Dee shouted at the now silenced door monster. It had exacted its revenge.

"What's up with him? Whad they do to ya?" Wholenut asked, but he didn't sound like he cared. I had not forgiven him for saying it was me who chucked the bottle over balcony.

"Let's get him up for chrissake." I said. Genghis was dead weight and really heavy.

"What happened? What the hell did they do?" Dee asked again.

"They, they, got me to the door and told me open it" Genghis sounded all teary and snatters were running out of his nose. We got him to the sofa and sat him down as quickly as we could because the snatters and tears were now falling in droplets onto the carpet. He bent over leaning his arms on his big legs and he must have relived whatever happened as he started to cry again without a thought about what it looked like in front of his mates.

"Get him some water somebody and a wipe for his face." Dee said. I took it upon myself to get him a glass of water and found a dishcloth for him to wipe his face.

"There you go Genghis. Some water to get down you and a cloth for your face." Genghis took the water and sipped. He wiped his nose and face free of the tears that were tripping him and tried to hand it back to me. "Naw, you're alright Genghis, you hold onto the cloth. Case you need it again."

"I crouched down on me honkers and got to look at them through the letterbox. I wanted to speak to them, get them to calm down and then one of the bastards shoved a stick through the box into my face."

For the next five minutes none of us could move for laughing. And when Genghis called us a bunch of 'no good bastards and no better than the people inside the door monster' our laughing started all over again.

I was smiling at the memory when Genghis opened the door with a big smile on his face. "Ah Squint my good man, come on in" he said in his loud voice that rolled out of the barrel of a chest he had. He sounded just like his da at the door and he seemed unsteady on his feet and a bit bleary eyed. The heavy lids of his eyes were lower than ever. He always looked half asleep and with his thin wee line of a moustache, that's what got him his nickname. "Duffer's here as well" He added.

I stepped into the hall closing the door that no longer was possessed of the monsters behind me. Immediately the house smelt different, even before I got near the glass fronted living room door that was lying wide open. I could hear music as I passed the bathroom door.

He was the biggest spoofer in the New Lodge, hands down. When I thought about our old primary school Edmund Rice, or as we just called it, Pim Street. It used to be a dam, Archies dam it was called. The story goes that a young kid younger than us drowned in it and when they built the school there he began to haunt it. Of course it was Genghis who saw the ghost one day when he was coming back down Churchill Street. He said the boy was looking for his mummy and he was wearing old style clothes with buckles on his shoes and when Genghis turned to look for his Ma the boy just disappeared into thin air. I remember everyone calling him a spoofing, lying twat, every name under the sun. But I found it unsettling, especially after all the stories from Granda Brady. There did seem to be something in it.

The living room was much bigger than ours in the Maisonettes, it was as wide as it was long. Duffer sat on the sofa beside Jesus and his sacred heart which was exposed to the entire room on one of those small mat type things that mum called throws. He was sat leaning forward with some papers and a line of tobacco. He looked up and made a smile that made his long nose look longer and his eyes look almost oriental like the monks in Kung Fu. He wore lime green corduroys and baseball shoes. He had a flowery shirt on that was red and blue in colour. The air was heavy and stuffy like the room hadn't been aired in yonks.

I was reminded of the incense used at funeral mass, like Lieutenant

Tim's funeral. The men in the uniforms and masks didn't enter the church, but handed him over to family and friends, who were dressed in ordinary clothes and who walked him up the centre aisle and placed him on the small shiny metal bars before the altar. I snapped out of that thinking and took a look at Duffer.

I knew they way he dressed must have something to do with what he smoked.

"You want some cookies Squint, there's plenty in the big Roses tin in the kitchen."

"Cheers Genghis, I'd love a Wagon Wheel. You got any cream soda and brown lemonade?"

"Soda pops in the larder. On the bottom shelf." Genghis said lazily as he dropped onto the armchair close to the electric fire which only had the lights of the whirling bulbs on. I went to the kitchen found the Roses tin the one mum used at Christmas for her pudding. I took a Wagon Wheel and sneaked a Breakaway biscuit out and into my satchel. I set the tin back and got two new bottles of Cream soda and brown lemonade and washed out a glass and poured in a mix roughly fifty/fifty parts brown lemonade and cream soda. A gulped a mouthful down, Jesus it was delicious, a bubbly mix of fizz that exploded like a starburst in my mouth. I drank half of that mix down and poured the same mix in filling the glass to the brim.

I went to stand at the kitchen door leaning against its frame. Duffer was on the big three seater sofa his back to Jesus' face and his sacred heart which was the throw over the back of the sofa. He was licking the rolled up cigarette he was making.

"What's the new album you got like?" I asked hoping they would play it for me.

"A cracker. Absolute gem. Jet Airliner and Jungle Love were the best ones for me" Genghis said. "It's a cracker album Duffer, isn't it?"

"Can I see the cover Genghis?" I asked, feeling they should have really picked up on my hint by now.

"Sure, it's down beside the record player."

I stepped across the round around the small coffee table with Irelands Own on it some the back page had been ripped off. I lifted the cover and went to the open balcony door and stood outside of the living room for the better light. Also I wanted to get away from the smell that burned at my nostrils and caught the back of my throat. It was leaping in there, really stuffy and with a heavy stale smell.

The cover was really class, a multi-coloured winged horse inside what looked like a Celtic band. The Steve Miller Threshold. Artwork by Alton Kelley and Stanley Mouse, I wondered if he was any relation to Mickey and found myself giggling at my thought of it. Recorded at CBS studios in San Francisco and produced by Steve Miller himself. I wondered what a wonderful place it must be to live in a place that had so many great singer s and guitarists never mind actors like Steve McQueen and people like Steven Spielberg. Hey they were all Stevens I thought and found myself giggling again. The album was now two years old, we were so behind everybody and not just in music I thought and found my serious thought amusing.

"You alright out there Squint?" Duffers voice was unfamiliar to me and I had to think hard for his name.

"Yeah." I said simply.

"Don't be having a whitey out there on us" He said and I heard Genghis laughing from way back in the living room.

"What time are you heading to the soccer game Squint?" Genghis asked.

I stepped up to the door of the balcony and placed a foot on the raised part of the frame. "I dunno, because I'm going to a football match." And Duffer laughed, letting out an explosion of smoke that looked like and smelt like the incense at mass for a funeral. Again reminding me of Lieutenant Tim's funeral when they brought the coffin in. His Da, Tim Senior leading the bearers and I felt as sad then as I did now.

"Keep yer kaks on Squint, I was only asking." Genghis didn't sound annoyed. He was smiling in fact and he made me feel kat about shouting back at him. After all I was here in his house having eaten a Wagon Wheel and drinking his lemonade. But the American stuff was getting on my nerves and I was feeling a bit sick in my stomach and I had come up to hear the album and I had heard diddly squat. The two of them just sat in the smoky room smiling, they looked like two morons and they were melting my head with their stupid grinning faces. I wanted out of the flat. I had to get up to the club and meet with Mister Hale and the other man and get to the match. I wasn't going to ask them to play it for me that would make me a crawler. If Ghengis was any kind of mate, he would have put the record on for me. The fat spoofer.

I heard Genghis say to Dufffer "this is the gear" and Duffer said back "Leb gold' and he nodded his head like he was gently head banging. He held the cigarette right down to the butt, he was holding it like it was made of glass or something really fragile.

"You want a toke Squint?" He asked, holding the burning paper out towards me. I could see the 'D' that was tattooed on his hand right below his thumb.

"No thanks, you're alright Duffer. I've to get on. Gotta get on and get to the match" I said, directing the comment at Genghis who didn't seem to care.

"It's not contagious" Duffer said. "Might make the match go a lot better as well."

"No, but I don't wanna end up a junkie. I don't wanna get hooked on that stuff."

They both laughed and made coughing sounds. Genghis rolled onto his fat side like he had been knocked over.

That was my queue to get across the living room and get out of the flat. "Look, I'll see youse later, alright" I told them.

"Keep 'er lit Squint. Hope youse win" Genghis said, recovered from his coughing fit and sitting up on the chair.

"Aye, cheers." I was happy we parted on good terms as friends should. I walked down the corridor towards the front door and had to skip into the bathroom for a pee. The bus journey would be a long one and I didn't know if it had a toilet on board. I hated the toilets in the clubs and pubs. They were stinking and full of oul lads smelling of beer and fags and wanting to talk to you while you're trying to pish.

The toilet was like ours, green and tiled but with the clothes horse in the bathroom it was full of damp clothes; mostly white shirts and black socks that his da wore to work. A big blue shirt I guessed was Genghis's. I looked to see if there were any girls' clothes, like blouses, bobby socks or knickers to confirm the existence of a sister for Genghis but I didn't see any evidence of a girl on the clothes horse. I washed my hands and looked at my face in the mirror, my face felt hot, but I looked dead pale.

I washed my face, rubbing it really hard with the soft towel trying to get myself back to normal. I left the bathroom as quietly as I could because I didn't want to speak to either of them in the living room and I was supposed to have been gone already. I could hear Genghis talking and I heard my name mentioned so I stopped dead in the hall, trying to control my breathing so I could hear what was being said. I could hear something about the artful dodger then da and then something about lights and fly killer thingys you see in the butchers. I heard him mention Wholenut and the bruises. I don't know why, but I felt sure he was slagging off all our da.

Genghis you fat numpty, why are you talking out of school to Duffer? He didn't care and he wouldn't even remember as he was a junkie. I was gonna tell this lads about when I got back, no fear. Now I had to leave as quietly as I could so Genghis wouldn't know what I knew. As I got to the door I opened it dead slow, thank God there wasn't any noise from the snib as it opened. I crept around the door and onto the welcome mat and for some reason the notion to slam the door came over me. To hell with it, let the druggies know. I should tell the boys down in Artillery and get them both tarred and feathered. I was giggling as I walked into the lift with the picture of Genghis all covered in feathers tied to a lamppost like some big fat black crow that had fallen from the sky and into the barrack. That would be hilarious, maybe the zoo could keep him as a rare exotic species of the lesser spotted New Lodge spoofer family.

I was still giggling about that image as the lift reached the ground floor and I stepped out almost bumping into young Gavin, known to all as Rusty because of his ginger hair.

"Whoa, ease up there Squint, you okay there?" He asked, his hands both up in a playful defensive pose.

"Sorry Rusty, didn't see you there. Aye, no probs Rusty. Just something I was thinking about made me laugh." He was wearing a QPR football shirt even though he was a mad Arsenal fan. He must have seen me look at it.

"Oh aye this, me and me brothers was up at the fields playing and this was the only shirt I could get me hands on. Can't wait til get home and get this shite off me." He slid past me into the lift and pressed the nine button. "Good luck this afternoon. I can't go, bloody skint mate."

"No bother I'll tell ye all about when I get back." I said walking towards the doors to exit the tower.

"Cheers, see ye later. You can tell me about the match." Rusty shouted to be heard over tthe rumbling noise of the lift door closing.

"Aye, see ye Rusty." I said feeling really tired and not really bothered about the match at all.

I walked past the railings to the nursery school that gave us a piece of grass to play football on. The swings that sat on the big bar acted as our goals. It was easy to climb over as the iron railings weren't in spikes nor anything. A flat strap of metal was on top right across the railing and you could even sit on top if you had good balance. I just got over as quick as I could and would kick the ball against the wall of the walled hut where they kept all the kids playthings like the swing chairs and the wee cars and skipping ropes all that kinda stuff. No-one ever tried to break in or else you'd get a kick in the plums. Everyone understood it was off limits.

Minutes later I was outside the Circle club where I had to meet Mister Hale and Mister McAleese. No-one was there, nobody outside the wire mesh that surrounded the entrance. You had to press the buzzer to get that's after whoever was on the door had a good gander at you. I had seen into the club loads of times, the stairs were really steep and there had been talk some man had fallen down and killed himself at the bottom. Looking at them stairs it was easy to see how.

I was tired and my mouth was dry I delved into my bag and took out the bottle of Fanta. I took a sip and swirled it around my gob. It was fizzing and felt burney in my mouth. I took a slug and gasped as it went down my throat. I had been to the bog at Genghis's so I wasn't worried about needing a pee for a while. But I didn't want to drink too much. I had no idea how long the bus journey was going to be and I was sure now that it wouldn't have a toilet on board. The buses usually don't, I was told. But there would definitely be a piss stop on the way. This was from a guy who went to all the away matches. That news was a comfort to me.

I thought about the last few days and Blackie and I knew as soon as I got back from the match I had to act quickly. I had my version of events thought out. It was Blackie who had touted on the tyres and pallets. He had admitted it to me and that's why I hit him. It made sense and it wouldn't give Blackie an opportunity to get his two bob's worth in. No-one would listen to him let alone believe what he said. I mean he wasn't even from the Barracks, so he didn't care if we have a boney. I felt bad for Blackie, but I had to do it otherwise it was me who'd be dumped out the gang and never talked to again. I couldn't risk that.

Then I heard my name being called.

"Ah, young man, you're here. That's good." It was Mister Hale coming out of the club beaming a great, big smile that showed both rows of his white teeth. He was wearing a smart jacket like you'd wear to mass and a white shirt open at the neck. You could see the holy medals hanging around his neck. His smile was really big and it made his eyes shine. "Bus not here yet?"

"No, not yet Mister Hale." I said, turning around to look up and down the road to be certain of my answer. "Be soon though" and I made a show of looking at my watch.

"Right, I got you this just in case" and he handed me a can of coke. "Look I'm going back in to get ready to come out. You wait here and I'll get Barney, Mr McAlea that is. We'll be out in five. If the bus comes wait for us here and we'll all get on together."

"Okay Mister Hale." I felt the chill of the coke freeze my hand it hadn't travelled up my arm. I was still feeling a little groggy and Mr Hale asked if I was okay.

"You look a bit peaky son."

"No, I'm fine. I've had a bit of a cold recently" I lied.

"Alright son. Here one thing. Call me Danny son. Never mind all that Mister stuff. You're making me feel ancient." He smiled again and he ruffled my hair to let me know he wasn't really telling me off. "I'll be out shortly with that McAlea one" and with that said, he disappeared back into the club closing what looked like a really heavy door behind him. I said okay and turned to face the road. The bus would be here any minute. I was starting to feel match nerves at the thought of a quarter final and the cup within reach. We were certs I thought, although I would never say it out loud. That would put the scud on them and get me a tanking if we lost. I mean our squad of players were better in nearly every department to the opposition mob. I could almost smell the semi-final. My only worry was that the final would be at Windsor and mum wouldn't let me go anywhere near there.

People had begun to gather at corners. There were quite a few at the corner of the New Lodge and Burlington Street just where the Celtic supporters club was. It was a long breeze block of a building. They must be getting their carry outs from there for the bus as they were coming out of the long entrance to the club with bulging blue carrier bags dangling from their arms.

I saw some of the smaller younger ones wave up towards me and I waved back in a weak, feeble way with my left arm. Most of them would be known to me, a lot of them were just slabbers and head melters who chanted 'SS RUC" throughout the games. A lot of them didn't even watch the match, they just came to shout abuse at the peelars and the opposition fans and their teams. I never told mum about them and their antics, she'd make me stay at home and have the neighbours watch the house.

I heard the roar of an engine and turned looking up the New Lodge and a single decker bus was turning off the Antrim Road and was rounding the tight space to get onto the New Lodge itself. I noticed straightaway that the bus was red and a dirty cream colour. I thought that would make us an obvious target. There'd definitely be no toilet on that, it was the same as our school buses and I now felt an urge to pee.

I pressed the buzzer on the gate. I waited with the tingle in my willy getting stronger. I pressed again. I knew they could see me in the big white security camera screwed into the wall about ten feet above me. Even that had a wire mesh to protect it. It was there because they said some of the IRA drank in there. There was coughing sound behind me, as if someone were clearing their throat. I turned round.

"Can I get past ye there son?"

He was an old man in his fifties, maybe sixty, with those shiny orangie coloured Chelsea boots, with jeans that had the biggest turn ups I'd seen. His da must have been a farmer, I smiled remembering the joke.

"Yes, sorry mister." I stepped aside. "Do you think I could go in and use the toilet? I'm heading off to the match and need to go before the off."

"Sure son, you don't want to be having any wee accidents on the way." The door buzzed into life and the old man who had with noticeably skinny wrists pushed at the door, grunting as he did so. He looked swamped in the giant overcoat. I followed him to the entrance door. He gripped the metal handle with both hands and pulled letting out a gasp that old people let out when they have to do something that requires any effort. "Too bloody old for this nonsense anymore son" he said with a smile, that was more of a grimace. I placed my free hand on the handle and held the door as he stepped into the club. I had to use all my strength as the door was a ton weight and it was fighting to get back to its closed position. "The men's toilets is down at the end. Just on yer right son."

"Thank you mister." I said back, watching my footing in the dark corridor.

"Good luck in the match son."

"Cheers, thanks." I said, as he slid open the door to the bar where there was a lot of shouting and laughing and the TV was really loud, you could hear the man on the TV talking very fast to keep up with the horses in the race. I walked the long hall to the door where it said 'Mens' in black marker. I wish I hadn't drank most of the coke as I opened the door and went inside. There wasn't any windows and the big metal urinal stank of piss and had cigarette ends and chewing gum all along it. I went into the single cubicle because I didn't want anyone standing beside me. I didn't see a bin on my way out, so I put the can I onto the cistern and left.

Mister Hale and Mister McAlea were outside looking around them. "There he is." Mr Hale beamed another giant smile in my direction. "We were looking for ye. We thought you'd given up on us and got the bus."

"No, no. I needed to use the toilet."

"Good thinking. Have you been yet Barney?"

"Catch you yourself on. Come on let's get on this bugger and get to the match."

"You've got everything?" Mr Hale asked.

"The essentials. Yes." I heard a rattle of bottles from Mr McAlea's long overcoat as he patted it with his hand.

"And you son? You've everything? Ticket. Drink? Something to eat on the way?"

"Yes Mr Hale all in my bag." I replied, patting my bag in an act that would convince him that I had.

"Good lad. Right. Let's get this show on the road then. We'll take the front. Don't want to near any of the back of the bus boys. Right hand side, just a few seats up from the driver will do."

We found our seats four up on the right hand side. I was given the seat by the window. I thanked Mr Hale for that, 'no bother, just enjoy the view son' he said. Mr McAlea sat behind us with a seat to himself. I reckoned there was about forty five of us on the bus and there was eight to ten buses going. There could be up to four hundred going. A Red Army indeed. The boys at the back were already chanting Red Army. Some tried to get a sing song started. I could hear bottles and cans being opened. There was a real buzz on the bus and a big cheer went up when the busman started the engine.

"You alright son?" Mr Hale asked of me. I said I was and held onto my bag and loosened my scarf as I was getting warm. I wanted to take my jacket off but it meant asking Mr Hale to move so I sat playing with the straps on my satchel waiting to get warm enough to open my bag for some water.

Some singing broke out about a broad black brimmer and Mr Hale turned to ask that they keep the songs to football. "There's childer on this bus lads, c'mon act the white man, behave yerselves." The singing died down and there was an outbreak of 'SS RUC' they chanted as the armoured Land rover joined the traffic just in front of the bus. Another bus load of fans joined ours at the bottom of the New Lodge and North Queen Street and there was a big roar. A bigger roar went up when someone shouted there's the Cliftonville and Ardoyne ones behind us. There was a total of four buses and I counted six police Land rovers.

"We're not in Kansas anymore Danny." Mister McAlea said his voice low and serious sounding.

"No Barney. But we've seen and done this all before and got the t shirt."

"And the odd lump" Mister McAlea added quickly, as he pulled out a large bottle of beer from his coat pocket. "This should make the journey that bit more tolerable." He smiled and used a bottle opener he had on his keychain to take the top of with a small fizz sound.

"Comes with the territory. It shouldn't take us longer than thirty minutes if we get lucky." Mister Hale sounded sad and I didn't care for the tone of their conversation. I was excited at the thought of so many reds fans gathering. There was ones coming over from the west as well. Nobody could stand in our way if there was hundreds of us. We always said the orangies were like bananas, they were all yellow and hung around in bunches. They'd shite themselves to see so many Fenians. I don't know why these oul boys were so down in the mouth about it. We'd roar them on to victory. The players themselves wouldn't dare let so many of their fans down.

Mister Hale took a swig from his giant sized bottle of beer. I could smell its sourness and wondered why people drank the foul smelling stuff. But I liked the way he had wiped the rim with his hankie and wiped his mouth after each swig. It showed he had class.

"Here Danny boy." It was a voice from the back of the bus where the main group of about twenty five had congregated like at the back of church. "Is it true that Barney boy there was watching the old firm match with you in The Phoenix when his wife barged in with his Sunday dinner and dropped it on the table saying 'I think you love Celtic more than Me' and he turned round and said, listen love I love Rangers more than you!" The whole of the bus erupted into laughter and bottles were clinked and cans raised in a salute.

"You should ask him yourself Bootsy" Danny said, without turning his head. I had decided to take Mister Hale's advice and see both men as my mates for the bus journey at least.

"That's not strictly true. It was Sunday lunch, Dinner was in the dog when I got home" Barney told them in a flat tone that caused another chorus of laughing and cheering.

Danny turned and offered the neck of his bottle over to his friend who clinked it with his own. "Here Bootsy, wait d'ye hear this one. We were on the boat heading to the Motherwell match."

"Is that the one we won two nil?" Someone at the back asked.

"Who the hell cares? Shut up and let's hear the man" Bootsy told the person who had dared asked. Bootsy was a very tall and lean fella and was known to be a good fighter along with all his mates, who were all sat on the very back seat. They didn't collect wood for bonys or hang around flats. They went to the clubs and some had steady girlfriends. I felt a lot better they were going just in case there was some trouble.

"Any way, we're on the boat going to the match. We're playing cards to ease the journey that bloody boat takes forever." There was a collective groan of recognition and agreement all round. "So we're playing cards, me and his nibs here. Wee Gerry Dodd, Doddsy and Co-Op from the Bone. It's gets called that 'cos he blew it up." There was a couple of barked out laughs at that. "None of us are getting the rub of the green except wee Doddsy. Barney here, he's been getting hands like feet all morning. Then he gets a prial. Three fives, I think wasn't it Barney?"

Barney nodded that it was.

"Well, he's got three fives, so he's all in. Doddsy sees him and Barney here throws the hand down thinking to all intents and purposes it's a winning hand. Not so. Doddsy throws down three tens. Ya bastard Doddsy, Barney shouts at him. As Doddsy is collecting his ill-gotten loot, Barney here shouts at him 'the only thing that came out the Bone was hoors and footballers. Behind us there's this kerfuffle and there's this big bastard, giant of a man standing up bristling with muscles and rage. He shouts up the boat 'here you, ya ballicks. My wife's from the Bone. Barney shouts back 'oh yeah, who'd she play for?"

There was another outburst of loud laughter roaring up and down the bus like a moving, living entity and there's shouts of "that's a belter" 'absolute gem and 'he is one cunny funt'. That line came from Teddy snatterface. It was his voice and his line he used, just like his punctured frenchie one.

Danny shifted in the seat. "Here son, you don't mind if you move over a touch."

I said 'no' but inside I did because I was losing him to the crowd at the back and his legs were so much bigger and muscly than mine. And I wasn't taking up much room anyways.

"Here. I've one more for ye, honest lads, the last one. Then you lot can get on with whatever. Here so, we're in The Mandeville having a game of billiards and this well-dressed gentleman walks in, stands watching the games walking around and then he stops and walks over to Barney here and introduces himself. Then he goes on to ask if his nibs here, if he's Bernard McAlea. Barney says, I am, I'm standing cue in hand waiting for something to kick off, but he goes on to say I was in your class at primary school in Saint Patricks. Now Barney looks him up and down takes a moment, then goes, there was nobody in our class with a beard."

The same result the laughing entity swept up and down the bus only it had grown in strength.

I had started to really enjoy being in their company as they were a real geg, they had become centre of attention and I was with them. It was only then that I clocked Teddy shithead. He sat two seats down from Bootsy and his mates. I hadn't seen him when I got on the bus. He obviously had got on before us. He made a show of the stubby brown bottle of beer in his hand, He didn't see me or he was doing a very good job of pretending not to. He was a real Ballbeg. He was sharing a seat with Matt McErlean, another nasty piece of work who led the Brusslee and Pinkerton Walk gang. I didn't turn back round because of them. I wasn't going to be yellow, a cowardly custard, a spineless, gutless wonder because of them. All the things I had said and believed about myself because of that shitehawk. He really was the real son of a punctured frenchie. The diddy-nosed glipe.

The bus trundled on and the singing got louder. It got more political except for a chorus of 'stop the bus, I want a wee wee', to which the bus driver shouted that it would be another ten minutes before a piss stop.

There was a loud crack on one of the windows I didn't know which one. Then someone shouted. "There's a few of the wee orange bastards and they're clodding stones at the bus."

There was a loud shout minutes later. "Look, there's more of the huns. Go on ye dirty bastards. Here, they're not Larne supporters. I recognise some of them. They're blues men. What the fuck." "Well, they were wearing the Larne football top and were mingling with the Larne supporters. Look they're all up on that flat piece of land on top of that small hill." I looked out across the bus and stood up. At the bottom of the hill there were two police Land Rovers.

"Here, the peelars are allowing them to get onto the top of that hill. Look, they've got bottles as well." Everyone went to the left of the bus to see.

"Come on sit down lads. I've to turn this corner and it's bloody well tight" the bus driver shouted.

"C'mon boys, sit yerselves down. Stop goading them. They'll put the windies in. Do what the busman's telling ya" Danny shouted down the bus.

"Knock it on the head boys." Barney shouted too. His voice lost in a host of other voices that filled the bus.

Windies. I almost smiled, but my feeling of alarm was heightened as I could tell from the shouts and cheers that the Orangies had got our bus in their sights.

The mob at the back weren't taking a heed to either man. They were yelling and shouting. Some were giving those outside of the bus the fingers and calling them 'bastards' and "orange cunts'. Some of them starting banging the roof of the bus and a loud chant of 'SS RUC' went up with it. Others went further and began chanting, 'I...I...IRA'.

"Sit down for Godsake. Do want to have riot on yer hands?" Danny shouted. His face and neck were red and he shouted. He was angry but also he seemed a bit afraid. That's when I became afraid.

"Ah, fuck off ya oul ballicks. Sure you played for the Lurgan blues long enough."

"And the Crues." That was Teddy fannyface's voice.

"Aye shut yer gob, you oul git" another shouted back.

"You sure you're on the right bus anyway?" Someone else shouted.

"Anything for a few bob, eh Haler?" Someone else shouted down.

Danny sat down. He went dead quiet and I could see he was rubbing his hands. They were big and strong looking. I heard him let a long, slow breath.

"Shut yer bloody gobs. None of ye could lace that man's boots, nor any of yer da's as well. If we'd a signed this man here, we'd have won the cup and the bloody league, no fear." Barney's voice was almost at breaking point.

"Yeah, only if the money was right." It was the guy called Bootler shouted back down the bus. He was a big gangly fella with big, long arms and a reputation as hard man.

"If they had paid him what he was worth. He's worth ten of any of youse." Barney stood up this time to shout back angrily. His face was red and there was spit flying from his mouth.

"Come on me old friend, sit yourself down. Calm yourself Barney. It's all drink talk" Danny said soothingly.

"Soup taker" Someone with a real nasty voice shouted down. "Sold your souls for a sausage roll and a slice of hairy bacon."

"Ya wee bastards. A bunch of toerags and hoods, the whole lot of yees."Mr McAlea shouted up the bus as he took his seat. The boys were now singing and making gestures at the windows to people outside. I sat quietly and prayed no-one would talk directly to me.

Suddenly the bus shuddered to a halt. "Right you lot. Sit the hell down or I'm walking off this bus." It was the bus man who was now shouting. He was big man, with a big round belly and the sleeves of his shirt were rolled up displaying tattoos of a woman with naked breasts and the other one on his left arm I couldn't make out. "I mean it. Sit down. And be quiet or there'll be no piss stop on the way back to Belfast. That's right I'll turn this crate round and head back to Belfast."

"You can't do that. We've paid good money for this bus" Somebody protested. It sounded like Bootsy.

"Any of youse got a licence to drive a bus? Because it's the only way you'll get 'til the match if ye carry on they way yer carrying on." The bus man pulled up his trousers that had fallen slightly below his waist. He sounded like he really meant it and he wasn't at all afraid of the crowd.

There was a silence that seem to last forever. You hear the shouts and the chanting of those gathered outside and it made it seem like they were really close and had the bus surrounded.

"Right, piss stop in a few minutes. Then the ground." There was good natured and relieved cheers and then three cheers for the busman.

Moments later Barney tapped me on the shoulder. "Here lad, who is that wee mouthpiece at the back; the one with the big gob and pudgy nabe on him?"

"Leave it Barney. Let it go. It's forgotten." Danny took a swig of beer and looked out the window. "No, I don't think we're in Kansas anymore, alright" he said, as the painted kerbs and the various fluttering flags on the telegraph poles raced past like we were on a life size scalextric set. I knew he had said it more to himself than to me or his friend Barney.

I really didn't want to get involved and I didn't turn my head as I managed, as quietly as I could, was able to say: "Teddy Scullion." I whispered it quickly as I could and then shot back to seated position and stared straight ahead to avoid any more questions.

I looked beyond the flags to look at the sheep dotted around the hills like scattered woollen breadcrumbs put out of the birds to feed on. I saw a brown horse chewing on the top of a pole that was used to fence it in. The horse was beautiful without a saddle and without being on TV for men to watch and bet on. I had the thought how horrible the people were here for putting up flags and painting their kerbs where they were surrounded by lovely countryside.

"Ah, that's Brian Scullion's lad. Looks like him. Bloody gormless shite." Barney said, staring back up the bus. "Sure, I knew his ma and da when they were just sister and brother" Barney shouted back up the bus, to the roars of laughter and approval from the crowd. I couldn't look round as it would make me accessory. Barney was clearly very angry at the attack on his friend Danny. For a moment, the thought that me and Dee and Wholenut, even Genghis would be friends like that one day. I would like to have included Blackie, but I had to be realistic.

"His da's a fitter, isn't he Danny? Here he played a bit too, didn't he? He had trial for the Crues. That's right. He wasn't good enough couldn't cut the mustard. He couldn't tackle a fish supper if I remember" Barney said, loud enough for everyone on the bus to hear.

"Works at the top of Oldpark if memory serves" Danny said, he sounded like me when I didn't really want to talk.

"There's more brains in a false face" Barney followed up and took a swig from his beer bottle.

I knew Teddy's da worked with his hands and with machinery of some sort. I saw him from time to time walk down the road in big blue overalls covered in oil. He was one of the few men I heard of who didn't drink and he never went into the pubs and clubs. You would see him out walking all the time.

I also knew Teddy skidmark head would feel wick about that remark and he would be out for revenge, so I was making sure of having nothing to do with it. I heard him tell someone to 'button their lip' for laughing at it and I kept my head down and ignored the conversation the two men beside me were having.

I closed my eyes. The last thing I heard was shouting and the smashing of glass.

The crowd moved as one as if bound by an invisible force that propelled them forward. A human juggernaut had been born; the individual had been bound and then broken and submitted to the will of the unyielding mass. I scrambled desperately to stay on my feet. I knew the danger was all too real of being sucked under and ran the risk of collapsing under the sheer suffocating weight of bodies that had settled like we were bound by brick and mortar. I fought with all my strength to find a pocket of air. I could not see the sky nor could I hear myself shouting for space, for help, when I knew I was screaming it out. I was enveloped by beer guts and belt buckles; my feet being trodden on or nipped by much larger heavier feet. I could not raise my arms up; they were fastened firmly by my side by the bodies crushing me on all sides.

I needed to get out and off wherever of this human freight train was going. It moved relentlessly, unmercifully; it was unmerciful on the flesh and bone. There was chanting and singing, the smell of beer and smoke and damp stained the air. I was drowning in a sea of dirty, greasy trousers, rough denim and heavy coats that smelt of body odour and soapy rust. There was buttons of every size and description pressed against my face. Metal ones from jean jackets scraping my face and people stepping on my feet and pressing my shoulders in. I pushed hard against those who hemmed me in, shouting for room, pleading with them to give me space.

Suddenly I found myself on the ground amongst the flattened cans and rolling, clattering bottles. I could taste the cigarette butts and chewing gum on the ground. There were some discarded scarves, blackened by the enormous human centipede that trundled on regardless of its individual parts.

I moved quickly to get on my knees and push out my arms, not caring what might be said or happen as I grabbed the jacket of the person in front and hauled myself up. I cursed my smallness, my puniness, my mum and da for making me this way. My fear overcame my natural timidity and I pushed, shouting 'move' over and over and within seconds I had a sacred half foot of space. I stiffened my back and looked right and then left to escape the crowd. I saw space to the right and heaved with all my might and an opening popped up and I fell into what seemed like a vast area of space.

I let out a deep gasp and saw markings on the ground. White lines like you see on the roads. I realised I was in the car park outside the ground. I knew that the crowd had moved on and I was being left behind. I didn't care at that moment, as I had no intention of re-joining them. The police ignored me and walked past shouting orders and guided the side of the crowd with shields and threats towards a destination I had no wish to reach.

I found myself being pushed towards the hill that overlooked the car park. I looked up and saw police officers in riot gear, their visors pulled open so they could talk and some men with the red and white opposition football shirts on. They weren't players, as they were all wearing jeans and they were pointing at the crowd and the police were looking towards them too. They were pointing, then one of them looked directly at me. I saw a firework fly into the air towards the red army and there was a roar and angry shouts. I really wanted to go home. I didn't care if I saw the match or if we lost. I wanted to get home and never leave. I wanted a warm bath and for me and mum to be sitting on the sofa at home watching Morcambe and Wise, anything rather than this. She'd be boiling mad if she could see me now. I will never get to another match, ever. And you know what, that's fair enough. I'll take that now, if only I could get out of here and get home. Where the hell did Mr Hale and Mr McAlea get to? They left me and I'd be telling mum about that, no fear. Jesus, I couldn't even remember getting off the bus.

I thought I heard mum call my name. But I knew it was just because I was alone and scared. That's when I saw the Larne supporters come down the hill, slowly watching their footing as the hill was wet and it looked muddy. They would be right on top of me in minutes if I didn't get off my arse and move. I found a natural path that had miraculously appeared right across the car park I gathered my courage and swallowed it inside of me and like spinach to Popeye, I found the strength to run. God only knows where I was going but I needed to get away from their fans and the weight of people gathered in the car park. I tried to figure out where the bus and the driver could be. I would beg him to let me on and I'd stay there for the duration. I didn't care about the match now.

I seemed to be in an open space where the things that made up my world appeared blurred and distant. I could make out cranes in the shimmering distance. I couldn't see the car park or the ground and the people going into the match. I wanted peace and quiet. Most of all I wanted safety. I then realised I had lost my scarf and I took my hat off too and threw it away from me. I could be anyone now. There was no-one near to me and it was really quiet. I thought I must have fallen asleep and this was a nightmare I was in.

"Are you okay?"

I nearly jumped out of my skin in fright at the voice behind me. I was shaking violently as fear gripped my entire body and I felt an irresistible urge to cry, shout for help and then run, run as fast as I could anywhere would do. Somewhere where I could be alone and think.

"Hello? Are you alright? Can I do anything to help? My name is Andre." The voice wasn't raised or threatening, but it petrified me.

Even though the voice sounded kind and it was offering to help I couldn't help but began to cry.

"I'm sorry, don't be crying. I didn't mean to frighten you. I just want to help."

The voice was calm, polite and sounded as if the person who owned it was sincere. I felt a strength return to my body and I turned and almost fainted with shock. It was as if the Robert Plant from the poster on my bedroom wall had come to life and was standing right in front of me. He smiled and brushed a curtain of long blonde hair back over his right shoulder.

Now that I knew I was dreaming I felt a wave of calm roll over me and massage my terror away.

"Are you alright now, young man?" I could see he was examining my face.

I had no words. I was in fear of saying the wrong thing, of upsetting the man, enraging him, as I was part of an outside crowd who were seen to be causing trouble in his town. Whether this was a dream or not, I didn't want to turn it into a nightmare.

"It's fine now. You're safe here, away from the trouble that's going on back there."

He did sound genuine. He sounded actually concerned and like he really wanted to help. I didn't think I had much choice and I placed my faith that he really cared.

"Thank you. I'm okay. I just needed to get away from the crowd."

"I'm not surprised. It's really kicked off. If you'll pardon my pun."

I knew what a pun was, so I smiled and turned to let him see my smile. He smiled back and moved his head to one side and brushed a thick layer of his long, dirty fair hair.

"As long as you're alright. Have you been separated from your friends? You may not be able to get back to them. The police have cordoned the area off and look to be forcing the supporters into the ground, away from those eejits throwing stones from the hill."

I was so relieved to hear him call the ones on the hill eejits. It meant he didn't agree with the actions of those who had started throwing of stones. He was not in support of them, by the sound of it, thank God.

He stood staring back at the car park where I could make out the buses and the police Land Rovers. I had no idea as to what to say next. I worried at what the man might say because I would have to think of a suitable response.

"Now only if you want. If you like and it's your call. I can take you to the nearest bus stop and I'll wait with you until a bus to Belfast comes and I'll see you off." He paused and I thought that was a great idea. Anything, anything that would get me out of the town and away from this match and back home. "Or," and again he paused, longer this time, "you could let me drive you home. My car is just over there." He stepped back to allow me full view. It was as if he were unveiling it to me.

It was beautiful. It looked like a crouched animal of sorts. Like the big cats you saw on widlife programmes and they were about to chase some poor critter for dinner. An actual, real sports car, in real life, like it too had come to life from the Matchbox collection I had at home.

"The Aston Martin, 160mph on the open road, if we had decent enough roads here," he winked and smiled, "16 cyclinder. And if you decide to join me, I'll keep to the speed limits, scouts honour." He smiled and made the signal with his hand that the scouts were famous for. I smiled a real smile without fear and my confusion and nervousness had disappeared. "What do you say kimosabe? I can have you home within the hour."

The thought of home almost had made me crying again. I composed myself and swallowed hard. "Your car is really beautiful" I said.

"Yeah, she's a beauty alright." He smiled. "Also, you can keep Andro company."

Andro? Who the hell was Andro? My alarm and fear was reignited and rejuvenated, electrifying my whole being in a new state of alarm.

"Who?" I ventured in a weak, scardey cat voice.

"I'm sorry. How remiss of me. Andro is my dog. You can just about see his large head at the back of the car. He just lolls there. He's a big softie really. He likes a bit of company. And you know what, I have some business in Belfast that I can do today that I had set aside for Monday."

"Oh." I said. I did not finish the 'thank Christ the night for that' for Andre to hear.

"Well, my young friend? What do you say to joining me and Andro on the road?"

He looked at me, kinda leaning to the side a bit, his head stretched as if he was waiting on my every word. What could I say to such a kind and generous offer? Especially as I was on my own and I'd look like a right wee, ungrateful shite and it might get him upset and I was on my own. He could set his dog on me and I'd be running for my life like I did from Dylan.

"Yes. I would love to, if you don't mind. I mean, if it's not too much trouble, I'm taking you way out of your way. But I have money to pay you for any petrol it will take."

Andre burst into a loud bout of laughing. "You're a hoot, a real one off." He held his stomach as if it were about to burst. "It'll be grand. Give me the chance to get her to open up on the road. It's been awhile since I have driven her any distance. Well, let's get the introductions out of the way. You know my name. Now it would be my privilege to know yours fellow traveller, if you will."

I had to think. I needed to answer. "Iain, it's Iain, with two i's" I answered and it sounded so like a made up name I felt ashamed and embarrassed for lying.

Andre started to walk in the direction of the car. I followed slowly and quietly behind.

"He's a Bernese mountain dog. The white cross you'll see on his chest is called the Swiss cross." Andre kept talking as he walked. I was nearing the car. It was a beautiful shade of green.

"It's Racing green, the colour of the car." Andre spoke, shocking me, as if he had read my mind. I saw the dog raise its head and I could see the white cross on its chest. Its head was enormous.

"It's a beautiful dog. Like your car" I said, showing my gratitude and thanks. I tried to imagine what mum would have me do in this situation when someone was being so generous and helpful. She would like me to be well-mannered and respectful. Up to a point she'd say. You can't be too trusting. I never could see how that advice balanced out.

"Yes, the car. The kind of car you buy with your heart and deep pockets." He said and I just knew he was smiling as he said it. "Ah Andro. We have company. So best behaviour. Try to keep the slobbering down" he laughed, as he patted the dogs head. "This is Iain, our guest for the journey. You'll get acquainted on the trip."

"Can you fit the seatbelt, you think?" He asked. "These can be a bit tricky."

"I think so" I said with a great deal of uncertainty.

"Good man. Give a go. If you're not able, I'll fix it in a jiffy.

He opened the door for me to climb in. I saw that the whole car was covered in leather, it was kind of caramel colour. I plumped myself down and found I almost sliding off the seat. It was slidey and polished to a shine I only ever saw when mum polished her brass ornament collection every two weeks. She would let me put the Brasso on and let me loose with a shammy cloth on the bigger figurines.

I used my feet to push myself back up, hoping Andre had not seen my clumsiness. I sat up and grabbed at the seatbelt. I had never put one on my life. I was ashamed to admit I hadn't been in a car before, well one that was moving anyway. I only got buses to the matches and to school. I shoved the metal piece down into a slot and wriggled and stabbed it in just as Andre got into the drivers side.

"Good man, I see you got the seatbelt in. You're a natural."

"Right, make some adjustments before we set off. We can never be too careful, eh Andro? Just think of me and Andro as two good Samaritans." He laughed, but this laugh sounded different, not as nice or genuine as his other laughs.

The car rumbled and shuddered like it had just woken up. I could feel the power charge throughout the car. It was rumbling like it was a living, breathing, metal beast.

"That is the sound of a 5.3 litre BOSCH fuel injection, it can do 60 mph in 5.9 seconds, top speed is 160 mph, not to worry we'll not be doing anything near that. Aston had to use Weber carburettors, they do good design, not so much the engineering. The English eh?" He laughed, and I smiled a small smile to appreciate what he was saying, without agreeing with it. "If you want to see the true face of human nature, put a man behind the wheel of a car I always say, isn't that right Andro?"

Stay neutral, I thought. You're Iain with two I's. But why would I be going back to Belfast? Only Reds' fans were coming from Belfast. I had to make up I was at the match or close to it as a fan for the other side from Belfast? My granda was from Larne, he had me support them. Thankfully, I had put my scarf in the bag. That was it. I felt better I had the back-up story. I could feel the dog breathing on my neck and moved my hand up to pull the collar of my jacket up. I did it without Andre seeing me do it.

"Andro, lie down." Andre commanded with a laugh in his voice. "He's a nuisance at times. He's generally okay, but they're a handful at times." He turned his head to quickly look back at the dog. "Aren't ya boy. He's more likely to lick you to death than anything. They were originally from the Swiss Alps. A Senne hund, it's taken from the German. They accompanied Alpen herders and dairymen."

Andre moved the gearstick and we were gliding along the road. You couldn't feel the road. I was glad of the big, large box separating both seats. I saw a sign similar to the one when I was on the bus saying entering Larne. I just knew this one said you were leaving it. I was feeling a lot happier than I had in what seemed like a lifetime ago.

"They are affectionate, intelligent and faithful. Aren't you old boy? He knows I'm talking about him. Be giving you an even bigger idea of yourself. They have such egos." Andre then reached down by his side and got a pair of sunglasses from somewhere and put them on. They were very wide and very silver and I could see my reflection in both of his shades. "Suns low, making driving that wee bit problematic."

I made no comment. I had an idea that there was a problem with the sunlight in his eyes.

"Although he drools a lot and you do." Andre said, it clearly directed at the dog. "And they shed like nobody's business. Their general health is not that good." He lowered his voice to say that, like he didn't want the dog to hear it. "No good in apartments or flats. You need space, don't cha boy? They need plenty of that these boys. Fortunately I have a large garden for him to run about."

I suddenly felt a force of shame attack and grip my body, as a clear wave of awareness engulfed me. I was poor, Catholic poor, the feeling swept over me. I couldn't have dog like that or any dog for that matter in the Maisonette. No dogs allowed in our Maisonettes, that's what annoyed people about Dylan and Duke, they weren't supposed to be there in the first place. Christ of almighty, we had to put newspapers up against the windows in the winter to try stopping the freezing cold get in. Da had to repaint the corners of all the bedrooms and bathroom because of the damp. He got this new wonder paint from work. We only just got the stairs carpeted.

But at least we owned our own TV and stereo, we didn't 'radio rent' them. We were also the only ones on the balcony to have a telephone, a cream one it was with a telephone seat that was velvet and dead soft to sit on. People would sit on that and phone relatives about emergencies; we, or I, got to hear all about the latest deaths or the babies born, who was getting married; who had got into trouble with the Peelars or the Brits. I would lie at my bedroom door, which I'd kept slightly open, to hear everything said on the phone. The staircase acted like a megaphone, even when they were trying to be quiet and whispering I could most of what they were saying.

Sometimes I didn't want to hear them, like Missus Maddens calls to her daughter who worked in Liverpool, as she spent the entire time crying and sniffing even after the call had ended.

Da wanted to install a meter for the phone but mum wouldn't hear of it. Da said they weren't there to provide a public service. About two days later a small wooded box appeared on the telephone seat right next to the phone with a slot to place coins in. On one side of it in black marker was written 'Talk is not cheap'. I burned inside with shame at the memory of that.

I watched the fields roll past like giant sheets of green felt. It was strange that they were all different shades of a green, lights and darks, with some cut into squares like the patchwork quilt Mum put on her bed in the winter. I sensed rain, but the clouds were clearing off somewhere and the sunlight was getting wider and wider, cutting through the remaining cloud, disappearing like the ice taken from the defrosting of the fridge and left in the sink for me to wash down the hole. There was a large white sign with the writing 'Jesus Saves' on it. Aye, and Pele scores from the rebound. I couldn't help but think those words when I saw signs like that.

"Are you okay Iain?"

"Sorry? Yes. Oh yes" I answered brightly. I was wary of discussing anything regarding how I was feeling right now.

"You were a million miles away there."

"Sorry, I was just thinking."

"Is that what that pained expression was?" He said in that smiley, friendly voice I had quickly grown used to and then he laughed. "What was it? You were thinking about? Hold the phone. Don't tell me. Let me guess. You're thinking," he paused and looked like he was giving it a lot of thought, "you're thinking, will I get home in time for the football results. No, no that's not it. You're thinking, how does a handsome young man like me, afford a car such as this. Isn't that it?"

I could say nothing in reply I was so shocked that he had read my thoughts.

"It's not that difficult to imagine what you're thinking. A lot of people have asked that question of me. I'll tell you Iain with two i's. I get vulgar amounts of money for giving people advice. I give advice that gives them reassurance. And it's usually people who have money but lack confidence, and a path they cannot see the road ahead. They are used to the feeling of control, to having a sense of power over their destinies. Once that is shaken or challenged they come to people like me. Ah, the human mind, an amazing organ. Once you have an understanding of the basics, you're made."

I twisted my shoulder to one side and tried hiding from his look. Even though I couldn't see his eyes behind the sunglasses I just knew he had made a wink.

Andre's voice had become serious as he talked about what he did for a living. It caused a quietness that made me stare straight ahead, beyond the road, and to the sky that was becoming lighter, and beams of sunshine stabbed through like torchlight. It was getting colder though. I looked across to my right at the fields that rolled out like a checked tablecloth. It reminded me of the big quilt Mum brought out for her bed in the winter.

I knew I had a quizzical look on my face as I sneaked a quick glance at him and then returned to my vigil, watching the road rise and roll past that somehow reminded me of the handrail on the escalators in Woolworths. That reminded me of the time I got lost, separated from mum and I rode those rolling stairs in tears until the staff took me to a big room upstairs that had television sets in it. They let me count the change on a big table from big bags of coins until mum arrived, with tears in her eyes, and that made me cry as well. The people in Woolworths got me a custard cream and Mum a cup of tea.

He leaned back in his driver's seat and I felt the speed of the car increase. I thought he felt I had insulted him. "And the people I give advice to, in some cases they even happen to be famous."

I stared at him in disbelief. "Famous? Who famous? Like TV, film star famous?"

"Unfortunately, I am never at liberty to say who my clients are. Sorry young man."

"That's okay. You're like those lawyers on TV, it's client something or other."

"Client confidentiality," Andre said, again reading my mind, "though a boy of your tender years would have no cause to need my services."

I didn't know what to say. Did he want me to say, yes, I do. Help me with Blackie and with the rest of the gang. I'm being eaten up with guilt that is making me angry all the time. Angry at my actions but angrier with others who put me in this place and made me out a dirty Judas.

"I mean, I couldn't imagine that you would have problems serious enough to merit professional services. Not at your age. It should all be about football, sports, using up all that boundless energy in having fun. Though I do acknowledge it can be stressful enough for young people with all that's going on. Perhaps a girl? Eh? Good looking boy like you must attract interest from the fairer sex."

I felt my face get hot and I just knew my face was taking a reddener.

"If you do, just remember, faint heart never won fair maiden. Go out and get what you want. And if you have made enemies, let's face it, we all do. Just think on the Japanese art of war, subdue your enemy without fighting. I think you know that already young Iain. Youth is so easily deceived, because it is quick to hope. To paraphrase Aristotle, that wise old buzzard. Don't be anybody's fool and even less their doormat. That's my tupenny's worth." He turned to look at me, his eyes staring straight through the dark screens of his sunglasses.

"That'll be fifty pounds then." He leaned right back into his seat he referred to as baskets and laughed.

There was so much going on in my head. What mum would say? How she's going to react? Where the hell did everyone on the bus get to? How'd I end up in the middle of the car park with a Robert Plant lookalike? Blackie made an appearance, his sad face with the look of shock, exposing me as a cheat and a liar. I didn't want to be that person, but now I hadn't a choice. I really didn't.

Everything was in a muddle. The only thing, the only real thing was being in this fancy car with this man who looked like my musical hero. It was all so weird and strange and it all felt so very far away from home.

I was really uncomfortable with the luxury of the car. It was easily the price of a house up the Antrim Road, the kind I dreamed of living in with mum and the one I wanted for me and Francesca when we got married.

How did you ever get enough money to buy something like this car I thought, as I wriggled in the seat to get my legs moving and the blood circulating.

My efforts at saving and scrimping seemed ridiculous now. My attempts to win 'spot the ball' in The Belfast Tele, it seemed was the height of stupidity. Da was right for once. It's a mugs game. But I never listened to him. I got the picture placed on the table in the living room and stared at the image for ages. I looked at the players' eyes and their movement frozen in the photograph, checking where their eyes were looking. I knew I had the ball and the centre of it couldn't be that difficult to mark. I carefully inserted the X's where the missing ball would be; confident one of them was the winning mark.

I had traced all the player's eye lines. I'd watched enough games and seen enough football to know where that ball should be. It was a cert. Plumb centre, no sweat. I handed over my finished work inside an envelope with my ten pence, ignoring Da's big sigh and his 'it's a con', like that crane claw for the soft toys.' I walked away and went upstairs. 'It's your money' he would say. I would skip up the stairs to my room and dream of winning the big prize and putting a deposit down on my dream home for me and mum and telling him to get lost.

Da was proved right every week. Every Monday, when I got the paper and thumbed through the pages to the names of the winners. My name never appeared. I was left feeling dejected. It was a con and I was a mug and I'd never have a house like the one I wanted, with a large garden that a dog like Andro could run about in.

"Do you like music Iain with two i's?"

"Wha...um sorry? What was that Andre?"

"Day dreaming again?" He cast me what I can only describe as a smirk. It was one of my favourite words and I was dead happy I could use it on this occasion.

"Sorry. Day dreaming. yeah. The air swirling about makes it hard to hear." I felt bad that I had gone into my head again and was ignoring Andre.

"Don't sweat it. Yeah, it can be a problem in an open top. If you want to, I'll put the roof up if you wish. It's good thing to daydream. Shows imagination. You're young, most natural thing in the world. So? You like music?"

"Oh no. I like the open air." I was quick to say as I didn't want the roof up. I was conscious we would be enclosed. "Oh, and yes. I love music. It's brilliant" I blurted out in a voice that sounded too keen. I was embarrassed by my babyish reply.

"You're enthusiasm is charming." Andre smiled. I smiled too because I knew I had pleased him with my answer.

"So. What are you are into? Let me guess." Andre looked ahead out onto the road. There were very few cars or lorries and you could sense the afternoon was going away.

"Barry Manilow, John Denver, that kind of thing perhaps?"

"No, no way." I was indignant. "I'm not into that." I was mortified and upset that Andre would even think that of me.

"Only teasing you. I bet you're a man of more discerning tastes. Like The Beatles or The Stones."

"They're okay. But the bands I really like are bands like Led Zeppelin, UFO, Bad Company, Free, Deep Purple, Fleetwood Mac."

"Woah, that's real heavy stuff for one so young. No Slade, T.Rex and the like?"

"Yeah, I like all sorts, but those bands are my favourite kind of music."

"Ah, the devil truly does have all the best music" Andre sighed.

I looked at him, smarting at him saying something that Da might say.

"What about local music? Home grown artists, like Them or Rory Gallagher, Horslips?" He continued, completely unaware of the silly thing he had just said.

I sat for a moment to find the right response, without sounding ignorant or stupid or both. "I really haven't heard their stuff."

"Who? Them?"

"All of Them."

Andre burst into laughter. "Sorry, but that sounded so funny. Them were a great band. Short lived, but hey, as they say it's better to burn out than fade away. Van Morrison was the creative force behind the band. He wrote songs like 'Gloria' and 'Here comes the Night'."

I could tell Andre knew that I'd never heard of the songs or the singers he mentioned and I felt embarrassed by my lack of knowledge of my own home grown talent.

"Don't worry. I can't sing a note. It vexes me greatly. Meaning that it bugs me. Bugs me a lot." Andre grimaced as he said the words. "If you like I could play them for you. I have them on cassette. The sound system in the car is, if I may be immodest for a moment, par excellence."

I watched as he reached into a concealed compartment and took out a cassette and slid it into the radio cassette player just above his knees. "Think you'll like this. As an old friend of mine once remarked, without music, life would be a mistake."

I glanced over to see Andre lean back in his seat and I could feel the car speed up. I could hear the intro and sense the energy surge through the speakers. I began tapping my foot to the beat and could feel a chorus coming. G,L,O,R,I,A! The letters were belted out in a scream, it felt tortured and anguished. It was brill. The next time the chorus came, Andre was singing along at the top of his voice. I felt like joining in, I felt Andre was inviting me to join him but I was too embarrassed, too shy and didn't think my voice was good enough. After the song ended I felt elated and excited, wanting to hear it again. I wanted to hear their next song too.

"I saw Them."

"Who?"

"Them. Not The Who. The band." Andre laughed again. "And Rory Gallagher. And Hendrix. He played Belfast back in 'sixty seven in the Whitla Hall. There's a great story about Hendrix and Rory. Hendrix, when he was asked, what it was like to be the world's greatest guitarist he replied, 'you should ask Rory Gallagher'."

"Wow, is he that good?"

"Let's listen and see. Shall we?"

I watched Andre push a button and despite the rush of air that swept past my head I could hear the whirring of the tape.

"Here's a good one. Song called 'Bad Penny'."

It was blues rock, the kind of squealing guitar sound I wasn't that keen on. But he was good, you could tell. His voice sounded hoarse and American, like Mr McSorley who smoked about a hundred fegs a day. He was a right rocket who was now in a hospice where most people were away for the tea. 'God's waiting room' da called it and made a show of shivering at the thought.

"I'll play you Zeppelin after this. It'll get me in the mood for Knebworth." Andre said.

"You're going as well?" I asked, feeling gutted that this was the second person in a week I had met who was going.

"As well as who?"

"A fella I know. He's called Frankie, but everyone calls him Enroe." I said glumly, knowing they were both going to be at the concert.

"I take it from your tone and demeanour that you're not."

"No." I said, in a simple statement of the fact.

"Oh, I'm sorry. I can see it means a lot to you" He said in a gentle and sympathetic manner that in a flash of mad, wishful thoughts, I thought I could ask Andre to talk to mum and see if I could go with him. We could take Enroe with us too. Mum liked him because he went to Mass and dressed in a shirt and tie on Sundays.

"Are they going to split up after this concert? My friend Enroe says so." I asked, in a dispirited tone unable to conceal my sadness at the very idea.

"There's talk. Sadly the talk is that they may disband. There's so much going on between Plant and Page, way too much. It happens with bands all the time, too much time on the road, too much time together. Too much indulgence in pastimes not fit for your young ears." He smiled and I knew that he knew it was over for the band somehow.

"Let's hear them and celebrate them while we still can. I'll put the sound up for this special occasion." Andre said. "Oh yes, when the Levee breaks. Great track" he said with a happiness I recognised.

We listened as the thumping drum and bass was punctured and pierced by a wailing harmonica.

I shook in a stab of fright, startled by Andre bursting into song.

"Crying won't help ya, praying won't do you no good."

He had a really strong voice, but he was right his voice was toneless, like mine. It sounded nothing like the song and I was glad he stopped a couple of seconds in. As the song ended I was about to ask him why he hadn't learnt an instrument and joined a band, he certainly looked the part. I didn't even mind he had those muscly forearms and them kind of thighs that had strength and manliness that I ached to possess.

Then he sat up and leaned slightly forward looking ahead. "Oh what's this up ahead? Looks like a checkpoint before we get into Belfast."

I leaned to one side but couldn't see beyond the small lorry ahead of us that carried things from Cork, Dublin and Belfast.

"Iain, it's a police checkpoint." Andre said.

I didn't know what he wanted me to say. I look at him blankly.

"The badge, the one on your lapel. You may want to take it off, or least conceal it." He smiled grimly towards me as the car began to slow down.

Holy shite. Oh for Chrissake! I'd completely forgotten all about the SS RUC badge. I placed my hand over it and felt for the pin and pressed down praying it would come off in one go. It did thank God. I took the badge and placed it in my side jacket pocket.

"Thank you." I mouthed, dead embarrassed. I felt humiliated; worse, I felt I'd let Andre down. He must know now I was a spoofer, just like Ghegis.

"No biggy." As The Stones sang 'just as every cop is a criminal for all the sinners' sakes.' He sang in a low voice and winked. I was dead relieved that he didn't seem angry or annoyed with me.

"You want another song on? I'll keep it to a civilised level until we pass through this checkpoint. What would you like to hear?"

The Sound of silence came into my head and I thought it was a good enough line to tell Andre who burst into laughter.

"Excellent choice Iain. Just excellent." Andre squeezed out between his laughter.

Then I had another great idea for a song. I felt sure Andre would like it.

"I shot the Sheriff." Andre wheezed and coughed as he laughed. "Man, you're gonna kill me. I'll put it on, it'll be a hoot to pass by with playing that song."

We approached the stony faced cluster of police, with their guns strapped across their stomachs. "They don't look happy, a policeman's lot is not a happy one. Let's be cool."

"Yes" I returned solemnly.

You could see them look the car over as we crawled up to the police officer in the middle of the road. He smiled and nodded in appreciation. And then he waved the car on.

"Sweet car sir, she's a real beauty." The voice was gorging full of admiration.

"Yes, thank you officer. Costly though" Andre commented and slowed the car right down to a point where you wouldn't have thought we were moving.

"I'm sure she's worth it. They're like women. You pay for what you get."

"What do you drive yourself?"

"Oh, nothing as grand as this bugger," the police man said looking the car up and down, "just a Ford Escort, 2000cc engine though. Need the speed, if you get my drift"

"Ah, get your meaning sir. Well, good luck officer. And be careful."

"All the very best sir. And a safe journey to you both. Stay away from the West of the city if you can sir. They're going buck daft up there." He added with the side of his mouth. He was dead young, pudgy and with freckles down the side of his face.

"Prudent advice Officer, I will of course take it on board." Andre and the police officer laughed and Andre, to my relief, picked up speed and drove away from the checkpoint.

The Clapton song had finished. "We'll just let it play shall we? It's got most of your favourite bands on anyway."

I nodded happily in agreement.

Bad Company by Bad Company just came on and I sat back enjoying the soft introduction and the expectation of the rousing chorus with its guitars electrifying the air around me.

"You want some ice cream Iain? I've to stop and get petrol and something to drink. I'm parched. Or lemonade perhaps?" Andre asked. "There's one coming up on our left. It's the final one before we enter Belfast proper as it were."

"I've drink and sweets in my bag thanks" I answered, thrilled to hear the word Belfast. Knowing the city would be coming into view soon filled me with joy and excitement. I couldn't wait to tell the boys about Andre and the car I was in.

"That's very mature of you to do so. Good man. I, as you will see, I am not like you in that respect. I never plan." Andre said and the way he said it, it didn't seem like such a bad thing.

"We'll be at a filling station in just a jiffy. And look, the sun's attempting to break out" he observed, as rays of sunshine shot through the clouds and onto the road and the fields. "So, what's your most favourite at school?" He suddenly asked throwing me into a state of panicked thought.

I rifled through the subjects I despised, French, Maths, Woodwork, Geography. I liked Religion, English. "History. That'd be my favourite." I blurted out.

"Oh, I love history. It's one of my favourite subjects. What era do you like best? I mean, modern, the middle ages, ancient?"

"Ancient." I said. Even though we did not study ancient history at school I read all about it at home from books I got in the Central library. "Like the Spartans, things like that."

"Well, I'm your man. I know quite a bit about that time in history. Like Lycurgus, a very clever man who when asked how to save Sparta from invasion answered 'remain poor'. What a clever answer and it worked for the Spartans. Philip nor Alexander attacked the city, even as they the Spartans defied them. Did you know that?"

"No, no I didn't. I just finished reading a book about Leonidas." I was raging I couldn't remember the name of the book or the writers name and it looked like I was just spoofing to please or impress him.

"Ah, the old Molon Labe, it means," Andre felt the need to explain as I must have looked as mystified as I felt, "Xerxes with his one hundred thousand men at his disposal asked the seven thousand Greeks and three hundred Spartans to lay down their arms, to which Leonidas replied 'Molon Labe." Andre bellowed out the words this time and then laughed. "It was come and get them."

"Wow, he was brave, as game as a badger as we say" I said, conjuring up an image of the Spartan King, tall and built like a Piercy, dressed in his armour.

Andro let out a bark that startled me and I cursed myself for letting out a yelp of fright.

"Sorry about that. It's Andro's way of telling me to stop showing off. It's alright boy. I'll stop and don't be frightening our guest again."

I wanted to tell him I wasn't scared but there was no point in that now. I was getting quite cold despite the sun strengthening and expanding its domain on the ground.

"Heads up, here's our stop coming up." Andre said. "You're sure you don't want anything Iain?" Andre asked as we took a sharp left into the forecourt.

"No, I'm fine honest Andre, thank you anyway."

"No problem. You're going to lose out on some of the finest Italian ice cream this side of the Tiber. And yes I'll be getting you a big bottle of water Andro. I know how thirsty you are." He opened his door and stood up and stopped and rested his hand on the rim. "You know, your parents should be commended for raising a young gentleman as yourself." He closed his drivers door and walked, off telling the dog to remain in the car without turning round.

I felt really made up after he said that. It felt great coming from a guy like that. I felt guilty as hell now refusing his offer of ice cream but I still didn't feel I knew him well enough to take a gift from him. Now the mention of Italian ice cream brought Francesca to life in my mind. I determined that when I got back home I was going to ask her out. Anything could have happened today and I may not have got the chance to see her again, or anyone. Life was far too short and far too precious to waste any more time. That's what I will take from all this today.

It was a large forecourt with six petrol pumps. One man was already out filling his car up. He followed Andre's car up to the pump where he parked at and nodded in our general direction. I saw Andre pass him a small wave.

"The men's room is over by the car wash Iain." Andre informed me and walked towards the petrol station, where you could there was shopping aisles and a counter. "You're sure you don't need anything? Or want something?" He asked as he dandered across the forecourt.

"No, thank you. But cheers though." I felt really made up that I was with him. He was the coolest guy I had ever known.

I got stepped out of the shade of the roof covering the pumps and into the sunlight. It didn't feel warm but it was nice to have a sense of it around me without being near the Barrack and the bonfire that would never be and Blackie. It was just then I sensed something beside me on my left side. It was Andro. He had gotten out of the car somehow. I looked back to check if the doors were open. They weren't. Smart dog I thought.

"Come on.." the word 'boy' froze in my mouth as I saw the misshapen shadow appear and zig zag across the ground. It moved like those giant moths we had in the house last summer. But it wasn't a moth, the head looked almost human. But it wasn't no human I ever saw, had what looked like antlers on a deer sticking out of their head. I swung around in terror. I stared up and around me, fearing it was hovering above me. Then I looked at Andro. I was hoping he would be able to protect us both. The shadow was coming right out of the dog. My heart was performing somersaults inside my chest. I couldn't feel where my next breath was coming from. I felt I was going to wet myself as the massive ice cube in my stomach plummeted into my groin.

I had to get away. I listened to the voice in my head telling me to run. Run. I ran. I was at the breeze block wall that was the perimeter of the petrol station. It was only four blocks in height which I easily jumped over and into the grassy area and a fence met my stumble. I grabbed the top post and hoisted myself over. I never once looked back as I was terrified Andro would be bearing down on me. I scrambled across the field that was bumpy because of the long tree roots that rippled across the ground. Ahead of me was a small open field. It rose up to meet a line of trees I hoped was the start of a forest. A place where I could hide, a place to think, gather my thoughts and try and agree what had happened. I was sure the dog wasn't behind me when I raced across the field again without looking back once. What if I was wrong? What if it was just a trick of the light?

Christ the night I'm gonna look like a right arsehole to Andre. He's never gonna forgive me for this. I'd insulted his hospitality. I'd be an ungrateful wee shite. I'd rode in his fantastic car of his, he'd been as nice as ninepence, asking me about school, laughed at my stupid jokes. What the hell was wrong with me? I'd got it wrong, badly wrong. Shite, I had to stop and go back. He'd laugh at the whole thing I know he would.

I got to the start of where the trees stood I was out of breath as the field was all uphill. I bent over trying to get my breath back to normal. I would take a large slug of water and then start to head back. I drank the water as my breathing settled down. I let out a long gasp and turned round to look back at where and what I thought I had ran from. There they were, standing inside the field, both of them staring up at me. Andre's face was like thunder, he looked different. His face looked greyer, his forehead was lined and he had this twisted smile on his face. I knew he'd be upset, but he was really savage looking.

He turned his head and looked at his dog. The air seemed to have stopped in the field. It was as if I could hear the very flies and insects in the field. Then I heard him say to the dog.

"Now, you go and get him back." The order was without feeling or mercy. It was harsh and brutal. I knew now it was his real voice. I knew that from experience. I knew people wore masks. I saw it all the time when they came off. I saw it with Da. When Mum was around he was all pally smiley and messing about. When she wasn't, he was different, like he couldn't be arsed talking to me, making sighing noises or ignoring what I said.

"Go!" He shouted, startling me. Then he leaned down and punched the animal in the face. I was shocked, horrified, despite what we had done to Dylan, but we did that in self-defence, that was to protect ourselves from its reign of terror. None of us really wanted to hurt the dog. We all felt shite about it and for oul Gerry as well. It was a right Judas punch, like Teddy skidmark face, like me I confessed. I looked down at them both. There was no sound. It was one of those moments in the spaghetti westerns when all the gunslingers face each other at the end. One sound would set everyone off shooting. Everything seemed to move in slow motion. I was caught up in it. I couldn't budge.

I watched frozen in terror as the animal moved, it began to shake like a dog when a dog was wet and drying itself. But this wasn't like those moments. The thing was changing shape. It's face, its body shook like it was being electrocuted. This is not real. This is not real. Please tell me this is not happening. It can't be happening. It just can't. A small voice shouted in my head run. Run. Get away from Andre and his monster the voice told me. I screwed the cap on my bottle of water knowing somehow I was going to need it later and shoved it into my bag and turned and began sprinting towards the trees.

I had to move, to get away from both these creatures. I turned to my

Guardian Angel one more time, to give me the strength, the courage to get away. I knew Andre was bad, really bad when I saw what he had done but also the enjoyment you could see on his face when he did it. I didn't want to swear, not when I was about to pray, 'O Angel of God...' I felt my legs move like they had been paralysed by an injection and it was now wearing off. 'My Guardian dear, to whom Gods love entrust me here...'

I fled towards the trees, brushing the branches I could away from my face and dodging those I couldn't.

"Hey, Iain with two i's, crying won't help you and praying won't do you any good!" The voice surrounded me and seemed close and far away at the same time.

I stumbled down a small hill sliding on a blanket of wet grassy moss that was like ice to walk on. I kept my legs straight and just allowed myself to slide down to the end of the wet moss, like someone from ski Sunday you'd see on those white snowy hills. My boots were drenched and I thanked God I got to dry ground still on my feet. 'To whom God's love entrusts me here,' I repeated loudly on purpose. 'Ever this day be at my side, to light...'

I ran across the flat ground taking big strides to get some distance from me and those creatures. It was getting darker and tighter to move. More and more trees appeared. I was grateful for them as they provided more cover and more hiding place. But I couldn't see that far ahead and it was getting so tiring fighting off the branches and my ankles went over a couple of times on stones hidden under the leaves and twigs. I winced in pain and let out a sharp yelp on one particularly pointed piece of rock.

Above me the sky had broken into hundreds of pieces as branches weaved together in a knitted pattern blocking out most of the light.

I went further, deeper into the forest, I had no choice. I fought an army of tree arms attacking my face. Sweat was pouring from my hair and dropping from my forehead. My collar was soaked through, my armpits were drenched and the shirt heavy with sweat. I stumbled, I climbed and scrambled my way along; clawing my way over the mounds as fell to my knees and moved along on all fours in parts. 'To guide. Amen' I gasped through my lips through a lot of spit that fell out of my mouth. I could feel the skin on my hands and ankles had been cut and grazed. I was exhausted, absolutely punctured. There wasn't enough air in the world to satisfy my lungs demands.

My chest burned inside and out, with the t-shirt soaked through and freezing my skin, rubbing against my nipples which felt red raw. I had to rest for a moment. I needed to get my bearings, find out where I was going. God knows I hadn't a clue. There was a large man sized boulder leaning against the guts of a hill that spilt out in thousands of tiny twigs and straggly long strings of stuff that was like Brillo pads to the touch all rough and scratchy.

I slumped down at the side of the boulder in an awkward position. My knees and ankles felt like they had been tied up in wet bandages. I knew some of it was blood but I couldn't catch my breath as if my nostrils and mouth were far too small to get in the air my lungs were screaming for.

I needed something to drink. Thank Christ I had just less than half a bottle of water left. I resisted the strong impulse to drink it all down as my mouth was parched and my throat burned and ached for water. I sipped and rinsed my mouth and swallowed.

"Here Squint, come on out ya winged nut wee skinny tout."

I jolted in a shiver of fright. I knew that voice right away, but I couldn't believe my ears. That was Teddy puss face! I almost choked back up the water. For a moment I was happy to hear his voice. At the very least he was someone I knew, even though I hated him. I put the bottle back in my bag. It couldn't be him. There was no way that ballbeg could be here. No way. Sure he had gone on to the match. Come on, wise up, think about it.

"Yeah, come on out ya wee ballicks. Let's get Dylan. He'd like a piece of him."

That was Dee's voice. In God's name, there's no way he could be here. What was this? Was this Andre walloper some kind of Mike Yardwood? Could he do impressions?

"Come on Squint, or we'll send Dylan in to get ye." Wholenut's voice was followed by that gormless laugh of his.

"Judas."

My heart sank at the sound of the quiet damnation. It was Blackie. It was him calling me that name. And he was right, he had every right to.

That's what made it the most hurtful of all the insults directed at me. I was sorely tempted to get up and apologise to him, to beg for his forgiveness. Go out and meet the fate I probably deserved. Tears fell off my face onto my knees making big, dark patches on my jeans.

Son, listen, listen to me please.. God knows I know I wasn't always there for you.

Da? Is that you? Da? I looked around me as if he were there to be seen. You clampit I thought of myself, he wouldn't be, he would never be there for me.

Listen to me, you have to fight this thing, it's very real. I've seen it. It's face, sweet Jesus. You have to fight this. I know you can. Christ knows, I couldn't, but you can. I'm sorry for everything. I hope you and your mother can forgive me.

Da! In my head I shouted his name. I could tell from the way his voice trailed off that he was finished talking to me. He never did say much to me around the house, except when he was slagging me off. Da, come back, please. I uttered in anguish as quietly as I could muster.

Da, you bloody arsehole. No, no, I'm sorry Da, I'm sorry. But I'm scared out of my wits. I haven't a baldy notion what the hell is going on. I need help, please.

That's precisely what is going on. That voice again. It was that lying ballbeg Andre. The fucker, God forgive me but to hell with him and all them fuckers. I looked around me and up the embankment ahead through the knitted pattern of branches and leaves I could see something that was not of nature. It was metal, the metal of the strips you saw at the bends on the roads. Roads. That meant traffic and that meant people.

"He's going to do a runner lads, he's making for the road." I heard a familiar voice from above me shout out. What the hell was going on? Why was everyone against me? Why was I here with my feet soaked from the wet grass and the mud stiffening on my jeans? My ankles and knees burned from the fixed position I had slumped into behind the boulder.

"Right split up. Here you lads from The Barracks, remain here and the Hallion Battalion" There was a joyous roar as the name was uttered. "Right," Piercy gave a laugh that made everything seem so much crueller, "cut across to that hill and cut him off from the road. He's not going anywhere."

Christ the night, that voice above me. That was Lieutenant Tim. He was telling on me, giving me away. His voice came from above my head, I looked up and on the big wide trunk of a tree about ten feet up was his poster with him standing up. He looked to be covered in dark brown bandaging I knew from the poster to be his skin. A disfigured arm was pointed straight at me.

"Cheers Mo Chara," Piercy shouted back to Lieutenant Tim. "Let's cut him off at the pass." Piercy shouted over and with his order there was a chorus of whoops and red Indian noises like you'd hear in them Westerns that were on TV on Saturday mornings. The ones where people died a bloodless, almost painless death and got to say their last goodbyes to loved ones. That was a load of ballicks. In real life, people died nasty, bloody, gaping deaths and never got to say fuck all, lying there with their shoes blown off and with holes in their socks and shite in their underwear.

I looked around, me scouring the ground for something I could use. I grabbed two rocks that that fitted comfortably in my hand. "Who's the tout now?" I shouted at the top of my voice in a total rage at him, at all them.

I got up, my limbs ached and burned with the strain and knocks of the last ten minutes or so I and I took aim. I threw the rock with all my strength at the poster. Bullseye! Right in the squealer's bake. The poster disintegrated, the paper exploded and rained down like confetti to the ground. Now for the rest of the bastards, I thought. I'd taken all the shit I could take. I grabbed another rock and found a branch that would make a great weapon. I checked it was strong enough to attack by tapping it hard on the boulder. Right. This is it. I steeled myself by thinking of all the times all of them had insulted me, hurt me, lied and betrayed me. That would be my armour.

"Alright! Alright! Ya bastards." I deliberately screamed out my fear and terror at the unknown. "Come on! Come on then, come and get me. You're all sons of punctured Frenchies. Let's have it, ya bastards." I stepped out from behind my hiding place. I knew the waiting was worse than what was going to happen, it was like being at the dentists, you sit there crapping yourself and then it's over in few minutes and you couldn't even remember the pain. I was in a bloody red rage now. I was furious that they had made me so scared that I had wet a part of myself. I tightened my grip on the branch in my hand and imagined myself splitting their heads in two, hearing them cry for a mercy that I was never going to give.

I was ready to confront my tormentors.

THE SECOND HALF

THE VENUE: THE CRUMLIN ROAD COURTHOUSE. 1979

Mr Justice O'Donnell paused, drawing in a breath determined to conduct the summation in the utmost professional manner. It was the very least the victims and their families deserved.

It was 10.30 a.m., the courtroom had fallen under a spell of heightened expectancy. This was now a place where phrases and words became ridiculously inadequate. Words had been made redundant in the nightmarish landscape they had fallen into in recent days and weeks. Expressions of outrage, disgust and sheer horror withered on the corrupted vine that had grown out of the darkest recesses of mans ingenuity and appetite for inflicting terror on his fellow man. He listened to erudite men, with formidable intellect, struggle to encapsulate and define events only to witness them crumble, their summations rendered ineffectual, comical. Nothing and no-one, could begin to articulate the catalogue of horrors that had been inflicted on the victims.

It had felt at times like they had been cast down into an abyss, to live out a tale scripted by the brothers Grimm, one they had made so horrifying and inhumane it could surely have only been the work of the most grotesque imagination. He felt at times they had all been blinkered and for the first time could see the world in its true dark light. You had to fight back hard not to lose grip on the world you had known.

He had never known such a depth of silence and the unimaginable sadness, that it was tangible at times. He was left with a well of despondency and despair that reminded him of being a child where control was beyond your grasp beyond human comprehension. The very idea of humanity was a delusion. He had an unparalleled gnawing feeling of helplessness.

Before him sat the men responsible for the crimes he had to listen to and make judgement upon. Their ordinariness was unbearably too close to human. They were just men, unremarkable, less than ordinary, with shave marks and wrinkles in their clothes. But beguiling as it was to see them as such, one had to keep in mind the extraordinary cruelty and wickedness of their actions.   If they had had breathed fire and looked like devils then he could have some grasp, some idea at comprehending their crimes and why they were committed.

Lempi had forgotten to listen any longer to the words. There were far too many, awash with statistics; 11 murders, 2000 years, 2 life sentences, 18 years, 8 life sentences, 10 years and one survivor and a Mr X. A numbness had settled into her being. They told nothing of the real story behind the words that attempted to box up and rationalise, to describe the indescribable, to rationalise the incomprehensible. There was nothing to be understood, this was just something lost to the human psyche.

He had grown a moustache since she had seen him last. He stood dressed in a white pullover and a black and white open-necked shirt. All brand new. The one beside him, the one who led Francis away to the car, he too was dressed in new clothing, a green and orange v-neck sweater over a dark blue open-necked shirt. He had grown a beard since the last time she set eyes on him. That time she stood in the witness box and recounted that night they had walked across Peters Hill, where they had lain in wait like a shark, in a deep, dark ocean, springing to life as prey approached; the lights of the car lit up and focused on them.

They stood in stony silence, staring straight ahead. Lempi's eyes were drawn to the one with the newly grown moustache. She scanned down his arm, down to that hand, the one with the blue letters tattooed near to his thumb. She now knew it was a crude anagram of the organisation the men in the dock all belonged and had sworn allegiance to. Those same letters that had been within inches of her face as she was held in his grip that night, one she could never, ever forget. The smell of leather, beer and cigarette breathed carelessly on her face.

What another inadequate series of words that was. Brought to justice, it was meaningless. It didn't feel like there was any or enough justice in this world. Not for the victims, not for their loved ones. Not for these men. She had often harboured thoughts of how they should depart this world. She felt no guilt on settling for them being hanged, drawn and quartered. Let their bodies be laid out for all the world to see the outrages perpetrated on their now ravaged, lifeless carcasses.

There they stood, the destroyers of lives, who had literally cut down the hopes and dreams of so many, leaving them in a living tomb of memories and the despairing thoughts of what could have been if they had lived.

There they were alive, safe and with new clothes, sharing smiles and secret words of solace and comfort with their families and friends as if this were in a normal state of affairs. It was devastating, crushing. Her heart lay bruised and open to repeated outrages. She had no idea how to heal, how to begin to live again, not without the unbearable weight of guilt, pressing down, crushing her.

She looked over at them again. Their lives had not been stopped. Their hearts were not broken and their souls, if they had one, were not crushed under the comfortless burden of the truth surrounding the deaths they had meted out.

Their loved ones had not died peacefully. Nor was it without pain or suffering. Those moments where the thoughts and images you had deliberately and forcibly stemmed, only for them to snake a way into your consciousness. The moment when you were held frozen and hell opened up to the slideshow of them, alone apart from the inhuman figures hellbent on death; terrified and tormented, crying out for mercy where there was none, crying out for help where there was none. And finally, for the blessed end and the eventual refuge in death. They were the moments to fear, they shadowed and they stalked your everyday and everynight.

She could not tolerate the thought of him stuck in that moment of horror. That place you cannot believe exists for you. She felt faint, breathless, her legs about to buckle under the terrible weight of those thoughts. She found herself getting up and moving as if it were not her. She watched the legs of the people moved to allow her out like when she was at church as child and needed to go to the loo. She could feel the disapproving eyes glaring at her; some hostile, some just curious and wondering, perhaps even sympathetic.

She got to the doors that were left ajar by the police officers gathered there. She mumbled an apology and heard one of the police officers say in a plain voice that it was 'alright' and she stepped out from the room and into a cold rush of air. She breathed in deep breaths, side stepping all manner of people who associated themselves with such events.

"Excuse me, sorry. I'm from......"

Lempi stared at the young woman. She gathered she was a reporter from her neat clothing and the recording device, the strap of which was draped over her shoulder. That was a bit of a giveaway. She wanted to ask her something. She was pleasant and well-mannered in her approach and Lempi felt sorry for her having to put herself in these situations for the job. She would have liked to help but she couldn't, she wouldn't. All she had to say was confined to that courtroom and that witness box. Anything further would be misconstrued as her seeking attention, publicity for herself and pity for her plight. His family's contempt for her would know no bounds.

"Excuse me," She began again, "could you tell me your connection with the trial?" She point the microphone at her. Lempi stared at her and suddenly became extremely angry at her. Angry at her blasé question, her casual manner and her hope and expectancy of an answer.

"Knulla av tik!" Lempi found herself shouting at the girl whose demeanour changed visibly to horror. Lempi stormed down the steps and towards the revolving security gate where more police were gathered.

"That's the girlfriend of the youngest victim." Lempi overheard a rushed, hissed voice condemning her entire being to the whole ghastly affair. She no longer felt she was herself but a composite part of the living nightmare they had so unjustifiably been set in. She hated those men for that as much as anything.

Lempi got to pavement outside, her vision blurred by tears falling from her face. She dabbed the moist handkerchief drying her eyes and blowing her nose. She had to get away from it all and fearing the reporter might follow she walked as briskly as she could without breaking into a run.

Those outside who were in support of the men in the dock had been a daily presence. They had gathered on the pavement outside, flags of differing colours fluttered, groups of them huddled together smoking and offering words of support and encouragement. She was baffled by their public support. She could not comprehend their stance. These were men guilty of the most inhuman crimes. Yet they stood in full view of the world's press in defiance, shouting and at times singing their support for these men. It was beyond words, beyond understanding.

She stared down at the concreted ground and pressed ahead down the Crumlin Road. She prayed for a break in the constant stream of traffic so she could cross. An opportunity arose when a police Land Rover had stopped to allow several police men out onto the road. It looked like they were about to set up a road block. She imagined that they were preparing for when the courthouse would clear.

The emotions were so intense, so nakedly on display that there had been several ugly scenes between the victims' families and the supporters of those in the dock. It was savage at times, with clear, unadulterated hatred in the faces and words exchanged. The police presence was large, it had to be, to keep the factions apart.

The police began stopping traffic on both sides. Lempi walked hurriedly across the road to the side the hospital sat on. She walked on down to the Carlisle Circus, a large disc of an island kept the traffic in a constant cycle of movement. In the centre stood a plinth without a statue that had been blown up in 1970, a statue of a Presbyterian minister known locally as roaring Hugh Hanna. Even the statues weren't safe she had said at the time. He said he was inducting her to all the things you wanted to know about North Belfast but were afraid to ask. He laughed at the absurdities, the sheer madness to it all. She missed his laugh and felt a deep sense of betrayal stab at her because she could not remember it clearly anymore.

There were other acts of treachery committed by her memory. She could not recall his smell, even though she had held onto his favourite t-shirt and socks after he had changed one night when they were going out to dinner. She said she would wash and iron them. "A proper little couple we're getting" he said, smiling his infectious, crooked smile. "Don't get used to it," she told him as she pushed him out the door.

She passed the Orange Hall, she did not look up at the statute that adorned its façade. Centuries of conflict and hate, endless war and countless deaths and what was it all for? Her mind was beset with the sting of thoughts and images harassed by her feeling of betrayal, of the punching guilt that she had her life and he had lost his forever. All her black days were a slap in his face. He wouldn't waste his time on guilt, on fear and pity. Live life! She could hear him shouting from wherever he was now. That moment when the bomb went off was his wake up call he had said. Live everyday, or life truly was too short.

What his family for all their posturing, their moral superiority, what they didn't know was his moments of pressing melancholy, when he spoke of death. She dismissed it, telling him to stop being so melodramatic. She hated him when he fell into that mood, he'd lie on the sofa, spellbound by the idea of it. He talked and treated death as a person, as someone he had encountered once and would be pursued by and would meet up with again in the near future.

"Oh that it is great. Tell me. Why did you want engaged then at Josef Reas, the jewellers?" She asked. He laughed a great big hearty laugh and she was happy to have made him.

"Oh Lempi, I just love the way you articulate things. It's so precious. Josef," he repeated laughing to himself, "and the way you have to describe it as the jewellers."

"Are you mocking me?" She asked, not in seriousness for she was relieved to have him back in the room with her. She went to the record player and put on a record to lighten the mood. Certainly not Patti Smith *Horses,* she hastily put that down and picked up The Allman Brothers *Eat a Peach*, she found the song Blue Sky on that album uplifting.

"Sorry for being a pain Lempi Olofsson, my beautiful Swedish meatball. It's an Irish thing." He said and he thought for a moment before he spoke. "The great Gaels of Ireland are the men that God made mad, for all their wars are merry, and all their songs are sad."

He liked to quote from G.K. Chesterton, she knew as he was a particular favourite of his. He was fortunate to live where he did. It was mostly quiet, very few foot patrols and she had never seen an armoured vehicle drive up his street. That was for the war zones of the New Lodge and Ardoyne. She hated the tone the people who lived in the South of the city adopted when they spoke of the people in those areas. They were condescending and demeaning. But most of all, they were ignorant.

Two young couples had been discussing a shooting on The Crumlin Road and Lempi could take no more of their witless drivel and called them 'Bourgeoise dullards, who knew nothing of those peoples' lives. They were asked to leave before they got served and she stood outside with her dad apologising. To her great surprise and happiness he told her never to apologise for what you believe. 'I'm proud of you. They were Bourgeoise. And vulgar. Chenin Blanc with Bolognaise', her father tutted and Lempi laughed and linked her fathers arm as they strolled off to find a more discerning restaurant.

The DM shoes she wore with the trouser suit began to chafe at her ankles. Bodies were starved of space in the seating of the courtroom and for her last appearance she wanted to demonstrate to all, the murderers and their families and fans, to his family, especially his sister who had been so hurtful and the obvious catalyst for the animosity and anger directed at her. She would let them know she had not been subdued or beaten and she could take her rightful place amongst the loved one of the victims. She had not wielded the knife that cut his throat post mortem, nor held the gun used to kill him. Nor had she any part in the hatred that inflicted the injuries to his body as he lay on the waste ground in some godforsaken area that she had never heard of.

She used her wait at the lights to look behind her as if she were naturally looking out for oncoming traffic. There was no-one following, no-one she recognised from the courthouse that is. She had been concerned the young female reporter would have followed in the hope that away from the epicentre of all that was happening, she might be more amenable to talk. She thought it was such an unpleasant and intrusive way to earn a living. They had no interest in revealing the truth or unearthing why this could have been allowed to happen. They were ghouls reaching out to grab headlines and find the most salacious and sensational stories no matter how painful and wounding those details were to the families. She knew too well how they distorted what you said and what they reported. She had made that awful blunder by trusting someone who assured their story needed to be told.

She learned a bitter lesson from that experience and allowed herself to trust no-one with her story. People were essentially self-centred parasites, feeding off one another. Tragedy was a currency and misery thought it priceless. Before, when she had Caelan, the world had been a much lighter, brighter place where breath and laughter was shared. Now her breath felt as if it was stolen and the laughs she heard seemed strategic, designed and hollow.

She did draw strength from the warmth and goodwill of people who knew of her situation, especially at Kelly's Cellars and she felt an invisible border of protection envelope her. At time that proved too much. Like that time just over two weeks ago a young guy joined their table one evening. He was fair haired and softly spoken and he made them all laugh with his observations on human behaviour. He had was in the second year of his art and design degree and was talking of his soon to be visit to the Gealtacht area in Donegal to try his hand at thatching roofs whilst he improved on his Irish.

He seemed to have so many interests and wanted to experience so many things. He was excited by life, like he wanted to wring every moment of it like it were a wet cloth. He was optimistic and his zest for life made her she instantly warm to him. He was like a breath of fresh air. He was fresh faced with his hazel eyes that sparkled with alertness and moved from face to face with intelligence. You could tell he was uncorrupted by life. It was quite beautiful and uplifting to look upon him.

Roma had noticed that she found him interesting and nudged her arm. "Here you. Are you smitten?"

Lempi did not understand the inference.

"Are you loved up or what?" Roma asked, smiling her wide mouth stretched as far it dared.

"Pardon me? No way." Lempi protested, her face feeling flushed with embarrassment.

After his visit to the toilet he arrived back and hurriedly drank his pint and made some quick goodbyes and good lucks and left hastily. She found out later that evening he had left the bar hurriedly because someone had warned him off the 'that wee girl and not to try your hand, she had been through enough'.

She stayed away from the bar for weeks. She settled in at the house dad was renting up in Sans Souci. She kept away from all the places and people who reminded her of the event. She consciously framed what had happened in that word attempting to box it and make it a fragment of her life not her life entirely. At times it worked.

Dad was out of town he was always travelling with his government job in forestry. They had some kind of emergency with Ash Dieback he recited on the recorded message service. It was serious. Down to Fer-man-ah. Will return in two days. See you then. End of message.

She crossed at the lights, knowing she was moments from the church where Caelan had been buried from. Close by was the spot she had concealed herself, along with Roma to watch his final journey. His family stood outside soaking up all the heartfelt goodwill and warmth that was possible in those circumstances and she longed to be with them to share in the life once lived amongst them. She wanted their understanding, even their forgiveness, But it would never come. They blamed the stupid foreign witch who had talked their brother, their son, their uncle and friend into taking such a risk that led to his death. That was the only conclusion they could reach to explain his being in that place at such an ungodly hour, Hadn't they offered them the money for a taxi? Hadn't they asked them to the party? Hadn't they told them they wouldn't walk home under any circumstances? Well, didn't you?

She could offer no defence when these questions were put to her so forcibly by his sister. Her confrontation that day in the bar was so abrupt and sudden, the anger pouring out from her entire body; straining to be unleashed to be understood. Lempi knew she wanted to understand. But how could she begin to explain the inexplicable. Briana stood like a wild animal her shaved on all side and a shock of pure, white hair combed up like the way the punks did. Lempi knew what she wanted. What she needed. She wanted someone to blame. Someone she could focus her pain on. And Lempi was willing to allow herself to be that person.

The white hair was the physical manifestation to her shock, her grief that could not be assuaged. Lempi thought unkindly that she wore her hair like a trophy. It was almost triumphant the way she drew attention to it and that angered her. She was ready for the inevitable onslaught, for words alone would not satisfy the rage Briana held. She stepped back and turned sideways and relaxed her arms.

But before any punches were thrown, Caelan's brother marched over and dragged Briana away without saying a word. His withering look collapsed Lempi's inner resolve and she ran from the place in tears.

She really needed to speak to her father face to face. The phone calls and the occasional fax from the machine he used for work that he used to keep up with her life at home would not do. He was in out in the field a lot, quite literally, as he worked a science officer for agriculture in the Forestry and Biosciences. He talked energetically about his job but Lempi could not summon the strength to show enthusiasm for a person dear to her father's heart. It hurt him she knew. That was another emotional crime she was guilty of.

God Lempi, I can still see the child you once were in that beautiful face of yours. Those tiny, delicate features and those big, wide innocent eyes still full of wonder. She fell against the sandstone of the church at the sound of his voice. She rubbed its surprisingly soft surface. It felt like very fine sand paper. She was the living dead, surrounded by people who thought she should have died that night too. Her life here was forfeit, she was as near to an accomplice in his death as you could be without being held legally responsible.

His face consumed by shadows. He jumped up on the sofa and shouted at her to turn off the radio in an agitated, angry voice. Lempi was standing by the record unit looking at the cover of The Alex Harvey band, its cartoonish cover amused her. She dropped the cover in a start of shock and almost immediate anger at his behaviour. Turn it off he said again his voice was alien to her it was full of hurt, of hate. She fumbled with the round stainless steel dials and managed to turn the sound completely off. He scrambled to his knees and jumped to his feet and they stood aimed at each other in the silence.

"What the hell?" Lempi was angry and she wanted him to know it. "Don't you talk to me like that. Don't you ever." Her voice rose to a level that could be heard outside the room prompting his brother to shout in if everything was okay in there.

"Yes. Just a quarrel, over music mate." Caelan shouted back through the door. "Oh God, I'm really sorry Lempi. I shouldn't have got on like that. I acted like a real nutcase there. I'm sorry." He said using his apology to approach.

"Don't." Lempi told him firmly, "don't come to me. I'm not ready, I'm not..." She did not know how to express the feelings that fought for her immediate attention to be addressed. She was primarily angered and upset at his behaviour and the manner in which he had addressed her. But a small worry also vied for a place in her consciousness. Why had that song on the radio given cause for him to act the way he did?

"The song was not that awful." She forced a smile trying to make an opening for them to talk. But knew she shouldn't have opened with that gambit when he flashed a look at her. It was as if he was another person. He visibly changed. His skin went taut and the colour deserted it. His shoulders slumped and fell back onto the sofa.

He sat up on the sofa and wrapped his arms around his knees. "That song brings me back to a time, to a place I never want to go back to. Never."

That's the day she found out about the pub bombing and his

interview at the police station and the day he believes he saw the devil himself. It had been chiselled into her mind. She saw him differently somehow after that admission, like he was a haunted being. Even when they were out and having great fun with friends she would steal moments to watch him as he talked or played guitar and looked at him as if were a stranger. How could he have kept hidden this traumatic event from her?

She had told him of her parent's separation. How her mother returned back home to Sweden; but her parents remained married as they loved one another, but her mother could not live in Belfast any longer. And it was not the violence, it was her work. And when an opportunity came she would not give up the research post in environmental technology at her beloved Uppsala University.

She had told him about her cousin's accident that left her in a wheelchair. It could so easily have been her had she not run faster and seen the car earlier. When she thought about him and his family he realised how little they told her about themselves. He had a brother who was 'alright, except he supports Leeds United', a sister who loved herself and thought the world revolved around her. His mother and father were ordinary people with ordinary jobs and had got their nice house in the nice area off the Cavehill Road when his father suffered a serious injury to his leg working as a bin man. It had been crushed when his work mate failed to spot him cramming fallen rubbish into the rear loader. Now he worked in their offices 'answering calls and stapling paper together'. Their father, Mister Deeny, managed well, he had a limp of course, but he could still walk to the top of the Cave Hill on a Sunday morning.

He had gone with them without a word. He allowed them to steal his life. Lempi took a deep breath hoping to fill her lungs up with holy, protective air. She felt foolish thinking it. But she needed intervention, someone; something outside of herself that would help. She stepped into the narthex of the church her head awash with a myriad of thoughts and images. She stole an admiring glance at the slatted wooden doors. They must be fourteen foot in length. They looked sturdy, capable of repelling any onslaught. How she had inwardly laughed when he had made his confession at the time. She thought it's so far-fetched, ridiculous, an absurdity from his youthful mind bombarded by violence and religion. But as he spoke she had never seen him so serious, so convinced of something and because she never knew when the people of this place were being serious or joking, or both; it was maddening at times but she held her judgement until he had finished. And when he had done so, she knew whatever did happen that night, he truly believed in what he had seen.

Like his stupid proposal, even that was treated like a joke he was playing on her. He got her to stare at the earrings in the window of jewellers and then placed his hands on either side of her head and moved her head gently towards the rows of rings. Pick one. Up to the price of thirty five pounds and fifty pence, he whispered into her reflected face. He had sold his guitar to get the money when she asked how he could afford it. She became enraged and told him to buy it back. She knew his family would think she had put him up to it.

She told she would only agree if they saved up and finished university, it would give them both time to have the resources to get engaged and then everone could see we had been mature and committed to the whole thing. Even my father wouldn't argue if we did that. When did you get so grown-up, he said, his face blank and emotionless. He spent the longest time with his eyes on the ground and his face as 'long as the spade in Lurgan is'. He laughed and he hugged her tightly. 'I didn't think it possible you could be as intelligent as you are beautiful'.

She pushed the large half door to gain entry to the church, her tears forming a wet trail on the mosaic floor. The tears were warm and bitter to the taste, blurring her vision, she didn't think it was humanly possible to cry this much. She used the seating of the pew to negotiate her way to the centre.

She sat down on the pew directly opposite the statue of St Anthony and used her feet to slide further up the varnished wooden pew. She was exhausted, drained of emotion. She yearned for peace and solace. She sought serenity and solemnity and the quietness of the church she thought would provide it.

But instead, she saw it as the setting for his last journey. Her presence was not welcome, there had not been any contact or solicitation from his family so she did not get to come and say her final goodbye or pay her respects or demonstrate to all that she had been a part of his life. She never got to pray and cry with all those who shared in the grief and loss engulfing their waking moments.

She drew great comfort from her friend Roma, who clutched at her arm as they sheltered at Unity Flats, close to a row of shops away from the road the cortege would take. She was relieved and glad her Dad was in Bristol for a meeting. He had told her to stay away and to make this, the day of his burial the point where she could move on. He went on to apologise for sounding harsh, crass even, but his responsibility lay with her: no-one else. She could see he was afraid, afraid for her and for their relationship. He didn't want lose her as well as his wife by his inaction, his inability to make time and show he cared. She knew that he loved her but was unable to show it in ways that were measurable.

They had argued and fought over her behaviour, his behaviour. They argued when she dyed her hair and took to wearing men's jeans and jackets. They argued over damp towels in the bathroom and unclean bowls in the sink. They never once in all their arguments argued about her taking a year out of University, of her sleeping until the afternoons and then going out to the pub; not once did they mention his name.

She thought this would an end to it for her and she would move on was he was laid to rest. Roma kept telling her it wasn't her fault and his family were acting like bloody bullies. A bunch of damn bullies she repeated and spat out onto the ground as there was movement around the entrance of the church. 'Here we go, babes. You be strong'. Roma's face tightened and hate lines formed on her forehead and around her mouth.

Lempi knew she was trying to be supportive, acting out the responsibilities of a friend but it was sour and ill-natured and not in keeping with the silent composure and respect of the funeral cortege as it spilled out onto the Donegall Road, stopping the traffic on both sides from entering or leaving the city.

She thought Roma must have realised her words were not right for the occasion and as his coffin passed, she crossed herself and said simply 'God rest you Caelan. Silent tears rolled down her skin. It was only at that moment, that it dawned on Lempi, that Roma and Caelan had been great friends, who enjoyed each others company. They were both lovers of music, Roma played the fiddle in the ceilidh sessions and earned her money from landscaping gardens, mostly in the good months of May, she was joking of course as Caelan and everyone around them laughed. And she grew all manner of plants and seeds she sold at her father's fruit and veg shop.

She had gone to Caelan's family home with a lush tropical peace lily and told Lempi she had to explain to Caelan's brother and his father that the dark green colors of most sympathy plants convey profound respect, while white flowering blooms symbolize purity, innocence, and re-birth. They had looked puzzled and hesitant accepting the plant at first but once she had explained the meaning of the gift they both hugged her as tightly as they dared and then returned quickly to the frozen state of pure grief.

Lempi had been in a fury of jealousy and resentment at her friend for having something so meaningful denied to her and it added to her deepening sense of injustice at his family. She felt terrible for her thoughts and feelings when they went into the Whites Tavern bar in town and Roma presented her with a Gardenia plant in a hand made box with the word 'Love' hand-painted on it. They both hugged for the longest time, and Lempi was sure she had permanently ruined Roma's suede jacket with the amount of tears she cried.

They both drank to one another and to friendship and enjoyed an evening celebrating Caelan's life and the lives of all their loved ones. They both joked about the insane and chaotic nature the experience of living was. They both promised to live life to its fullest knowing it was the mostly the drink talking.

Lempi forgot Roma's present that night, leaving it behind in the bar and had to return the next morning and sheepishly retrieve it. The bar manager had said the girls in the bar had wondered what it was for. They all thought it was beautiful and that the person who had left it behind would most certainly come back to reclaim it. She explained to the bar manager what it represented and he said, the girls were right then, and also about whoever gave it. You've a good mate there, he told her and she had to agree.

I hope these thoughts counts for prayer, I cannot pray in the conventional sense, she muttered under her breath. I shall sit and rest for a while. I will light candle before I leave for all who have suffered. But not for those responsible, that would be the Christian thing to do. But I am not a Christian at this time. It felt like healing when she ventured to forgive. But she only could get so far before the anger and bitterness swamped her. The images of his suffering and all that had been taken from her and his family firmly shut that door. I will light one too, for my father and mother I know they worry for me. And secretly she felt good about that, because she knew they had been in regular contact because of it.

As she bowed, somewhere in her mind, her spirit from somewhere it found her humming 'Rescue me sang by Aretha Franklin and as she hummed she found the tune so comforting and so appropriate she began to softly sing the words 'Rescue me, Oh take me in your arms', she sang to the station of the cross above her on the walls of the church, 'rescue me, I want your tender charms', and for those moments it felt like the only possible prayer she could say. 'Coz I'm lonely and I'm blue I need you and your love too'. She sobbed, knowing that she needed the peace she yearned for if her life was to reassemble, this time without the missing parts that hollowed out her being.

It was just at that moment that Lempi found her contemplation disturbed by the sound of loud clacking, like metal clashing with the tiles of the church floor. It was regular and rapid. It spoiled the serenity she had fallen into and she resented the presence of it. It was discordant, inappropriate and at odds with the quietness of the chamber. She looked up wiping her eyes and took a moment to focus and home in on the moving figure nearing the altar.

A shiver of freezing recognition pierced her body. She recognised the well dressed man, who continued to click clack his way up the central aisle. He was from the courthouse. She had seen him on the occasions she had been compelled to attend. She shrank back in the pew concerned that he had followed her, perhaps another reporter. He had come in on those occasions with the minimum of attention from security. He was always very well dressed and always had a seat near the front just behind the lawyers. She thought he was something to do with law, then security like the intelligence services or from the press. It didn't matter which, they were all insufferable parasites, constructed and organised for exploiting the continuing misery of its people. He sat staring ahead without taking notes, his face set like stone and on the are occasion she felt her eyes drawn to him you could swear he wore the faintest smile on his lips.

She watched as he approached the altar and took a sharp right and walked towards the elderly priest who was at the sculpted life-sized Calvary scene. The priest was taking the dead candles from their metal plates and dropping them into a red plastic bucket apparently oblivious to the approaching figure.

FATHER VINCENT'S JOURNAL: PARISH OF SAINT PATRICKS.
MAY 1979.

Earlier in my priesthood, I would not have been able to write this and I certainly would have looked askance at anyone who broached the topic of demonology. Though I was aware that the teachings about demons, prayers to ward off the evil spirits and the official rite of exorcism have long been part of the official teaching of the Church, I doubted a modern priest could take such a pre-Enlightenment topic seriously.

However, now with more than 35 years of priestly experience under my belt and some growth in the Spirit's gift of knowledge infused through the sacraments of Confirmation and Holy Orders, I no longer doubt the reality of malevolent spirits. As a matter of fact, I would be displaying great hubris to even entertain such doubts. The Gospels are filled with stories of Jesus' encounter with demons. It is first necessary to define what a demon is and how it acts then explain misidentification of demonic possession as mental illness or simply the free will of a bad person being acted out. Finally, I will attempt to show demonic possession and the effects of demonic activity.

Traditionally demons have been described as beings without bodies that possess intellect and free will (Aquinas, p. 450). This description does not sit well with modern people since it presumes metaphysics which uses reason to know things that are not immediately available to the senses. Aiding reason, faith provides another vantage point for validating the activity of the spirit world. In Ephesians 6:12, the St Paul says, "For our wrestling is not against flesh and blood, but against principalities and powers, against the rulers of this world of darkness, against the spirits of wickedness in the high places."

A demon's influence, according to St. Augustine, can change the cognitive part of the person by changing his internal and external sensory powers. The demon says, "creeps stealthily in through all the avenues of the senses, it gives itself shapes, it adapts itself to colours, it adheres to sounds, it appends itself to odours, it instills with flavours" (Aquinas, p. 526). By its very nature "a demon intends to lead men to falsehood. He does so by inciting a man to cogitate about a particular thing and impedes the use of reason: this is commonly known as possession" (Aquinas, p. 535).

In a discussion of the demonic, it is important to be sure that certain psychological disturbances, whether chemically caused or due to an imbalance from emotional distress or trauma, be ruled out before demonic possession is considered. Of course professional diagnosis must be made to determine the potential causes of certain behaviours which may be indicative of, for example, schizophrenia, multiple personality disorders or other mental illnesses. It should be noted, however, that Satan does not like to be revealed. It is therefore conceivable that he may hide behind the facade of a psychosis.

This appears to be case with Samuel, who is currently in the care of Staff at Purdysburn Hospital. They in turn contacted me when they attempted to contact Bernadine, his wife. They were informed by Greta, the sister that she was residing at the Presbytery temporarily. Due to a recent estrangement within the relationship she has declined any persuasion to see him.

Samuel was discovered two days ago in a state of undress and extreme distress in the Sailortown area. The police assumed he was drunk and perhaps drugs and left him in the cell for the night to presumably sleep it off as they were convinced he had taken a cocktail of drinks and perhaps drugs. During the night he was found to be foaming from the mouth and violently moving backwards and forwards. There were outbursts of vile language and perceived threats to his personage. One police officer remarked that he sounded more like an animal than a human being. The police doctor was called in and he was sedated.

He has since been transferred to Purdysburn Clinic, who was contacted by the police seemingly at a loss and struggling to keep Samuel from harming himself or others. I have been contacted by the police to make enquiries about anything I may have heard in relation to a missing person.

By sheer good fortune Greta, sister of Bernadine and regular worshipper had come to report her brother-in-laws disappearance and the lack of police interest. The woman was distraught but after calming her down I managed to get a brief description and phone call to the hospital it was clearly established that the person they had under their supervision was indeed Samuel. We thought it a good idea that Greta talk with her sister and left them alone in the presbytery front room for several hours. We did not venture out and remained in the office across the hall with the door open.

Staff have had to keep him sedated and under close observation. Senior Staff Nurse Lewis, whom I have been in contact with; informs me that staff have not encountered anything close to the deep level of anxiety and psychosis. Father Stephen and I have been to see him and we are now convinced that this is beyond psychosis or psychological trauma. What troubles both of us greatly is that he will only say one word repeatedly.

Just yesterday I contacted his employer who confirmed he had been absent from work and I explained the circumstances as best I could. I again stressed the nature of this apparent breakdown most likely should be attributed to their son's injury and hospitalisation taking its inevitable toll. His employer, a Mr Cowan confirmed that Samuel's son had been in hospital for some time due a head injury and that everyone in the company was thinking of him and his family. I assured him that he would get an update as soon as I have something to report.

Bernadine, Samuel's wife, had recently made a visit to a city centre bar with some of her work colleagues after work. She explained that she needed to talk to and to relax for an hour. I told her she had no need to explain herself. Significantly that evening a man introduced himself to her at the bar calling himself Andre. After a short introduction he said he could tell she was preoccupied, worried. She felt she could talk to this stranger for some reason and told him everything regarding her child.

This man claimed he could return this couple's child to them.

During the course of their conversation he claimed he could restore her child to full health in return for certain conditions being met. Bernadine assures me she dismissed his claims as some form of block-headed, outlandish wooing. She insists she dismissed any ideas of entertaining that and informed him that she was a happily married woman.

She states that before her very eyes he killed a fly that had landed on the surface of the table and killed it. He asked to check if it were dead she states that the fly was definitely dead and then he placed a hand over it for several seconds and the fly was revived and flew off. She states that is when she got unnerved. He pressed on with his claims to be able to revive her child. She admitted then that she had been vulnerable and desperate enough to listen to the man and agreed to allow him to help.

1. Stop attending church 2. Stop attending confession and 3. Stop my visits to the child as hospital Chaplain.

She point blank refused and re-joined her friends before getting the bus up to hospital for her nightly visit.

That night she was plagued with terrible headaches and a mysterious blue light that pervaded the house and settled in their child's room. She entered the room and fled in terror as the light had taken the shape of the man who had approached her in the city centre bar, this Andre. She has come to us at parochial house and has remained since. That was four days ago.

My real concern is after hearing her confession that she has placed herself in very real peril. She confided that her faith broke after her novena to St Anthony, said every Tuesday for nine consecutive weeks, had in her mind, failed. I cannot go into any detail of what she did next, suffice to say that someone or something has heard and has entered the scene with evil intent. At this moment in time she is safe within the Parochial House, where now prays and fasts.

I have spoken to her employer and they have been quite sympathetic. They only know that she has fallen ill because of the toll her son's hospitalisation has taken on her health, both physically and psychologically.

Now I fear this is more than mere coincidence, as we know the word he has been repeating is known to us as that of a high level demon. Adrammelech. The high Chancellor of Hell. Or in Bernadine's encounter 'Andre'.

Her son is at this moment in critical care at the Mater Hospital under the care of consultant Mister Kidney and Doctor Hooper. As hospital chaplain, I have prayed for the child at his bedside on a number of occasions. Doctor Hooper provides me updates on any progress regarding the focal contusions the boy suffered when the bus he was travelling in to a football match was attacked. Doctor Hooper fears the brain oedema from this significant contusion will lead inevitably to clinical deterioration due to swelling and brain stipe. I have been noting down our discussions in great detail. They are keeping the boys oxygen levels above 10 K PA with arterial oxygen saturation. Care has been taken to ensure endotracheal tube tapes are not causing venous compression around the neck and that the head and neck are kept in neutral alignment to optimise venous drainage and return. There are machines of all types that are continuously monitoring arterial blood pressure, core body temperature, respiration rate and ICP monitoring for ventilated patients where neurological deterioration cannot be easily observed clinically.

They are careful to avoid dehydration, treating it with Dextrose and serum electrolytes and osmolality are regularly monitored. There is a pulse oximeter, endotrachedral tubes, chest and urinary IV's and a central venous catheter. He goes on to list ventilators, monitors, dialysis, feeding tubes and IV pumps. There is pain management, monitors for haemoglobin and an Apnea monitor for breathing, an intracranial pressure monitor and the crash cart stands ready at any time.

The boy has been positioned with his head elevated 15 to 30 degrees to decrease ICP, 60 degrees can produce stronger results. The effect of environmental stimuli on ICP is limited, so the presence of unpleasant stimuli is reduced as much as possible. To this end, they have indulged the mother and allowed for his favourite posters to be placed above his bed and his favourite music is played on a record player. Dr Hooper is bemused, almost exasperated at the lengths the boy's mother will go to. But Dr Hooper tells me all of this at a cost. He feels there is no hope for the boy to recover. If the child were to defy insurmountable odds, he and the consultant believe the child will be extremely limited in terms of brain activity and would in effect result in a vegetative state until an inevitable and untimely demise.

He entreats me to tell his mother of these facts as their words have fallen on deaf ears, as his mother clings onto the forlorn hope as only a mother can, that he will recover. This has been stressed to me in no uncertain terms that it is not medically possible. That is the reality she must face, Dr Hooper presses.

I rebuked Dr Hooper for embroiling me in this design to enable what I cannot and will not do as a priest and a Catholic. Namely aid and abet them end the child's life. Where there is life, there is hope, I have impressed upon him and I reminded him of his Hippocratic Oath. He angrily refuted my argument as mere sentiment and plain wishful thinking.

Just yesterday I contacted his employer who confirmed he had been absent from work and I explained the circumstances as best I could. His employer, a Mr Cowan, confirmed too that Samuel's son was being treated at The Mater and was of great concern to them all.

Now I fear this is more than mere coincidence as we know the word he has been repeating is known to us as that of a high level demon.

I believe this family has been directly targeted and been in direct contact with this demon.

I am making arrangements for myself, Malachai and Father Stephen to visit with him. I hope to convince those in authority there to allow him to come with us so that we can cleanse him from the unclean spirit. We will of course be giving the authorities a more secular reason for taking him into our charge. Father Stephen has a doctorate in psychology and rather fortuitously for us, and has practiced in the UK and Ireland. We shall be endeavouring to have him treated privately.

I believe Samuel is a case of a demonic encounter and a possible intrusion, a case worthy of exorcism. However, I realised that talking to health care professionals of this possibility, then and even now would, in most instances, be impossible. If I mentioned such ideas they may even have suggested that I needed professional help. This man is in great mortal danger, as is his wife. Their son too, as I believe him to be the source of this contact having looked at and discounted contact with the occult through séance, Ouija boards and black magic or a religious cult or trauma through domestic violence, abuse or divorce that can lead to alienation and loneliness.

My instinct tells me that it is the last in a line of possibilities that someone, most likely the boy because he hovers between the conscious and unconscious worlds, that he could well be the source contact with this evil.

Although there are other reasons for this behaviour, I have found nothing in his background from his wife, his sister-in-law and some work colleagues that he is an evil person. Deeply flawed yes, like most of us. It is important to note that evil people will use any means they can, even seemingly unrelated things, to bring down an opponent or anyone in whom they perceive a threat. It is either, "everybody is doing it" or "if they try to get me in trouble, I can make trouble for them too." It must be made clear, we are not talking here about a sociopath of a person who has made a conscious choice for self and knows the difference between right and wrong.

This leaves the last category of the person, possessed by demons. It is obvious from what I have said above that recognition of demons is not at all easy, since Satan often works in disguise and evil may be of a person's own making. But there are some indications that perhaps what one confronts in some instances is just slightly beyond typical abnormalities.

The possessed person senses the presence of an unwanted other intelligence that is directing them to certain thoughts and actions. They may even report hearing internal voices and sometimes these voices (demons) identify themselves by name. These peoples' behaviours do not necessarily have to be off the charts or even bizarre. Nevertheless, they are not happy with these alien forces which are causing unhappiness and disruption in their lives. As a matter of fact, they feel caught up in "untruth" about themselves, life, the world and reality in general. The traditional definition of truth is the conformity of mind with reality. In the process of exorcism, the exorcist confronts the lies the demon speaks, which sometimes causes the demon to flee. After all, isn't Satan the father of lies? This very much coheres with what Augustine and St. Thomas say in their description of the demonic described above.

The distortions presented by the demons may be as simple as confusing one's obligations and performance, for example, in the tasks of marriage and parenting, or causing an inordinate desire for material things, which prevents a person from attaining true love and friendship. The key here is that the demon has some control over the possessed person. It is felt or recognized to be a power beyond the individuals' control.

Another indication of a demonic presence is addressed by the French philosopher Louis Lavell in *Evil and Suffering* (1963). He says that evil causes a separation of harmony either in the same being or between beings. This, he says, is:

Because every bad will pursue isolated ends which, sacrificing the whole to the part, always contaminate the integrity of the whole and threaten to annihilate it.

In my own experiences with the demonic it is often the backlash when the demon is outed or confronted by truth that has been the strongest indicator of its presence. To speak the truth in love is abhorrent to a demon. This is especially true when the demon is recognized or Satan is identified as the root of the problem. The reaction is sometimes subtle and sometimes violent, but an attack will follow. I do not mean physically, although sometimes this may happen, but usually by an assault on the person's character or some other diversion that will remove the protagonist from doing battle with the demon. Priests are especially susceptible to this since Holy Orders which configures them more radically to Christ makes them bearers of the Truth in a most powerful way.

This is a warning; every priest is a prime target of Satan. Speaking truth, however, is not limited to religious matters. It may be simply articulating ethics for good human behaviour. Once again, through the Holy Spirit's gifts of understanding and right judgment, insight and good advice on life's issues that will bring about peace and goodness is a thwart to Satan's plan.

I do not make these observations to encourage the unprofessional to begin to exorcise all those they may deem to be possessed. At times, no doubt all of us might be diagnosed by others as being so disposed. But I urge serious reflection on the topic by those professionals involved with human physical, emotional and spiritual well-being.

Psychiatrists, lawyers and priests should work together on these cases to make sure valid criteria are met for exorcism, that proper legal and medical precautions are taken to protect the Person being exorcised, and that competent persons are assigned to perform the ritual. The rites of exorcism, a long part of religious tradition, would not exist unless the truth of Satan and his demons were recognized as being real.

This is what I have been at pains to impart to Father Stephen and Malachai and all those who have chosen to join us. I have made my plans to thwart this evil and have been open and honest to all those I have sought to help me in my endeavour. We have fasted and prayed, we have made and heard confession for ourselves and all those involved. We are certain that our people are in a strong spiritual place. They are aware of the potential dangers but their faith has committed them to our cause. If all goes as I have planned we will be in a position to confront and contain this evil sooner, rather than later. Otherwise it strengthens.

Deus det mihi ad robur spirituale.

Father Vincent took off his round shaped glasses and rubbed his eyes which ached from the lighting on his desk. He closed his journal and lifted himself from his chair and bent down to place it in the large safe they had for all the important documents, letters and church funds. He dared not think on what the next entry in the journal could be.

SAINT PATRICK'S CHURCH, DONEGALL STREET, BELFAST

"Ah, asimus tuus, equos fecerint, erepta mortis." A quiet, but strong voice interrupted the priest's chore of collecting the burnt out candles.

"I'm sorry. What was that you said?" The priest said in a tone that highlighted the affront. He stopped collecting the last of the burned out votive candles and looked up at the tall, well- dressed figure. The priest stood with the bucket resting at his arms-length and stared at the stranger before him.

"Surely you understand the Latin? Perhaps, if I used Aramaic?" He smiled diffidently at the elderly priest and then at The Calvary where the life size figures of Christ on the cross, Mary the mother of Jesus, Mary Magdelene and St John situated in the South Transept of the church.

"No, no. I understood what you've said," Father Vincent cleared his throat and looked at the stranger, "just taken aback somewhat, that you should say it in the house of God."

The man moved a hand to his lips to conceal a smile. "Why Father? To anyone who was there this is a complete insult to the actual events. The pain and suffering was unendurable for him. He screamed out his curses on mankind as he pissed himself at the thought of what lay ahead. This is a mockery if ever there was." His smile closed on his lips and he stood impassively staring ahead.

The priest stared at him at length. And he made a short prayer.

"What are you muttering? A damn prayer?" The stranger sneered, his voice soaked in derision and contempt. "If I'm not correct worm then, se non e vero, é vero, é ben travato." He said with a theatrical Italian accent

Father Vincent looked up at the figure. He was an impressive and imposing man, well dressed in a grey three piece suit. He had a strong, handsome face and wore what looked like an expensive watch and cuff links. He was muscular, one could tell from the cut of his clothing. The back of his hands clasping the walking stick were hairless, his fingernails tapered and immaculately clean. Father Vincent noted the head on the stick was of an animal which he could not identify. He was easily six foot two or three with long braided fair hair that cascaded down to the small of his back like a waterfall that had been captured and represented in hair.

"What are you doing here? You're not here to give prayer or praise, clearly."

The stranger choked back a full, gleeful laugh. "No, no, that I'm not. I'm here for an item of my property that you have taken from me. I'm here to collect it. So be good a shepherd and go and get it for me, thank you."

"A good shepherd would never knowingly or willingly walk his flock into the hands of a wolf. Don't give orders in my own church. I will most certainly not take instruction from the likes of you. I instruct you to leave at once." Father Vincent was greatly disappointed he had raised his voice to a level where it had travelled around the church.

"Listen worm. I won't ask again, get me the woman you have hidden around this tomb for a dead man. Now." The stranger demanded, leaning in to the face of Father Vincent who could see now what he was confronted with. His breath smelled of death.

Now, Father Vincent wanted to know who he was confronted by. "In the name of Christ, I demand to know your name."

"Is that all, worm?" The stranger stepped back pulling his face away from the priest's and breathed out. "I have many names; murder, rape, abortion, incest, bestiality. Shall I go on? There are many, many more." A scornful smile erupted across his face, his eyes blistering with malcontent.

"Oh, I believe you have many more, of that there is no doubt," Father Vincent replied calmly to counteract and contain the build up of menace, "as long as it's not Nybbas." And Father Vincent made a small chuckle. "That would be of a great disappointment to me," Father Vincent remarked, and made a show of resuming his task by collecting some more of the cradles that had held for a time the flickering moments to the hopes and prayers of someone. "To be host to such a great buffoon would be the ultimate in insults."

The priest turned to face the altar. "I believe he's a standing joke amongst even his own kind. A fatuous oaf with..." Father Vincent felt his throat gripped by a stingingly powerful hand.

"Shut up! You worm. You know nothing of our kind." The stranger seethed with uncontrolled rage. "You piece of dogshit. How dare you insult us."

"I know. I know," Father Vincent wheezed his words out, "an imposter when I meet one." He felt himself fall to the ground, unaware that he had been lifted from it in the first place.

"What is this? Who dares to attack me?" Nybbas turned in fury to face the assailant.

"Get your hands off him. Get away from him." It was a young woman. Lempi had watched the two men as soon as she heard the raised voices and launched into action when she saw the man from the courthouse reach out at the priest.

She stood before the priest's assailant, all the training she had undertaken flooded into her mind and memory muscle. She adopted her pose, her knees bent very slightly. She heard the trainers shouting : Never rest weight on a leg with a completely straight knee! Her rear heel raised with the weight placed on the ball of her foot. She kept a small amount of tension in her abdominal muscles, once she had been hit when her stomach was relaxed. You do not want to be hit in a relaxed stomach! She was ready for him.

'Chin down! Hands up! She again could hear the trainers shout as they confronted their opponents. The head should be slightly tilted forward with the chin practically glued to your collarbone. She was an attentive student and was prepared. Make sure your cadence contains no rhythm, use constantly repeated movements. If it does, it becomes easy for your opponent to time you with counter shots.

"My dear, don't. Don't involve yourself. Not on my account. Please." Father Vincent implored in a weakened voice. He tried to get to his feet but held in his kneeling position by the stranger.

"Stay dog. Stay on your knees you bag of dust." The stranger barked at him. "Too late for that old worm. This supperating wound of puss has involved herself." Nybbas sneered at Father Vincent.

"Take your hands off him. Lempi shouted mindful not to lose all her composure, as that could prove fatal in any encounter.

"Welcome," he said with a wide smile that warned of deadly intent, "you've no idea what you've got yourself into you, you whore."

"Go to hell, du jävla fegis. I hate bullies, you are so damn pathetic." Lempi moved from side to side on her toes preparing to attack or be attacked.

"Ah, Svenska! Välkommen pissstain." The stranger replied, startling Lempi that he could have instantly known her insult in her native tongue.

"Malachai! Stephen!" Father Vincent collected himself and stood up to shout out the names.

A figure appeared at a door near to the shrine to the Virgin Mary at the north transept, another priest, younger and looking startled, afraid even. From behind him a much smaller man, powerfully built and with a full beard.

"Ah, you've got the whole raggletag gang together. Quite the rancid little crew I see. Good to see what we're up against." The stranger said in a quiet, understated voice nodded and smiled again intimating that he had little or nothing to fear.

"I don't need it for the likes of a lickspittle like you." Father Vincent lowered his head in one deft quick move and pushed himself back from the hand of the stranger.

"That is very courageous of you worm. But know this. We will be back." He said this and straightened up and as suddenly as the violence erupted, a calmness prevailed. He clicked his heels and made a low bow to father Vincent and turned to face Lempi and did the same.

"I don't want the monkey, bring me the organ grinder." Father Vincent said in a rasping voice that burned at the walls of his throat. "Tell him to come himself if he has the courage to. Tell him, tomorrow, here at five when the church will be shut to the public. But it'll be open to him. Go tell him. Tell your master." Father Vincent fought against the pain throbbing in his inflamed throat to shout out his demand.

"Oh, I'll be delighted to." Still facing Lempi, he spoke quietly, politely. "I look forward to renewing our acquaintance, you bleeding bag of excrement." Lempi stiffened, raised her arms and was about to strike.

"No, please young woman. No, please don't pander to his vanity." Father Vincent called out.

Nybbas gave a low bow, turned to face the front of the church and with astonishing pace raced down the centre aisle through the double doors of the church, which he flung wide open and disappeared out onto the street, his figure merging with the distant passing people and traffic that moved outside.

"Vincent, are you alright?" The small man with the blackest of black beards asked, anxiously guiding him to be seated. He was small, not dwarf small, but he was powerfully built.

"Yes, yes Malachai. No small thanks to our friend here." Father Vincent was clearly hurt and was helped to his feet by the man called Malachai to the front pew.

"You were very brave. Thank you." Malachai said and nodded his head in an act of gratitude.

"Brave? Brave?" The younger priest's voice was shrill and brittle. "You could have gotten yourself killed! Are you insane? All of you?" He looked around him at each of them in turn. Lempi relaxed her stance, although she felt like sweeping the young priest's legs from under him. "This madness ends here and now. It has to end before someone's killed. I have written a report on what I seen up to now. I have not as yet sent it to the Bishop, but I have no other recourse. Don't you see Vincent?"

"You damn coward." Malachai denounced. "Get your report off to Bishop Philbin, he'd love nothing more than to rid this parish of..."

"Of what Malachai? Of what? Anarchists? Oh, don't tempt me because I will. This church and its presbytery has become a hotbed to all manner of ne'er do wells."

"Ne'er do wells." Malachai repeated sarcastically. "It'll be scallywags next." He added derisively. "It's called practising what you preach. Instead of currying favour with the great and the good to further your own career, why don't you join us in helping, in reaching out."

"To who? Murderers and gunmen?" Father Stephen stated in a raised, agitated voice.

"God placed no doors to Heaven. Though you would put bars on the windows too. I have no doubt."

"Listen up Deacon," Father Stephen's voice had grown cold, his face had become set in un-expunged anger and he edged towards Malachai with his fists clenched.

"Stephen, Malachai, please. Stop this unedifying behaviour. It is not becoming of either of you. Stop it. Not in front of our guest." Father Vincent demanded.

Both men remained in stony silence staring at each. Lempi thought it her opportunity to say something and leave. "Well, thanks for the show. Been an experience. I'd no idea attending church could be so..." She struggled for a word.

"Eventful?" Malachai offered with a wide smile small displaying his white even teeth.

"Yes. Eventful. That is adequate. I hope you'll be okay Father." She aimed her voice over to Vincent. "I had better scoot. Got things to do, people to meet, you know how it is." She said light heartedly to cover her steps down from the altar.

"Ah, young lady if I may," Father Vincent struggled to get up. "I'd like to speak to you just before you go."

"Rest, Father." Malachai advised him.

"It's alright Malachai. Thank you, but I'm not for the bone yard just yet."

"I never..." Malachai began his explanation but was cut short.

"It's no matter Malachai, I know, I know. Young woman, if I may. I should like to speak with you before you leave. Would you grant an old man an indulgence?"

"I really should be going." Lempi insisted as delicately as she could.

"Let her go, don't be embroiling the girl in all of this." Father Stephen said his face reddening with irritation. His voice was shrill and brittle and full of self-preserving fear.

"I'll stay then, just for a few moments. I'll hear you out." Lempi crossed her arms in act of open defiance to Father Stephen.

"Is your hand alright? You hit him quite a whack." Father Vincent enquired studying the young girl.

"Yeah, I'll live." She answered, rubbing her hand self-consciously. "Though his skin felt strange, rubbery, like it reminded me of an iguana I touched once. I hit him right in the Vagos muscle. He should've gone down." She said to herself more than anyone else in the church.

"Stephen, Malachai." Father Vincent said quietly and calmly. "I know you both have duties and chores to do. I suggest you do them. There is little time."

"Yes Father." Both men said in union and Father Stephen walked towards the north transept and disappeared through an oval wooden door. Malachai remained until he had gone from view.

"Been nice meeting with you...what is your name warrior?" Malachai asked, tilting his head slightly at her.

"Lempi." She replied simply. "But I'm not a warrior."

"Oh but you are. You just don't how much of a one you are, yet." Malachai turned swiftly and nodded to Father Vincent and followed the same path Father Stephen had taken moments earlier.

Father Vincent and Lempi were quite alone.

"Oh hello." Lempi greeted, feeling immediately awkward as she encountered Malachai who was leaning against the outside of the church he levered himself from the wall that divided the two large entrance doors. He was feeling slightly absurd in the open and in the daylight where the everyday surged. "Father Vincent. He's a great priest and an even better man, you know. The words spilled out in a torrent of praise.

"Yes, he seems like a nice man. A genuine man."

"Not a dry old biscuit then?" Malachai laughed a deep playful laugh that Lempi found pleasant.

"You listened?" She asked without feeling offended.

"Only to the shouty bits, I couldn't help but hear those. Which was mostly you. I was up in the choir loft. I had a few things to attend to up there."

"Was eavesdropping one of them?" Lempi attempted to sound jaunty in keeping with the tone of their conversation but it came across as sour and accusatory. She placed her hands in her trouser pockets taking comfort from the feel of her own legs.

She was very satisfied that Malachai was speaking to her in a normal way. Most people on first meeting her assumed she was without a word of English using hand signals and long drawn out syllables for very small words. 'She's foreign, not stupid' flashed across the landscape of her mind. That was the first words she had heard him say as he introduced himself 'Hi, I'm Caelan. I'm with the stupid' he said introducing his brother who had been explaining to her how to order a drink at the bar in 'Irelande'. She liked him instantly.

"I apologise but it wasn't my fault. I had duties to attend to." He answered recovering his ground lost to him with her observation.

"Why are men so presuming?" Lempi asked trying not to sound bitter. She hated the very idea of projecting the image of her as defensive and slightly unpleasant.

"Presumptuous." Malachai heard him correct, shaking his head allowing his black curls to fall forward cursing himself for being pedantic.

"I'm sorry my English isn't perfect, how's your Swedish?" She countered not caring how she presented herself.

"Mea culpa, mea culpa, mea maxima culpa." Malachai kept his head bowed as he spoke. "We appear to be getting off on the wrong foot." He looked up without smiling.

"Well, no matter. I must go. I've had a crazy day. I need to get home, get changed, get some rest and some food."

"Before you do, please would you give me a few more minutes. Just a few minutes. I swear. It could be important."

"Who to?" Lempi snapped back. She stared up at the Statue of the Saint the church had been named after to avoid eye contact. She felt awful, she was tired, and she was hungry and vexed by all this talk that made no sense to her life. She had already had the clear intention to jettison the prayer given to her by Father Vincent as soon as she found the first bin on her walk back home. She wanted a drink and she needed Roma for company. She would ring her as soon as she got away from this small man who was starting to grate on her nerves.

"Did you receive his blessing?" He asked.

"Yes, I did. It would be rude not to. I told you he's a nice man. But he's old and his ideas about the world are old. I'm sorry, he means a lot to you I know but outside your church, there is a big world." Lempi tried not to offend and tried to sound sympathetic.

"Yes, and the dangers are big also. Just let me give you a background to Father Vincent."

Lempi let out a theatrical groan and let her arms fall limply by her sides to intimate her suffering. "Do you have to?"

"Just let me say this. He accepted me in as his Deacon fully aware of my past as a fanatical anti-cleric. I despised the church and its authority, secretly hated those who pursued wealth. I saw Christ only as the source of authority and only answerable to him. Christ was against human leadership. We argued long into the night me with my big ideas about breaking down the church selling its possessions to feed and clothe the poor. I would cite the edict of Milan in 313 AD when Christianity became legalised and transformed a humble top-down sect into an authoritarian top-down, organised global religion. It's what they call the Constantitian shift' and how it now identifies with the will of the ruling elite."

Malachai sounded bitter and harsh. He stood and stretched himself letting out a gasp. "Oh I am tired." He admitted. Lempi surmised his height at about five feet and no more.

"As am I, that's why I must go. I'm had a really long day so far and I need food and rest. I had no idea church could be so entertaining, thanks for that." Lempi made to leave when Malachai spoke up.

"Just give me one or two more minutes, please." He implored. "I want you to know this man who holds meetings with both sides of the great divide we have here. A lot of them have killed because of it, but he does not judge." Malachai smiled again. "He's the only one I know who practises what he preaches. He has a room that contains a chair, a bed, four books including the summa of St Thomas and has been awarded a Master of Sacred Theology and is indefatigable when it comes to working for the poor in his parish."

"Thanks for that. Now I feel real shit for what I said." Lempi admitted without feeling apologetic for her language, "I won't be apologising for that, for anything. I told you that I'm tired and hungry."

"Okay, peace. I just wanted you to know that someone cares. And there is a welcome for you here at anytime." Malachai fell silent and stared up towards the thickening clouds.

"You know he did say something that was true. Unless you have already heard." Malachai open his hands and made a slight shrug of his wide shoulders to intimate that he had not. "He told me I had forgotten to be happy that I had lost the mind map for it. That I have fallen in love with sadness. And he's right. Maybe I like to be this way now." Lempi found herself back at the edge of the bottomless well.

Malachai shielded his eyes from a spotlight of sunshine that punched through the clouds. His hands and forearms looked remarkably strong as did the expansive chest that was covered by his checked shirt. "You have the strength to fight that and get back to the path that will lead you out of the sadness engulfing you at this moment."

"Thank you." Lempi smiled, she did not argue this point. She wanted to leave and had already established in her mind that she would bin the prayer she had been given in the first bin she encountered

"And, believe me. I saw real passion not that long ago in those fists. I saw a true fighter. As brave and as true as anyone I have ever seen."

Lempi sniffed and dragged out the hankies fused together by tears and snot from just that day. It wasn't even dinner time she thought. And with that thought she felt another wave of despondency and despair wash over her.

"I'm not lying to you." Malachai leaned his head to angle where he could see Lempi's face as she bowed her head to wipe her eyes and then her nose.

"I'm the opposite of brave. I'm a coward. I'm a... I can't find the word. 'But it's not a good one. Heaven's not for the likes of me." Lempi, looked up and stared straight at him. Her face as firm and fixed as her voice.

"Oh, but you're so wrong." Malachai unchained himself from the church wall he had fallen back against whilst he talked. He stood up to his full four foot and ten inches. "My motto in life is toil and a peaceful life. I'm from a long line of Doukhobors, we believe God dwells in each and every human being, not in bricks and mortar and I know he dwells in you for a heart as good as yours could only be made to feel this bad. You think your soul is in abeyance. No soul is lost."

"How do you know that about me? You don't know me at all. No way do you know me. What I've done." Lempi shouted back, causing people walking past the church to stare over at them. "What?" She snapped at the passer-by, "Why don't you photograph me, it would last longer." This caused the middle-aged man to scurry quickly on up the road.

"You know you return to being a native of your mother country when you get angry." Malachai's wry observation and smile wrong-footed Lempi and prevented her from turning her full rage at him.

"You're not the first to tell me that." She said sadly and Malachai could tell now that she was returning to whatever, whoever it was that was wounding her soul.

"You're going to be fine. I know it." He said and he meant it. She possessed an unusually strong presence and despite it being shallow and decorative, she was unusually attractive with that clear skin unblemished by make-up. He enjoyed her smart trouser suit with the red DM boots. That just smacked of character.

For the first time in a very long time Lempi believed she would. But she'd had several false dawns before.

"Here, please take this." Malachai proffered to her a sheet of paper. She could see it was embossed with the image and address of the church.

"What is it?" She asked, staring at the image.

"That is the private number of the church presbytery. If you need to contact us, call at anytime. If you need to talk or if you notice anything unusual, anything like lights or a feeling of unease that something's or someone's not right."

"You're talking demons? Like the Father? Look, in my experience and believe you me, I have the experience," Lempi's voice rose like an emotional burp, "the demons I know are not horned or have clov..."

"Cloven?" Malachai suggested the word that Lempi was at a loss to find.

"Yes, cloven. Thank you again." She said without a trace of gratitude. "In my experience they are just men. Evil fucking men, animals. They act like demons of the imagination but they are human and not at the same time. I'm sorry. I don't need this. I must go." She made to hand the paper back to Malachai who immediately noticed the multiple tiny scar tissues on her forearm.

"Are you are harming yourself Lempi? But why Lempi?" Malachai asked his face riven with concern and compassion.

"To get the black blood out." She bit back. "It's inside of me. Men put it in there. Not demons. Letting it out helps me, makes me feel better." She retracted her arm and the paper.

"Take that number please. Use it when you feel like that." Malachai implored, he stood up a look of grim determination set in his face.

Lempi felt shame now for her actions and folded the paper in half and placed it in her jacket pocket with the prayer Father Vincent had given her. She had nothing more to say. Her sense of shame ended abruptly when she saw that Malachai appeared to be mouthing a prayer and she felt annoyance at her admission and his intrusion by asking.

"Lempi, I know you must go now but hear these words as you do. There are two kinds of mourning, one that has lost hope and become mistrustful of love and truth. The other, the shattering encounter with truth which leads us to undergo conversion and resist evil. This mourning heals, it teaches us to hope and to love again."

"You finished now?" Lempi asked in a tight, sharp voice. She could feel that the skin of her lips were dry. She was talked out and too tired to listen anymore.

"Yes."

"Thank your God for that." She stood and looked herself up and down. "Adjö Deacon." She said quietly and turned her back and walked from the church feeling weary and worn down.

"Pax Vobiscum Lempi." Malachai shouted after her as she became subsumed into the people and traffic that constantly fed the city centre.

Lempi sat in McElhattons bar and took out from her jacket pocket the telephone number and prayer she had been given. It had been an unusual day to say the least but not her worst by a country mile. She had liked that expression as soon as it was uttered and then explained to her. She flattened the paper the prayer had been written on. She took her pint of Carlsberg and sipped. She had rang Roma as soon as she entered the bar and cajoled her to come and meet her at Kellys. Roma whined that she had bouquets to do for a wedding, it was a rush job for her Da; but was soon changing her mind when Lempi told her of the fight in the church in the church. 'Fuck off, what are you like? You can't take you no-where' she laughed down the phone 'give me an hour I should have these finished by then' she told her down the phone. Lempi went to the bar and ordered her drink.

There were several men in the booths, drinking and watching the horse racing. The building itself sat at the corner of Donegal and Union Street where there were several bookmakers based. She noticed one younger man stood at the bar drinking what she guessed was a vodka and coke. He watched her as she took a seat near the entrance. To avoid his gaze she had taken out the papers from her pocket. She stared at the prayer without reading it. Then she could see the younger man with the moustache and double chin release himself from leaning on the bar.

"Knulla." She simmered beneath her breath. She leaned into the paper she held up to her face and read the words.

O Divine Eternal Father,
in union with your Divine Son and the Holy Spirit,
and through the Immaculate Heart of Mary,
I beg You to destroy the Power of your greatest enemy - the evil spirits.

Cast them into the deepest recesses of hell
and chain them there forever!
Take possession of your Kingdom which You have created
and which is rightfully yours.

Heavenly Father,
give us the reign of the Sacred Heart of Jesus
and the Immaculate Heart of Mary.

I repeat this prayer out of pure love for You
with every beat of my heart and with every breath I take.

Amen.

To her great relief the younger man turned and walked out the side entrance into Union Street. She placed the prayer back in her pocket thinking it to be a load of shit.

Father Vincent cleared his throat and drank from the glass of water he had brought with him onto the altar.

"Good afternoon everyone." He said in the microphone. His voice seemed to travel around the speakers within the church one at a time circulating clockwise.

"Good afternoon Father." A chorus of female voices echoed back at him.

There was an excitement that was palpable in the church. He could feel it come from the body of women. They occupied the first three rows nearest the altar on the gospel side of the church. They were all from the parish. The first row had fourteen women from the New Lodge Road, they said the rosary for peace in the area known locally as the Barracks. Amongst their number was Mrs Toal, their housekeeper, their gatekeeper really. She sat centre front row.

She was a formidable woman, efficient, organised and hard-working. She would not be out place as a secretary to a captain of industry. Behind them sat the women of Carrick Hill, eleven of them sat, some whispering along the row. In the last row sat women who had attended the regular rosary at church, women from around the surrounding district, whose faith and commitment could not be questioned.

"Thank you again for attending and at such short notice as I know you all have families to attend to. This is an extraordinary paroctius testimonus for me, for us all no doubt. I don't wish to bore you all, so I shall move quickly on. Please take your tea whilst I talk." He stood at the podium and arranged the sheets of paper he had written his speech on.

"With Calvary before Him, the Lord spoke these remarkable words – 'Now is the judgment of this world: now shall the prince of this world be cast out.' He was referring to His imminent suffering on Calvary's cross, which would immediately accomplish salvation for His people, and judgement for Satan. From the time of Calvary, Satan would be curbed in his power, a defeated enemy, still able to work much wickedness until the final day, but severely limited." He paused. He had made sure everyone had been supplied with tea and biscuits as they arrived. He had ensured that it was father Stephen and Malachai who served them.

"Christ came as the representative of His people, and in every conceivable way obeyed His Father, even to the death of the cross. And through that perfect obedience culminating in Calvary, His people were saved from condemnation. By His righteousness and atonement, a continuing human race was purchased, so that a glorified earth could be thronged by ransomed people. The human race would no longer be a failed concept, and God's design would be restored and redeemed." He heard his voice rise and fall as spoke marking the moments he wanted to emphasise.

"Satan's apparent triumph was crushed, leaving him susceptible to judgement and curbing. No longer would he be able to keep people from the Truth." He stared around him, watching Father Stephen and Malachai patrol opposite sides of the nave of the church.

"Demons themselves knew that Christ would end their liberty, and this is seen in their anguished cries as the Lord cast them out. Possession was common in the time of Christ, but His ministry marked the end of demonic liberty to occupy human souls at will. We are aware that today there are still some reports of New-Testament-style demon possession, but only where people have voluntarily and strenuously invited demons into their lives by deep involvement in occult practices. Satan, via his demons, can no longer enter uninvited into human souls to possess them since the work of Christ, this being one aspect of Satan being 'cast out'."

"Another of Satan's limitations is that he is not allowed to reveal or show himself, being forced to work entirely by secrecy and stealth. Satan is now a spiritual vagrant, powerful," He paused, and gestured to the women with a sweep of his hand that they were all in the firing line, "yes, with a vast host of fallen angels doing his bidding, but he must tempt us From 'outside', and secure our co-operation for everything he wants us to do. He is certainly the prince of this world, but a prince with no palace or rights – a dispossessed and a doomed prince."

"We know a good deal about Satan from the fact he is an angel, though a fallen one. As such he was created without a body or physical aspect, for angels have no bodies, unless God clothes them with a temporary appearance in order to send them as messengers or witnesses into the world, as in the case of the angels that sat in the tomb of Christ. Angels evidently have an appearance in Heaven, but are not normally visible to human eyes on earth."

"Angels are immortal only by God's sustaining permission and power. We read in Scripture that they have mysterious differences in 'rank', so there are higher angels. Though spirits, they operate in dimensions of time and space, for they are not infinite and outside time, as God is."

"Angels clearly have powerful intelligence, and although the day will come when believers, as glorified people in Heaven will be greater than the angels, while on earth we do not have their powers of mind."

"Angels have great knowledge but it has a limit."

"Angels cannot tell the future, apart from knowing the Word of God, as we also may know it. When Old Testament prophecies began to be fulfilled with the coming of Christ, they observed with wonder these events, things which 'the angels desire to look into' *(1 Peter 1.12)*. In this they are not like God, Whose knowledge is infinite, and Who continuously knows all things that happen throughout eternal history."

"Angels clearly have power to communicate with each other. They cannot create anything or kill anyone at will, though they may sometimes be appointed by God as His agents to terminate life. Even Satan is shown seeking the express permission of God to inflict disease and take life in the book of *Job*. Angels cannot change earthly substances, altering one element into another, nor can they alter or override the laws of nature, except at God's direction. They are bound within these limitations. It follows that angels cannot work miracles unless God empowers them to do so."

"As fallen angels, Satan and his demonic hosts share all these limitations. And here is another limitation," Again he paused to emphasise the point, "common to both good and evil angels, and one which is of very great importance to us in our battle with the devil. Angels cannot search our hearts and read our thoughts. They cannot enter into the innermost recesses of our thought-lives. An old Christian adage runs –Demons can speak to the soul, but not search the heart.' We will say more about Satan's inability to read thoughts in due course."

"Satan cannot make us do anything. He cannot so dictate to us that we are bound to do his bidding, but must work by deception and persuasion. It is therefore wrong to say, 'Satan made me do it.' He may urge us, suggest things to us, press us, and lie to us about the outcome, but he cannot make us do anything. We must never ascribe to Satan powers which belong exclusively to Almighty God; and while we should be very aware of his power, we must never fear him as invincible."

"Satan means adversary, and he is described as a dragon, indicating his great ferocity, and also as a serpent, expressing his cunning and subtlety." He stood for a moment to collect his thoughts and to allow what he was saying to sink in. He sipped from the glass to moisten his lips.

"He is referred to as the father of lies, indicating the method that he has always employed, and also as the murderer of souls, the prince of demons, and the prince of this world who guides the minds of unbelievers open to atheism and ready to show hostility to God. He is called the tempter, and an angel of light making evil appear good, and suggesting justification for selfish, covetous and other wrong actions."

"Satan was cast out of Heaven for challenging God, and hates Him with all his being, opposing and frustrating His plans if he can, and keeping souls away From Him. Satan is intensely jealous of human beings and hates them also. He acts to tempt into sin both the lost and the saved, particularly striving to lead God's people into error and failure. If Satan can get into churches, inserting false teaching and bringing believers down in sin, how he triumphs!"

Father Vincent found himself walking form the podium where he made his sermon. The church was a natural amphitheatre that amplified his voice. "He therefore constantly seeks to discredit the church and the Gospel in the eyes of the world, and also to thwart and hinder Gospel work by tempting believers to worldliness, laziness, and indifference to the plight of lost souls."

"Satan is always working to erode the faith of believers and spoil their assurance, peace and joy. He does these things by a process of attrition, causing believers to give way little by little to doubts and temptations, until he has gained victory over them. He also inspires false prophets and evil workers, putting into their minds ideas that are unbiblical, and succeeding wherever they fail to prove all things by the Word."

"He controls people who are opposed to the Gospel, blinding their minds, and through them, shaping society." He said holding his hands up to his head suggesting physically the binding effect.

"When we see the world today," he continued, "ruled by aggressive and vindictive secular humanism, with immorality legalised and encouraged, and laws passed to punish those who oppose these things, we see the orchestrating hand of Satan. How similar is the 'script' justifying these things in all parts of the world! Thus Satan is 'the prince of the power of the air'."

"How do we defeat the devil?" Some of the women found themselves attempting to answer.

"We pray. We give ourselves to Christ. To the Virgin Mary." Several voices broke out.

"Submit yourselves to God. Resist the devil, and he will flee from you. It is an amazing thought, is it not?" A number of women voiced their agreement with him. He continued making his way back to the podium. "To think that this mighty evil being will run from us, the weak believers. He is powerful and invisible to us; he will tempt and suggest evil things constantly, and is armed with unimaginable cunning. Yet, if we know how to resist him, he will flee from us. This is what I have impressed upon Father Stephen and Malachai and to those of you who have bravely come to help us in this endeavour. We must have no doubt."

"He can hear us and see us, but not read our thoughts. By his deep knowledge of human nature and behaviour, and by close observation of us, he is able to discern or guess many of our reactions to temptation, and to seemingly interact with us, but he cannot see our hearts. If we speak to him and we should not, whether by word or thought, he will 'hear', and some of our thoughts may be very 'loud' and obvious to him, such as hatred to someone, and great pride, but in the ordinary way he cannot read our minds. If a person's temper is rising, or if he is looking at things with lust, the devil is very shrewd, and will read the signs and know what is going on. But never think he can get into the mind and actually read our thoughts from the inside."

"Satan watches us," Father Vincent put his fingers up to his eyes to suggest that he was watching as he spoke, "he has his host of demons assigned to follow us and to notice every omission of spiritual duty, every neglected prayer, every missed reading of God's Word, every ignoring of a sermon, every delay in carrying out a good work, and every act of worldliness or of uncommitted conduct. Under scrutiny will be the things we look at and engage in, and by these things our vulnerability to temptation will be ascertained by the tempter, and the next assault upon us planned. But, once again, he cannot succeed unless we let him. Will we let him?" He asked in a loud voice.

"'No'." The chorus of voices shouted back.

"The devil is more intelligent than mere mortals and should never be argued with. He is not a mere metaphor or a nebulous concept but a real person with dark powers. He's not like mist, not a diffuse thing. You must never converse with him or you will be lost."

"Oh he will be polite," Father Vincent made a smiling face and the women laughed, "and with that pretence he will enter your mind. I pray for the people in my charge that they will not fall prey to him. I realise now, beyond human doubt, that this family have for whatever reason attracted the interest of a demon, one with great power who is as near to Satan himself. Are we going to help this family?"

A rousing chorus of "Yes" reverberated around the church.

"Our adversary believes us to be divided and therefore weak, but we will show him that we are united in our aim, in our desire to confront this evil. We have the greatest defence. That is our faith and we have the greatest weapon, which is prayer."

The women stood up and applauded. Father Vincent motioned for them to sit down.

"And as for tomorrow. I have no doubt our adversary will turn up. We will be ready. We are prepared." He told them forcefully as the women sat back down in the pews.

Roma laughed helplessly as Lempi described her time within the church.

"This Malachai character, he's like a midget?"

"No, not a midget, he's small but perfectly built." Lempi did her best to capture Malachai without sounding insulting.

"Like the soup, condensed?" Roma laughed again swallowing down her Barcardi and coke. "Is he good looking? Do you think all of him comes miniaturised?" Roma ventured running her long fingers down the side of her empty glass. Who'd have thought chapel would be so entertaining. Roma mused.

It was her fifth pint to Lempi's reckoning. Lempi did not bother to answer as Roma held no real interest in hearing it as she turned and hissed over. "Isn't that wee girl Ainé? Coming in now with that creep Tom whatshis face?"

Lempi stared over at the girl who had come in. She had the most strident red hair and shining hazel eyes. It was Ainé. Ainé Magill, she was a lovely girl, a primary school teacher. Lempi waved and Ainé waved back at them both with a heart-warming wave.

"She is quite the beautiful girl." Lempi observed.

"What's she doing with that tosser Tom? Big lanky gobshite." Roma asked sourly her face fell in a look of utter disdain. "Can't believe I snogged that cockroach."

"Come you. Let's have another and cheer up." Lempi said breezily. She had been entertaining the idea of asking Roma to stay over with her. But every time she moved to ask she felt stupid, superstitious and angered that these men with their mediaeval nonsense had made her feel under some kind of threat. No. She thought I've survived worse than stories to scare children. After another round of drinks Roma had to tell her of party they were invited to that night.

"We meet in the Blackthorn. It's Danny Wilson's cousin, it's a twenty first. It'll be a laugh. Danny's great craic, so's his mates."

"I don't know," Lempi replied, "I've had a really, really long day. I'm wearing a trouser suit for flipsake."

"We'll get a Joe baxi over to yours, get you out that outfit, why you went over there today, but that's another story for another day. You'll have a shit and a shower. Then a taxi back to the Blackthorn. I got paid today for those bouquets. Come on." Roma cajoled and Lempi felt a pang of guilt for doing the same to Roma hours earlier in getting her out.

"You're so eloquent Roma." Lempi teased.

"Shut up. What do you say?" Roma asked in big, inviting smile.

The idea of a party appealed to Lempi. It would take her away from the house and give her a distraction from all that occurred during the day. And it would make a great story in the pub. The Irish loved that.

"C'mon, what do you say to Ceoil agus Craic? Eh?"

"I say yes." Lempi smiled back.

"Good girl. You know it makes sense." Roma smiled back a large wide smile. Her deep set dark eyes she accentuated with dark eye shadow shone and glistened like her long black hair.

Roma almost fell out of the taxi onto the road outside Lempi's house. She had badgered the taxi driver all the way over to wait outside for them.

"Are you mental? I'm not waiting around for two wimmin to get showered and changed. I'd lose fares all night. Catch yerself on darlin'." They agreed that when they were ready to leave the house, he or someone from the depot would collect them.

"Where you going?"

"Over to The Blackthorn bar." Lempi answered as Roma staggered and almost stumbled over.
"She'll be goin' nowhere that one. She's a full as a bingo bus." The taxi driver dryly observed handing Lempi her change.

"He's a cheeky wee turd. I know him." Roma breathed out raising her arm to send two fingers after the departing taxi.

"Come on girl. You need something to eat."

"Got anything to drink Lempi babes?"

"Let's get in and see." Lempi was anxious to get her friend off the street.

"Yeah! Let's go, it feels like it's going to bucket down" She said staring up at the night sky.

"Jesus! Shit. Roma. Look!"

"What? What's up? Roma closed her back and turned round to look at the house.

"The light in the halls on." Lempi felt a rivulet of fright bubble up and mask her mind. "Somebody's in my house." She hissed.

"It's your da, is all. Come on." Roma slurred out the words unthinking.

"No, it can't, he's out of town. Away on business."

"You sound so like your in a movie when you said that." Roma laughed. Then she gave herself a visible shake and said. "Right, it must be hood then, a stinkin' wee shite trying to rob your house. Let's get him." Roma stepped forward but was held back for going any further.

"No. No Roma, we don't know who's in the house. We'll get to a phone and ring the police."

"The peelars." Roma attempted a raspberry sound spitting out saliva onto her chin.

"Yes. There's a phone box just around the corner." Lempi reached into her pocket searching frantically for the prayer she had been given. She gripped it in her hand and thought now to ring the number Malachai had given her. She heard the words of Father Vincent and Malachai blend and echo in her mind. Roma had no idea of the potential danger they could be in. Looking at her as she held her arm and made to drag her to the telephone box she couldn't have cared less.

"Ya wee shite. Robbin' peoples' houses." Roma shouted out into the night air.

"Shhh Roma! For Godsake, you'll have the whole street out."

"That's it. We'll get everybody out and give him a community beatin'." She proclaimed triumphantly.

"In San Souci? I don't think so." Lempi said failing to smile at her wry observation.

"Lempi? Är det du?" She heard a familiar heart-warming voice shout out.

Mama? Är det du? Lempi turned to look up at the raised figure at the top of the three steps to the door. She viewed the outline of the figure and although she felt a rush of elation that fluttered inside her chest, it was tempered with a healthy dose of mistrust.

"Vem annars? Min litt swift."

There was no doubt now that it was really her. She had called her by the pet name she had given her when she was a child as they walked the Dalby Söderskog National Park. Lempi grabbed her friend and dragged her along back towards the house. "Mama." She cried out happily.

"Hey! What's the craic? Who's a mama? Are we going to get him now?" Roma's voice sounded hoarse and she stumbled in her high heel which she rarely wore.

"Yes, Roma. That's right, we're going to get him." Lempi indulged, smiling at her friend as she brushed Roma's long hair from her face.

"All's well that ends well as they say."

"Yes, that's what they say." Malachai said quietly. "We can get home now James. Don't spare the horses. It's been a long day for all concerned. Thanks for coming when I called you."

"Thank you for calling me." Father Stephen smiled back and indicated left and pulled slowly away from the space they had parked in having followed the taxi up from Castle Street. "They live to fight another day. Our fight is coming all too soon." Father Stephen observed.

Malachai for his part said nothing.

Malachai cracked his knuckles as an act to tell Father Stephen he was ready.

"You have arrived early."

"Yes. I thought it prudent of me. I see you're having work done." He observed staring up at the balcony of the Gospel side of the church.

Father Vincent sat down near, but not close to him. He let out a small groan as he took a seated position on the pew.

"Sign of old age Father. You need to slow down. Take more rest." The voice was gentle, kind in an extremely disquieting way. "No need for introductions."

"No need." Father Vincent answered simply. "Yes, were having the walls repainted on each of the balconies. The smell of paint bothers you?"

"No, no." He replied, sniffing the air, "I prefer it to the smell of the human filth." He said staring up at the large dust sheets that hung up on hooks from one wall to the other. The man dressed in jeans, t-shirt and a waistcoat turned to him. "You knew I'd come. How?"

Father Vincent glanced over at him. He could see the t shirt bore the words 'Jesus loves you, but I think you're a wanker'. "Vanity." He announced. "And conceit." Father Vincent tried not to sound derisive. Keep an even keel but give no quarter.

Without a sound or sense of movement the man had saddled up close to him. Close enough for Father Vincent to look beyond the handsome face, framed in long hair cascading down to near his waist. He could see into the eyes, that were not eyes but black inkwells of fathomless darkness that opened up a soulless wasteland that offered only despair. He was staring into the abyss. Father Vincent gathered himself and shifted himself to stand.

"Not at all. Just why did you feel the need to send an imposter in your stead?"

"You felt insulted, I hear." He laughed a laugh only someone who took great pleasure in pain would make. It was ugly and distressing to hear. "My curiosity piqued when Nybbas told me what had transpired. I thought, my, this priest seems to have above average intelligence. Rare, I must say in your kind."

"You flatter me. I meant someone of your standing. A Minister of the Office Grand Chancellor and The Grand Cross of the Order of the Fly. Where is he, your cohort?"

"Oh, I have given him time off to get his jollies. Some child or whatever died. Knocked down by an army vehicle, head squashed. I'll spare you the details. He enjoys the burials so much. He loves that kind of mishap, like miscarriages or abortions. He has a penchant for innocence lost." The creature smiled again and tilted his head forward as if to bow. "Whatever gets you through the day or night."

"Why the need for such subterfuge someone as great in the echelons of power as you are."

"Careful Father, now you're in danger of flattering me."

"Weren't you a god to some? The Assyrian city of Sepharvasm, wasn't it? They would sacrifice their children to you in acts of obscene worship." Father Vincent did not hide his disdain.

"Yes, it was glorious." The creature stood up and made a show to yawn.

"It was murder." Father Vincent snapped, vexed at his casualness.

"Such an ugly word, vulgar, not worthy of you I am thinking. I, unlike your god, delivered on the demands made of me. Their harvests were abundant, they were protected and importantly, free peoples, as such they could do as they pleased without fear of damnation."

"It was ignorance, superstition and fear. You gave nothing in return and took the blood of the innocent." Father Vincent felt his anger rise and tried to calm himself as his hands shook with rage.

"That's rather rich coming from your belief system based as it is upon the blood soaked carcass of that woodworker slave you hang to your walls. Oh daddy, didn't I do good? Aren't I a good child as you watch me be slaughtered. He was butchered. And it certainly wasn't slow neither. Oh how we did enjoy every single moment. And here you are hiding in your theatres of death and denial, worshipping fear and self-denial, afraid of life and afraid to live it." He countered, his face contorted in contempt. "He is as bloodthirsty and capricious as any of us. More so, dressing it up as good for the soul and the empty promise of life everlasting." He laughed into his hand.

"His was a death that was willingly given and one that gave life to countless others." Father Vincent countered.

"It never ceases to amuse, what you humans choose to believe in. I thank him for that, otherwise I wouldn't have such an interesting and enjoyable environment to dwell in. All thanks to your beliefs. They have given such joyous moments of mayhem, the murders, the injuries and the despair and grief. Even Sheol and Abaddon could not aspire to some of the acts perpetrated in his name." A rumble of laughter echoed around the church. "That's the delectable irony and truly, it is something to be savoured."

"The path to peace and salvation is not an easy word. It is through suffering we develop and grow in God." Father Vincent said in a quiet voice. "And through it we participate in the redemptive suffering of Jesus."

"I don't think I've heard that shit said so convincingly, not in a long time, bravo. There is nothing for you or for anyone. He has made it impossible for you. You are like us in some ways. You are inherently selfish and self-centred, thinking only of your own salvation. You talk of peace and that is all it remains. Talk. Your nature enjoys inflicting pain. You crave power and authority over your fellow man. I have had the most enjoyable sojourn not far from here in your local courthouse. A litany of crimes of what you would call barbarity. To me, to hear the statements on how they died, how they cried, pleaded for mercy, pleaded on behalf of their families, for their wives and their children. It was, well, enchanting." He said with a flourish, he looked around him as if he found the words and images delectable.

"Of course, they all cried for their mummies towards the end. What's wrong Priest? Surely you were safely tucked away from all the horror? Oh yes, protected behind these thick walls and your garb, your frocks and dresses." The creature laughed, spitting the words out dismissively. "Where was the good shepherd when his flock was is peril?" He asked, throwing his arms up in the air like some theatrical device.

"No-where! That's where. And where was your merciful,

compassionate god as the knives stabbed, cut and slit and the fingernails were ripped out; their eyes gouged and teeth ripped out. And beautiful as it was on one occasion, the very baubles of faith placed inside his sliced heart. The cries of your flock begging for mercy where none was given, begging for a quick a death and none was given."

"Stop! Desist from your sacrilege!" Father Vincent shouted at him. "That was man who has abandoned his God. That is what you can only offer. Death and damnation. To revel and relish only in anguish and pain." He shouted into the air but directed it to all those concealed behind the dust sheets.

"That is your god manifest. He demands, he commands. It's all him, him, him. And that obedient unto the death slave child and that, that," the creature's voice rose in anger, "that dick dodging cosmic doormat of a mother." He stopped mid-sentence and coughed. He placed his hands to his throat coughing violently. His face turned red almost puce as he bent over still coughing fiercely opening his mouth trying to expel whatever was obstructing his airway.

For a moment, one ridiculous moment, Father Vincent almost gave into a natural human impulse to go to his aid but suddenly, he doubled over emitting a rasping hoarse cough and then, an explosion of what Father Vincent thought were butterflies spewed from his mouth. But they floated to the floor gliding gently to rest on the floor of the church. Father Vincent could smell a powerful aroma of flowers and he realised then that they were flower petals, rose petals in fact. The type associated with Our Lady.

The creature raised his head and straightened up and exhaled loudly and breathed in a deep breath, turned to the priest and winked. He rested his hands on his waist. "You never did develop a sense of humour did you Miryam?" He shouted out breathing heavily.

"Why don't you leave and leave that family in peace?" Father Vincent asked of him.

"Not much of a family anymore," the creature rubbed his throat, "not in the conventional sense Father." The creature grinned wickedly.

Father Vincent noticed that the creature was stepping away from the petals that had rested in a pile on the ground.

"I mean, the boy, if you'll forgive me, is as close to a vegetable you'd have with your dinner and the mother is whore who seeks comfort where she can find it and the father is a prolific thief and gambler. Oh, and who is now gone, having shuffled off this mortal coil this very morning. By his own hand. Not ours, I hasten to add. So he is even beyond the forgiveness of your church and loving god."

The creature walked along the pew his hand gliding along the top rail. "After all, you cannot say mass nor can he be buried in your consecrated ground. So you're saved a viaticum. Is it not the case that your lives are not yours to dispose of?" He asked rhetorically. He waved a hand dismissively. "No matter, he was weak. I showed him his true face and he buckled under the weight in recognition of his true self. He never wanted the child you know. Just her. He resented the boy everyday of his short life. And the boy knew it of course. He's a wonderful piece of work. Such an adept liar and charming liar," the creature walked clasping his hands behind his back, "with such rage inside and hatred for his father that we know only too well. Think that's why I like him and he likes me. You can keep the woman. She is ruined now, damaged goods by all your jiggery Popery." He laughed at the joke he made.

"He belongs to God." Father Vincent told him adamantly.

"He belongs with us!" The creature returned at him with equal force. "You priests are so tedious. It's like your garb, everything is black and white. Just remember he came to me. He wanted things that your god could never deliver."

"It was pride that changed angels into devils, it is humility that makes men as angels," Father Vincent cleared his throat and sang out, "Heavenly Father, I love you, I praise you and I worship you. I thank you for sending your son Jesus who won victory over sin and death for my salvation. I thank you for sending your Holy Spirit who empowers me, guides me and leads me into fullness of life. I thank you for Mary, my Heavenly Mother who intercedes with the Holy angels and spirits for me."

He stared straight at the creature who made a yawn and then smiled.

"Heavenly father allow your son to come now with the Holy Spirit, the blessed Virgin Mary, the holy angels and the Saints to protect me from all harm and to keep all evil spirits from taking revenge in any way."

"Not very likely Father. Now I bore of your performance." The creature was vehement. "Now you leave us alone, leave the boy. Let him determine who he wants to be with." He smiled, he rolled his hands making a performance out of being obsequious. "Please Father." He said in a child's voice.

"In the name of Jesus I rebuke you spirit, Adramelech, vice Chancellor of Hell. I command to go directly to Jesus, without manifestation and without harm to me or anyone so that he can dispose of you according to His will."

"I've had enough of this." Adramelech moved menacingly towards the priest.

Father Vincent crossed himself and began reciting "Ex orcizo Deo Immundissmus..."

At that moment a host of voices filled the church.

"Cede, Cede." Father Vincent directed his order at the approaching creature.

"Mai! Mai!" The voice growled back.

"Recede Ergo Nac..."

"You old bag of piss and shit." Adramelech screamed into his face gripping him by his throat.

The disembodied voices grew louder, they were above him and on all sides.

"I believe in God the Father Almighty, creator of heaven and Earth..."

"Shut up! Stop! Stop praising him..." Adramelech let go of Father Vincent's throat and held his hands over his ears falling to his knees as he did so.

Father Vincent stood over and joined in the prayer "conceived by the Holy Ghost, born of the Virgin Mary...You know the foundation of the world is love, so that even when no human being can or will help us, we may go on, trusting the One who loves us. Will you place yourself under oath to leave. Leave and return to the dark recesses from which you came." Father Vincent commanded. "Do you?" Father Vincent bellowed at the kneeling creature.

Above the voices began their prayer, concealed behind the dust sheets and masked by the smell of fresh paint. They recited the Rosary as one amplified voice that reverberated around the empty and closed doors of the church. That had been left to Malachai who was by the far the swiftest of them.

"You aren't above a little deception yourself priest I see." The creature said his head bowed into his chest.

"Do you place yourself under oath?" Father Vincent asked again.

Adramelech looked up at him, his face without colour. He looked visibly weakened and frail, the force removed from his body. "Woe unto me. Woe to the proud and my ingratitude, to the disobedience that led to my damnation." His voice was weak and submissive.

Father Vincent approached. He then demanded again in an authorative voice that punched through the prayers that enveloped them and the entire church.

"Do you place yourself under oath?"

"Yes." He lied.

As Father Vincent had envisaged. But this was a skirmish only. An introduction. And as such they would part to evaluate and plan their next move. His intention had been realised, to let this creature and his kind know that faith was till alive and strong. That they were willing and able to challenge and even thwart their scheming.

And with all that achieved, he let the creature leave, with the sound of worship ringing in his ears.

EXTRA TIME

Artillery Youth Club is two tier structure topped by a feature cantilevering the two-storey lantern. It was pebble dashed and painted white once and on a Thursday evening, after Top of the Pops, children from fourteen and upwards went to the disco.

"Squint! Squint! Open the door. Come on!"

I heard the pounding on the door and instinctively reached for my branch, the weapon I had found to bash my enemies with. It had disappeared and one of them was at the door. What door? The door to where? Where the hell was I?

"Come out of them bogs, you glue bag." It was Dee, another bastard. The enemy was at the gate, quite literally.

"Fuck off Dee, you and the rest of you bastards. Leave me the fuck alone." I shot back at the door as I stood up and clenched my fists. All of them were bastards and I knew how they felt about me.

"I told ye, he's off his nut, leave him." I heard Wholenut tell Dee.

"Come out of the bogs for chrissakes. There's somebody who wants to see ye." Dee hissed through the door.

"Oh aye, who? Piercy and his mob?" I shouted back feeling my face get really hot. I looked around the toilet wondering how I could get out of there without any of them knowing. I checked to see if there was something I could use as a weapon to hurt anyone who came near.

"It's Francesca." Dee said softly. "She's been asking where you got to. I think she likes you mate and the slow set is coming up in a couple of minutes." Dee hissed through the space between the door and the lock. "Swear to God mate. I'm not spoofing. Am I Wholenut? I wouldn't, not about this."

"No, he's not. Get out of them bogs, ya wingnut." Wholenut said.

"It's up to you, but I'd get out there if I were you. And pronto mate. She's not gonna wait around. Look, Ghengis and that dope head Duffer put some of that wacky tobaccy in your drink and you've been off yer nut ever since you got in here. Ghengis told us. It was us who got you to the bogs and got you to shut the door."

Could this be true, any of it? The whole thing's been, what do they call it, when you're off your nut with drugs? All of it an hallucination? I sat back down on the toilet seat and put hands up to my head. Those fuckers! They drugged me. I'm gonna kill that fat spoof. Then I began laughing, laughing hard. I was no longer in a living nightmare. Did I even go to the match? Did we win? I laughed again, not really caring.

"He's lost it." I heard Wholenut comment and I wanted to throw the door to the cubicle open and hug him.

I was back amongst my friends and the living. I was young, alive and a girl, the girl of my dreams wanted to dance with me, so I'm told. Jesus, I'd better get me skates on and get out there. The slow set only lasted for four songs. Though when you're standing with your mates it was like an eternity.

"I'll be out in a minute. Youse go on in. I'll be there, just need to wash me face and make meself beautiful."

"It closes at ten." Wingnut said. "You don't have enough time."

"Piss off you and let him sort himself out" Dee laughed.

I still was not entirely sure about what had happened and I wasn't going to just trust what they said.

"Alright, Squint. Here Squint." Dee said, I could tell he was right against the toilet door.

"What is it?"

"Don't be doing anything I wouldn't."

"Like what?" I asked not having a clue what he was saying.

"You know."

"Don't be trying to feel her wibbly, wobbly, wonders." Wholenut answered.

"What he said." Dee said. "She's a really nice girl."

"Chance would be a fine thing. No way mate, I won't. She probably won't even dance with me."

"I think she will alright. Right, we're going back in. See ya in there."

"Yeah." I said. I waited until the door to the toilets closed and opened the cubicle door. I looked out both ways like I was crossing the road. I was definitely in the youth club. I went to the mirror that someone had scribbled marker pen on. My face exactly the same. I washed my face and dried it with the rough cloth on the dryer, pulling it to get a clean piece. Jesus, Francesca. I knew they were spoofing. They were taking the hand out of me. Probably Wholenut's idea, that's the kind of stunt that fucker would pull. But Dee wouldn't go along with that. But then, half an hour ago they were all chasing me and wanting to kill me. But that was the wacky tobaccy. Fuck. I didn't know what to think or do. Then it dawned on me. Dee was Francesca's cousin. His mum's aunt or somebody was related to the Fuscos.

The door opened and one of the young Moffett boys came in.

Hiya Squint."

"Hiya, Thomas." The name just came to me.

"Bloody slow sets started. I hate it. That's why I'm going to hold up in here"til that shite is over."

"No girl you fancy a dance with Thomas?" I asked unable to stop a smile on my face.

"Are you crackers Squint? They're all bloody stupid and never stop talking about make-up and about pop stars they fancy." Thomas pushed himself up and onto the ledge between the two sinks. "And me mates just stand there like a bunch of glipes, pushing each other and giggling about who they're gonna ask to dance but never do."

Oh, to be that age again I thought, as he was about ten. He was part of the Quo fan club, the headbangers they were known as. All dressed in jeans and the DJ would play Down, Down and 'Sweet Caroline' for them every week and they'd all head bang to it. I could hear the strains of the slow set with 'Love don't live here anymore' by Rose Royce. I liked them because they had a song called 'Wishing on a star' that was out around the same time as the film Star Wars and it always reminded me of that film.

"You going out into the slow set?" Thomas asked, almost gasping at the very idea. His eyes widened to match his mouth.

"Yep, got a dance all lined up. I hope." I said and as I said it I doubted the whole thing.

"Ya jammy bastard." He smiled towards me and turned on the cold water tap.

"You're turn will come mate." And it would, he was a good looking kid, with a mop of blonde hair and a nice way about him. "Here, tell me Thomas," I looked around to the other cubicles, to make sure the toilet was empty but for the two of us, "this is going to sound well, a bit bloody bonkers. But see the match today? Did we win?"

"Yeah," he replied Thomas looked at me uncertainly, "weren't you at it? You're a Reds man like. Have you been on the happy apples?" He asked slyly smiling.

"Must've been." I said, smiling back, as admitting to too much cider was better than what I had been on. I heard of guys getting tarred and feathered and given a real good beating for smoking that stuff. And I had been eating it. "I just can't remember."

"Two one they won. There was a bit of trouble, but you probably didn't see much of it, or anything." He commented smiling again. "See ya Squint, after all them froots have finished dancing with the birds." He looked up at me. "Good luck with the slow set mate."

"Cheers mucker. See ya after then." I said, again smiling at his shake of his head that registered his disgust. I walked out of the bogs and into the entrance area where football nets and the red plastic seta all stacked up in tower blocks. I could feel my heart pounding and my hands began to tingle like they were being tickled by a hundred invisible feathers. I looked instinctively at the exit door, where several of the big lads stood smoking. They paid me no heed. They were always there, standing guard, staring through the peephole on each of the two doors when anyone rapped on the stainless steel on the outside.

I thought about the journey to the match, none it made sense to me. Did I even get to the match? If I did I can't remember anything about it. The last thing I remembered was talking with Mr Hale and Mr McAleese. I do remember now. I had been sipping some of the beer they had with them. Christ the night and day, drink and drugs, mum would go off her nut.

I opened the door to enter the dance hall, where we played pool and table tennis, that was before we got asked to join the Fíanna, me and Dee and Wholenut. They said we'd first dibs on the table tennis and pool if we joined up.

We never went back during the day or the evenings, only for the disco. I could see my mates in the left corner, all them bunched up for comfort and protection against the slow set and the love songs. That's where we stood screaming out the chorus to Clout's Sam, when it went: I'll be your substitute' we'd all go 'Prostitute' instead and end up in a wrinkle laughing our heads off.

I looked around beyond the number of couples shuffling on the floor to the song. It was weird that no-one ever kissed during the slow set. Or if they did I'd never seen it. I looked for her staring around the hall. She wasn't in her usual place. Everyone found their place to stand. Our spot was the left hand corner and the back of the hall where there was a steel shutter where they put the tables in for safe keeping and space for the disco where the Quo lads gathered. Near to the DJ and the record decks, that's where Francesca and her friends stood.

That's when she appeared. She had been talking with a girl much taller and I couldn't see her. She returned to her friends who huddled together for a moment and then she turned round and looked directly at me. Then she smiled. It was the best smile I had ever seen. The whole world seemed to melt away. She wore a green v neck sweater with two yellow lines around the neck and the whitest white open-necked shirt and the tight navy-blue pin-striped trousers I loved to see her in. I couldn't budge. I had no power in my body. I was like a Burton's dummy. I concentrated and focused on my feet. I walked slowly, deliberately towards her, my heart felt like it was on fire, my body electrocuted by an excitement bursting through my body.

"Hello." I managed to say. My tongue like it had been nailed to the roof of my mouth.

"Hello. You're Connor?"

Her voice was sweeter that I could ever have imagined and she smelt of summer holidays like she was dipped in suntan lotion. Her skin was perfect like her white teeth and shiny brown hair.

"Yes. And you're Francesca." I said dumbly. My voice was failing me over the music.

"I know." She gave a little laugh and I was overjoyed I had been the cause of it. I realised that the Rose Royce song was coming to an end. I was dreading what the next song would be.

Then the DJ, who was known as Tojo because of the big, giant glasses he wore like a Japanese sniper would, placed the stylus down on the vinyl plate and said something stupid about star crossed lovers everywhere. It was MR Big and that song's intro went...'You are the morning.'

"Would you like to dance? I asked, my voice crumbling like Rich Tea biscuit in my mouth

"Yes. That would be nice." Her velvet voice made her words sound like clouds of poetry.

She didn't say 'that'd be nice', she said the full words, mum would love her, she was pure class. I reached out my arms and she placed the softest hands I had ever felt into mine. We stood inches apart. I had no idea what to say next.

"I like this song." She said softly.

"I do too, it's by MR Big." I said in dream like trance.

"Do you know a lot about music?"

"A bit." I said trying to be modest, but now I think I could well impress her.

"You dance very well." She complimented.

"Thank you. It was me mum, she taught me." I said without a trace of embarrassment.

"She taught you well. I like a boy who is close to his mum." She commented and laid her head on my shoulder.

We moved slowly in a clockwise circle. I looked away from the antics of the lads who were waving and showing me the fingers when my turn came to be facing them as we rotated in time and space. I did not flinch when I could see on the wall that her shadow was almost identical to Andre's from my hallucination. Instead of being afraid and running for my life, I listened to her sing along to the song.

'I am the darkness, you are the light." She sang in the sweetest of voices.

I waited for a moment and sang back

'Oh lady of the land.'

'Come to me, take my hand.' We both sang that part.

'Until tomorrow I'm your man.' I sang back, not even caring that my deepest held feelings were on display.

I wished the greatest wish that tomorrow would never come and I could stay here with Francesca forever.

INJURY TIME

Father Vincent had scooped up the precious petals and as he did so, he counted them. There were exactly the same number as the ladies of the Rosary. Plus one, for one special mother who had endured much suffering recently. He would issue each of them in the little glass boxes they had in the storeroom, where they had kept reliquaries that were no longer useful. Now they had something truly precious and relevant to the faith.

He would gather all of the ladies within the presbytery and speak with them on the issue of secrecy and remind them of the oath they took. He would remind them to be ever vigilant, as there was incontrovertible proof that sinister and dark forces, outside and beyond the everyday kind they had to battle, had come. And remind them the goal is peace. Without which the dark angels would be here for an eternity, as the IRA bombed the heart out of the cities and towns and the Loyalists claimed retaliation, even if in many cases they got it in first.

The real battles were yet to come.

Printed in Poland
by Amazon Fulfillment
Poland Sp. z o.o., Wrocław